Dear Reader,

We've got three *sizzling* stories in our
Silhouette Summer Sizzlers this year from
Annette Broadrick, Jackie Merritt and Justine Davis!

Melody Young's life is looking good in "Deep Cover"
by Annette Broadrick. She's about to get a promotion
and get married—that is, until her fiancé gets another
woman pregnant! And things don't improve when a
wounded man turns up demanding Melody's help....

The temperature hits boiling in Jackie Merritt's
"Stranded," when vacationing Loren Tanner gets
her motor home stuck in the Nevada desert. Then,
when handsome local rancher Ty Ruskin tries to
help, he gets stuck right along with her!

Former corporate raider Gunnar Royce had left the
cold business of takeovers for sun and surf...and
was concentrating on wooing lovely, sheltered Jill
Brown. But to protect her, he needed his ruthless
skills. Could the dragon win the damsel in distress?
Find out in "The Raider" from Justine Davis.

Give yourself some time off this summer and let
these three talented storytellers sweep you away to a
passionate world of possibilities....

Wishing you a delightful summer.

Best,

Isabel Swift
Editorial Director

Silhouette®
SUMMER
Sizzlers
'94

ANNETTE BROADRICK
JACKIE MERRITT
JUSTINE DAVIS

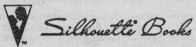

Silhouette Books

Published by Silhouette Books
America's Publisher of Contemporary Romance

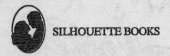 SILHOUETTE BOOKS

SILHOUETTE SUMMER SIZZLERS 1994

Copyright © 1994 by Harlequin Enterprises B.V.

ISBN 0-373-48321-X

The publisher acknowledges the copyright holders
of the individual works as follows:

DEEP COVER
Copyright © 1994 by Annette Broadrick
STRANDED
Copyright © 1994 by Carolyn Joyner
THE RAIDER
Copyright © 1994 by Janice Davis Smith

CONTENTS

DEEP COVER

Annette Broadrick

Chapter One

Sweat collected on Ryan O'Roarke's brow and trickled down into his eyes as quickly as he could brush it away. Although the sun had been down for hours, the claustrophobic heat of mid-July in Dallas wrapped around him like a blanket, suffocating him.

He crouched beside the metal wall of the old warehouse and listened.

He ignored the heat because he could do nothing about it. He ignored the throbbing pain in his side for the same reason. It was a healthy reminder that he was alive, despite being hit before he'd managed to get out of the line of fire and fade into the protective darkness. He'd been lucky. The blackness of his surroundings was the only thing that had saved him tonight. He wiped away the beads of moisture again, forcing himself to concentrate. He had to stop the flow of blood before it left a trail. If they were looking for him, there was no reason to make their job any easier.

He continued to listen, concentrating on keeping his breathing shallow while straining to hear any nearby noises over his own heavy heartbeat.

The weighted darkness was eerie in the silence, the all-pervasive heat guarding its secrets. Ryan could hear nothing that betrayed the recent explosion of harsh lights, deadly gunfire, and excruciating pain.

After several minutes of tense concentration, he heard the faint sound of an engine being pushed to its limits and the shrill squeal of tires. More traffic noises echoed through the deserted industrial streets before he picked up the far-off sound of a siren. Another one soon joined in a disharmonious duet.

He felt along his side in an attempt to determine the severity of the wound. It felt as though he'd been branded by a hot poker. His hand came away wet. He knew the wound couldn't be too serious or he would never have made it this far.

He needed to make a pressure pad and stop the bleeding, but he couldn't afford to sacrifice his shirt at the moment. It wouldn't do for someone to notice him and his injury before he got out of this area.

He pulled a handkerchief out of his back pocket and shoved it against his side.

He couldn't go to a hospital. They'd call the police. Somehow he had to figure out a way to get out of town before he attempted to contact Tuck and tell him that despite all their precautions, his deep cover had been discovered and exposed.

Someone had betrayed him. He was furious enough to live and find out who the bastard was. Life was tough enough, trust too hard to come by, to be betrayed by someone who was supposed to be working with you.

They must have known who he was all along, but didn't reveal their knowledge until the crucial time of exchange of money for cocaine.

He'd had a split second to realize that something wasn't right before all hell broke loose. He'd dropped and rolled toward the deeper shadows close to the building. Once he'd reached the inky blackness he'd jumped up and sprinted away without looking behind him.

Neither the cocaine nor the money was a priority when each breath he drew could easily be his last.

In the relative shelter of discarded boxes in an alley somewhere in south Dallas, Ryan continued to wait and listen to the sounds of muted voices and car engines that carried in the night from two blocks away.

He wondered who had called the cops. He also wondered who else had been the target besides him. If he hadn't sensed that something was wrong, he could easily have been on his way to the morgue, the hospital, or the police station. He considered himself pretty damn lucky to be methodically losing his life's blood in this black alley.

Ryan tore off the tail of his pullover knit shirt and hastily folded it, shoving it against his side as added padding. His arm was beginning to throb. The bullet must have grazed the inside of his arm, as well.

What was he going to do now? There was no one in Dallas to contact. He was on his own. He'd always known that. How ironic that this latest exchange was in his hometown. Other than quick visits to see his folks, he hadn't been back in more years than he could remember.

His folks. Wait a minute—hadn't they told him they intended to visit his sister Carmen in Atlanta about now? His mother had wanted to be with her daughter when Carmen went into labor with their first grandchild.

The family had long since given up on Ryan producing offspring, which was just as well. It was bad enough having parents and a sister who could be used as leverage against him in the event he was exposed in his line of work. He couldn't afford to take a chance with a wife and family.

With his folks out of town, he could use their house for a couple of days, maybe more. Only two men, well placed officials in D.C., knew that he had parents living here. No one else would think to check out the location.

That's what he would do. Somehow he'd manage to get himself across to the north side of town, give his wound a few days to heal, then figure out a way to reach the coast and make contact with one of the ships offshore.

Adrenaline—still with him from his recent escape—pulsed through him, urging him to get as far away as possible.

Ryan moved like one of the shadows, slipping from the alley and following the back streets of the warehouse area until he reached a major intersection. Before moving on, he used the reflected light to check his side.

The blood had stopped dripping, thank God. The inside of his arm, just above his elbow, had a jagged tear that had also stopped bleeding. If he could keep his arm close to his side and keep his shirt over the wound there, Ryan thought he could catch a cross-town bus and reach the residential area where he'd been raised without drawing undue attention to himself.

He had little choice. He'd just run out of options.

Melody Young knew that today had not been the worst day of her life. At the moment, however, she couldn't recall a day any worse than this one in all of her twenty-nine years.

About the best thing that could be said for this Friday in mid-July was that it was just about over. It couldn't end soon enough to suit her.

After overtipping the cabdriver who had brought her home from downtown Dallas, she let herself into her house, grateful to be home.

She wasn't particularly proud of her recent behavior. She would have liked to have dealt with the situation with a little more grace and style than she had shown. Her mother would have been appalled by her betrayal of all the social niceties she had spent years drilling into her.

Thank God her mother hadn't been there.

Melody kicked off her shoes just inside the doorway, another habit her mother deplored, and padded down the hallway toward the kitchen in her stocking feet.

She flipped on the light and paused for a moment to adjust to the brightness. Sheba, her cat, sat up from where she'd been curled on one of the kitchen chairs and gave an elaborate stretch and yawn.

"I know, I know," Melody muttered, putting water on to boil for tea. "I'm home earlier than you expected. Sorry to disturb your nap, your highness."

She'd had the forty-five minute taxi drive out to the Dallas suburbs to think about what she was going to do now that her plans for her immediate future had blown up.

She didn't have any answers and, at the moment, she didn't care. She'd taken action by walking out. She hadn't sat there passively waiting for the next round of humiliation to be heaped upon her. For that she was downright proud of herself.

Sheba leapt daintily off the chair and sauntered over to where Melody stood leaning against the counter. "You know, Sheba, I should have listened to you. I realize that now. You never did like Winston, did you? A clear warning if I've ever had one."

She leaned over and scooped up the cat, stroking her.

Melody didn't want to think about how she was going to break the news to her family that the wedding was off, nor did she want to think about having to face the office staff on Monday morning.

What she wanted to do more than anything at the moment was to run away... far, far away.

A brief vision of childhood flickered in her head... of visits with her grandparents at the beach. Her grandmother had always understood Melody when no one else had. She had always listened without judgment, loving Melody unconditionally. Melody recalled those days with longing, wishing she could return to the innocence of childhood. She'd had such fun during those summer visits, taking long walks on the beach, playing in the shallows, picking up shells, talking with her grandmother.

Unfortunately for Melody at the moment, her grandmother wasn't at the beach. Her grandparents were visiting Melody's aunt in California.

She stood in the kitchen of her home and stared out the window. Instead of the night and her reflected image in the glass pane, she saw a soothing view of early sunrise over the Gulf of Mexico.

Her grandmother wasn't at the island at the moment, but the beach was there... the water was there... the serenity of the island was there, all waiting for her.

The kettle sang out, startling Melody and causing Sheba to leap out of her arms.

After making her tea, Melody's thoughts returned to the possibility of escape, at least for a few days. She had some vacation time coming at work, especially now that she wouldn't be taking time off in September. Why not take a few days and drive down to the island?

She sat down at the small table and sipped her tea, thinking about the idea. The more she considered it, the more it appealed to her. She didn't want to be in the office where she would have to see Winston, at least not until she'd had some time to work through the confused knot of feelings that had been raging inside her.

What better place to go than to the island where no one knew her? She could get away from the world while she tried to deal with the mess that was her life at the moment.

She looked down at Sheba, who was now munching on food in her bowl. "How does South Padre Island sound to you, Sheba?" she asked. "How about a little surf, sand and sea air? It's always cooler on the island in the summer than any other place in Texas. Sounds good, doesn't it?"

Her grandparents would be delighted to have her make use of their retirement home. They liked to spend their winters there and travel over the United States the rest of the year.

She'd be doing them a favor, checking on the place.

She'd be doing herself a bigger favor.

Knowing that she wouldn't be able to sleep anyway, Melody decided to go tonight. Traffic would be light and the drive would be more comfortable without the summer sun beating down on the car. Taking action once again soothed her into believing that she could take at least some control over her life. She couldn't take responsibility for someone else's behavior, but she could make some positive changes in her own life.

With something like missionary zeal, Melody marched up the stairs to her bedroom and began to pack. Sheba followed her and jumped up on the bed, eyeing the open suitcase warily.

"Yes, I know you don't like the sight of a suitcase. A suitcase means traveling, which you hate," she said to the distrustful feline. "However, you always enjoy yourself once we get there and you know it. By the time we hit the outskirts of town you're sound asleep, so don't give me any trouble, okay?"

Melody went into the bathroom and gathered the necessary toiletries. After she placed them in her cosmetic bag she paused, studying herself in the mirror, trying to be objective.

She certainly wasn't anyone's idea of a beauty, that's for sure. Her eyes were too big, her nose too short, her mouth too wide. At least she'd outgrown her freckles, which had been the bane of her childhood. Her hair had thankfully darkened into a deep auburn. It lay in quiet waves around her face. Yep, her hair was her best feature, she decided, ignoring the cobalt blue of her eyes and her clear complexion.

Why hadn't she realized that Winston had lied to her when he'd told her she was beautiful and that she was the only woman who could make his life complete?

Ha!

She returned to the bedroom and placed the spill-proof plastic bag containing her cosmetics into the suitcase. As soon as she closed the suitcase, Sheba leapt off the bed and ran out of the room.

"You can run but you cannot hide. I'll find you, you know," she reminded her roommate.

Just what she needed to finish off a perfectly rotten day... chasing the blasted cat around the house instead of being on the road headed south.

She carried the suitcase downstairs and let herself out the kitchen door that led to the garage. Since she still had to bring the kitty litter box, the cat food and her highness out to the car, Melody decided to back the car out of the garage to make loading easier.

When she returned to the kitchen, she heard the phone ringing. Out of habit she reached for the phone before it occurred to her that the call might be from Winston.

She had no desire to speak to Winston Townsend III at the moment. She might never have a desire to speak to him again, she decided with a painful sort of honesty.

So she waited until the ringing stopped and her answering machine clicked on with its cheery message. She was glad she hadn't answered when she recognized Winston's voice.

"Melody? Are you there? If so, please pick up the phone. At least let me know you got home safely. I realize how clumsily I handled this evening and for that, I'm sorry... Melody? Oh, this is ridiculous, trying to explain to a blasted answering machine! Look, Melody. We have to talk. We can't just pretend this thing never happened, now, can we? Call me when you get home, all right? We'll get together tomorrow. Just name the time. I'll be glad to come over there where we'll have some privacy. I realize that was another error in judgment on my part... Melody, if you're there I want you to pick up the phone, do you hear me? Melody?"

When nothing else was said, the machine disconnected the call. She smiled to herself. It was kind of fun to have a machine that would hang up on people. Maybe she'd write a letter of customer satisfaction to the manufacturer.

She turned away and gathered up the dry cat food, the canned cat food, and the doll blanket Sheba liked to sleep on, and took them out to the car.

As she stowed Sheba's things in the back seat, a sudden flash of light in the house next door—where there should only be darkness—caught Melody's attention. Slowly she straightened and frowned, peering into the darkness.

There was no light. The windows were dark and the shades were drawn.

The O'Roarkes had been gone almost a week now and were expected to be gone for several more. There was no reason for a light to be on in their home. Was it possible someone had broken into the place? She stood by the car and watched for several moments more but saw nothing suspicious.

Maybe the light had been a reflection on one of the windowpanes from a passing car. Of course. That's probably what she had seen from the corner of her eye. Their neighborhood was patrolled frequently and the crime rate was low. Despite living in a large city, Melody felt safe here.

She'd lived in the same house her entire life. She'd insisted on buying it when her dad retired three years ago and her parents had decided to move to Arizona.

Well! Was she going to stand here caught up in her memories for the rest of the night, or was she going to finish packing the car and head out of town? She closed the car door and trotted to the kitchen door. She would put the box of kitty litter in the car next, then start her cat hunt.

As soon as Melody opened the screen door, Sheba shot out of the house as if her tail was on fire and dashed into the shrubbery next to the O'Roarke home.

That did it! So Sheba had decided to widen the area for hide-and-seek, had she? Melody grabbed the kitty litter and marched back to the car, placed it on the floorboard of the passenger's side of the front seat and headed for the house next door.

"Here, Sheba," she called softly. In the same soft, sweet voice, she continued calling. "Once I get my hands on you, you ridiculous piece of cultured fur, I'm going to wring your beastly little neck," she cajoled.

Sheba was a house cat. She'd been a house cat for all of her five years. Therefore, Melody knew from experience that the big, black outdoors would eventually convince Sheba to seek safety with her human roommate.

The question was when.

Melody wanted to leave. Now. She did not want to crawl under bushes on her hands and knees looking for the darned cat.

Sheba gave a soft mew and Melody smiled to herself. "I thought so," she muttered. "You're not quite so brave as you thought, my fine, furry friend."

She reached into the bushes. Instead of Sheba she felt one of the glass windows of the basement move slightly. Oh, no! She couldn't have gone inside. Surely she wouldn't have.

She had.

Sheba was inside the neighbors' basement, sounding pitifully alone and miserably abused.

"C'mon, Sheba. You got in there. You can get yourself out. The window's too small for me. C'mon, Sheba. I'm right here. All you have to do is climb out the way you jumped in."

Nothing but plaintive meows answered her.

Great. This was just what she needed. She was going to have to break into her neighbors' house to get the stupid, idiotic cat out of there.

Otherwise, the cat would go without water and food while Melody was gone.

Melody knew that sooner or later Sheba would come out, but if Melody wasn't here, Sheba's chances of survival were very slim.

Melody leaned back on her heels. Technically, of course, she wouldn't be breaking into the house. The Youngs and the O'Roarkes had lived side by side as neighbors for as far back as Melody could remember. She had a key to their house, just as they had a key to hers, in case of an emergency.

All right. She could deal with this. It was just one more thing in a day that had been filled with a series of humiliating disasters. But hey, she could deal with this one, too. She could. She would.

Refusing to allow herself the luxury of letting go of her hard-gained self-control and screaming with frustration, Melody stomped into her house, grabbed the key she needed and strode back to the house next door. She knew the floor plan as well as she knew her own. She wouldn't do anything suspicious, like turning on lights, that might call attention to her presence. She would go through the back door, through the kitchen, then into the basement. She would find her cat, consider the pleasure she'd relish by donating her to the humane society, then get out. Melody would leave the house, the city, and the mess that was her life at the moment.

With her plan clearly thought out, she crept up the stairs to the back porch, unlocked the back door and let herself into the kitchen. Luckily her back porch light made the kitchen window shades glow, giving her enough light to see.

See? Nothing to it, she reassured herself. Melody reached for the basement door. She was turning the knob when she was grabbed from behind. A large, muscular hand clamped over her mouth while an equally muscular arm wrapped around her waist, lifting her off her feet.

She tried to scream, but no sound came out. A hard, lean body seemed wrapped around her. There was no escape.

Melody knew she'd been wrong after all.

This really *was* the worst day of her life.

Chapter Two

"Who are you?" a deep voice growled menacingly in her ear.

She was shaking so hard her dangling body jerked and quivered in his arms like a marionette's. She squeezed her eyes tightly shut, then opened them, hoping that this wasn't happening, that it was something her crazy imagination had conjured.

No such luck. She could feel the man's warmth emanating from him and surrounding her in its heat. The arm around her middle tightened, stopping her from taking a deep breath.

"Mumph," was the only thing she could say around the hand covering her mouth.

"I want to know who you are and what you're doing in here!" the deep male voice continued. She nodded her head vigorously and tried to reach the floor with her feet. Instead he kept her pressed against his body, so that she felt singed through her clothes.

She couldn't budge. She could feel the well-defined chest muscles where her head rested, the corded ripple of his stomach and abdomen muscles, and the unmistakably masculine bulge where her bottom was touching. This was no kid getting his jollies from breaking into homes for the sheer devilment of it. This was a grown male who showed no tendency toward releasing the firm grip he had on her.

She tried to remember some of the self-defense moves she'd been taught. Wasn't there something she was supposed to be able to do with a hold like this?

Who was she kidding? At the very least, she needed to have her feet on the floor.

The man muttered something uncomplimentary and, still holding her inches off the floor, strode down the hallway to the small bathroom that was in the center of the house. He shoved the door open and stepped inside.

As soon as he closed the door, he brushed his elbow against the light switch, filling the small, windowless room with sudden blinding light.

Their eyes met in the mirror they were facing and they both stared in shock. He let go of her as though he'd been electrocuted and her feet hit the floor.

"You!" Both spoke at the same time.

He shoved her away from him with unflattering haste. "What the hell are you doing in here?" he demanded.

She turned, facing him, and continued to stare at the man as though she were hallucinating. Melody hadn't seen him in years, but she would have known him anywhere, under any conditions. His hair was as black as ever. He wore it long and shaggy. He looked pasty white except for dark smudges beneath his silvery blue eyes. She mentally inventoried the thick black lashes she'd always envied, the high cheekbones, the strong jaw, and the devastating dimple in his chin. Those things had stayed the same over the years.

Only then did she see the bloodied rag against his side . . . the faded and ripped jeans, scuffed sneakers, and the black knit shirt with a ragged shirttail.

"Answer me, damn it! What the hell are you doing here?" he repeated through gritted teeth.

She couldn't seem to make her brain work . . . or her tongue. She swallowed. "I, uh, I was trying to get my cat out of the basement. She, uh, I was . . . that is, we were—"

"How'd she get into the basement?"

"She pushed open one of the windows wide enough to get in, I think."

"Then why didn't you wait for her to come out?"

She couldn't seem to think, bewildered by his demanding questions, unnerved by his appearance, and shaken by the unexpected and frightening encounter.

"I, uh, I didn't want to wait. The car's already packed and I just wanted to—"

"Packed? Where are you going?"

"To my grandparents' place—"

"On the island?"

"Uh, yes, that is—"

"Do they know you're coming?"

"Uh, no. But it doesn't matter since they aren't there, anyway. I just needed to, uh, get away for a few days and I decided to—"

"Who knows where you're going?"

"Well, nobody, since I just decided to—"

"Good." He took her arm. "Go get your cat and I'll meet you at the car."

He wasn't making any sense. Melody swallowed, feeling as though she'd missed something rather vital in this conversational exchange.

Ryan reached over and turned off the light. "Keep the lights off, remember. I don't want anyone to see me."

She heard the door open, but nothing else. The atmosphere of the room shifted, the tension eased, and somehow she knew he was gone.

"Ryan?" she whispered, stepping into the hallway. There was no answer.

Melody raised a shaky hand to brush her hair off her face. Ryan O'Roarke here? How could that be? Hadn't his parents told her something about him working somewhere back east?

He'd been hurt. She couldn't tell how or the seriousness of it. However, from the grip he'd had on her, the injury mustn't be too severe. He'd looked awful... exhausted, unshaven and angry.

Obviously he hadn't wanted her to find him there. Was that why he was going to wait at her car, to give her a lecture about coming into the house?

Well, how was she supposed to know he was in it, for Pete's sake?

She felt her way along the hallway, relieved to reach the brighter kitchen. Once again she reached for the basement door, this time feeling her way down the steps. "Sheba?"

"Meow." Sheba brushed against her ankles in a conciliatory manner.

Melody scooped the cat up into her arms and hurried back up the steps. After making sure the back door locked behind her, she darted down the steps and over to her car. Ryan was nowhere to be seen.

"Ryan?" she whispered, looking around.

He was gone.

Startled and more than a little confused, she tossed the cat into the car and went back into her house to lock up. She made sure everything was in order before she grabbed her purse, turned off the lights and let herself out the back door. According to the blinking light on her answering machine, she'd received two more phone calls. She didn't stop to find out who had called.

She had a hunch she already knew.

When she reached the car once again, she looked all around, wondering where Ryan had gone. For all she knew he could still be in the house, sitting there in the dark, watching her.

She shivered, wondering what he was doing in Dallas.

She knew it was none of her business and that she might never have an answer. Knowing Ryan, he'd probably deny he'd ever been there and insist she'd made up the whole story.

She certainly wouldn't put it past him.

Jerking the car door open she quickly slipped inside before Sheba decided to make another nocturnal journey into the wilds. With a brief sigh, she turned the key and started the car, then let out a yelp when a voice from the back seat said, "Let me know when you get sleepy and I'll drive for a while."

She stared over her shoulder and saw Ryan lying on the back seat of her car.

"What are you doing in here?"

"Hitching a ride south. Don't mind me. Just pretend you're alone. You and this damn cat!"

"What did you do to my cat!"

"Nothing! Absolutely nothing. It's what your cat is doing to me! She won't leave me alone. She's cleaned my ear, sniffed my hair and has become inordinately interested in my chest hair! I'm so pleased to be able to offer her some feline entertainment. Now then, can we get the hell out of here? Please?"

"But where are you going? Why do you need—"

"Look, Tiny-Toon, I'll answer all your questions before this drive is over, but I haven't had any sleep in almost thirty-six hours. Give me a break, will ya?"

Now that her porch light was off, she could no longer see. Melody turned on her headlights and from the reflected glare off the white garage door, she could see the strain in his face and the pain in his eyes.

"You're hurt," she said, stating the obvious.

He closed his eyes. "I'll live."

"Shouldn't you have that looked at?"

"No way. Emergency rooms get real nosy about bullet wounds. I just want to get out of town."

"Bullet wounds!" she echoed faintly. She swallowed, feeling a sense of unreality sweep over her.

"Actually, they're more like grazes. I was lucky. Both are flesh wounds. I bled enough to have cleared out anything that might have wanted to linger to cause infection. Come on, let's get a move on, will ya?"

Numbly she put the car in reverse and backed out of the driveway. She drove automatically, her mind racing with conjecture, to Interstate 35E and took the on ramp heading south. Her head swam with unanswered questions that she wanted to ask her uninvited, unwanted passenger.

Ryan O'Roarke was lying in her back seat with a bullet wound to add to his already disreputable looks.

Ryan O'Roarke, her childhood nemesis.

She should have known that Ryan would show up today—of all days. He'd always had a positive knack at being present during her most humiliating experiences. More often than not, Ryan managed to engineer most of those humiliating experiences while she made that traumatic transition between blissful childhood and disciplined adult.

"Ryan?"

"Don't talk to me. I'm asleep."

"Oh, yeah? Well, you're talking back."

"I talk in my sleep."

"Sure you do."

"All right, what is it!"

"Are you escaping from the law?"

"And everybody else."

"Does that make me an accomplice to whatever it is you've done?"

"Don't worry. I'm sure you've got enough sterling character witnesses to get you off with a light sentence. You might only get a suspension."

"Ryan!"

"Damm it, Tiny-Toon, you don't have to yell! I'm not that far away."

"You're never far enough away as far as I'm concerned . . . and stop calling me that ridiculous name."

"It's no more ridiculous than the name Melody."

"My parents happened to like the name. That's why they chose it."

"I like Tiny-Toon better."

They were barely past the city limits of Dallas and had already fallen into the habit of wrangling as they had when they were growing up next door to each other.

"What did you do, Ryan?"

"You don't want to know."

"You got *that* right! However, since you've now chosen my vehicle as your getaway car, I'd like some idea of how serious the consequences are going to be for me."

"Don't worry about it. Nobody saw me. There's nobody to say I was in Dallas. There's no way you can be implicated."

"Lucky me." Well, that exchange had been a great big waste of time. He'd told her exactly nothing. Melody couldn't remember a time when she'd managed an even exchange with Ryan, much less one where she got the best of him.

She'd spent many an hour during her childhood plotting to pay him back for some of the things he'd done to her, but it had never been enough. No matter what she thought up to do to him, he was diabolically clever in getting his revenge.

Wait a minute—he'd said he was exhausted. He needed some sleep. So, why didn't she wait until he was really out for the count, then pull into one of the cities along the interstate and find the local police? She could tell them that he surprised her in her car. That was no lie. She could tell them that he forced her to take him with her— Her thoughts slowed... On her vacation? Nah. They'd never buy that one.

Okay. She could tell them that he'd forced her to drive him out of town. That was it! She could say that he'd looked and acted like a desperate criminal, insisting on avoiding the police.

Melody continued south on a highway with little traffic other than the eighteen-wheelers moving their products from one long distance place to another, smiling to herself. She was delighted with her scenario, envisioning the look on O'Roarke's face at the moment he opened his eyes and found himself surrounded by stalwart men in blue. She could see him now—every last expression on his face, every emotion sweeping him to the only conclusion there was.

She had finally bested him.

What a feat. After all these years, she would have won. The mere thought of the victory made her sigh with pleasure. For the next several hours she embellished her plan, adding little bits of creativity to the scene. At one point, she almost laughed out loud.

She luxuriated in her dream of revenge during the small hours of that night, then carefully, reluctantly, placed them—unexposed to the harsh world of reality—into the deep recesses of her mind.

Ryan O'Roarke was a well-known adversary. Unless whatever he had done was so bad that he would be locked up forever, then someday he would come looking for her for pulling a trick like that. Even if he *had* done some awful deed, O'Roarke had the uncanny ability to talk himself out of the blackest situation. He'd probably get out of the whole mess within hours and come looking for her.

No, it was better to dream and to savor the dream without having to deal with the complications of the reality of such a plan.

However, spending hours plotting what she would like to do with O'Roarke had taken her mind off of Winston Townsend. She hadn't given him a thought since she'd discovered O'Roarke in her car.

That realization was a shock. How could she have been so distracted that her own personal problems had taken a back seat to her current situation? O'Roarke had jarred her out of her self-absorption.

He'd always had a knack for doing that, for minimizing her pain, for being insensitive to her trials and tribulations. For that matter, he'd generally been the *cause* of most of her trials and tribulations.

No two men could have been more opposite than Winston Townsend III and Ryan O'Roarke. Even the idea of a comparison was laughable. Winston was the kind of man that Melody had hoped she would find someday, if she took her time and refused to be carried away by unreliable reactions.

She'd always known that what she didn't want in the way of a life mate was a swaggering macho male. Unfortunately, in her home state of Texas, the swaggering macho male tended to dominate the scene—and was damn proud of it.

Yessireebob! Despite the number of times she'd heard it, she still ground her teeth when some good ol' boy referred to her as a "sweet little lady." It didn't matter that she had all kinds of degrees, or was working toward becoming a full partner at the firm of certified public accountants she'd worked for these past several years.

It didn't matter that she knew more about business and the tax laws and the current economic situation than most of the men for whom she worked. She was still running into men who considered a cute remark filled with sexual innuendos their highest form of compliment to her.

Oh, no, she had no use for this kind of man.

When Winston had been hired by the firm a little more than a year ago, she knew that he was different from the men she'd been exposed to her entire life.

To begin with, Winston was originally from Chicago. Everyone knew that people from Chicago were completely different from people in the south—or more specifically, from Texans.

For starters he'd called her Ms. Young—not "little lady," not "honey," not "sugar." He spoke to her as though he saw a person—an intelligent person—not a redheaded, blue-eyed, long-legged female who had been holding her breath waiting for him to come dashing into her life to make her a...*a woman!* He treated her with respect. He treated her as an equal. Because of his polite manner during the first several months at work, she'd been unprepared for his invitation to have dinner with him.

For the first time in her life, she hadn't spotted a man's planned moves several leaps in advance. She'd been intrigued by his subtlety. To be honest, she'd found herself wondering about him at various times. What would he be like in a social situation?

He handled his job with obvious competency. Rumor had it that the firm felt lucky to have gotten him. He was on the fast track to a partnership and she'd had to weigh how she felt about dating a person she worked with, one she would possibly be in competition with.

So she'd been very, very careful with him, politely agreeing to dinner as though they were no more than two business colleagues who wanted to get to know each other better.

She had always said she would never get involved with a man that wasn't her friend. Winston became her friend in the following months. Since they were assigned different clients, their work didn't overlap. They had the same pressures, had to meet the same deadlines, had to deal with the same temperamental personalities of their employers.

They were comrades together in the trenches, and the feeling of an embattled business war zone pulled them closer together. Winston understood so much about her, what she wanted and how she intended to reach her goals, because he had the same ambitions and knowledge.

As the months went by, she became more and more relaxed with him, more in tune with him. He began to share his life and background with her. He let her learn who he was, what made him tick.

How could she resist such a perfectly wonderful man who wasn't afraid to be open about his weaknesses, who didn't mind being vulnerable with another person, who didn't have to flex his male, macho muscles at her?

The truth was, she couldn't resist him. When Winston had proposed to her on Valentine's Day that year, she knew she had found the man of her dreams, her soul mate.

He'd suggested that they marry in September, on the anniversary of their first date.

A romantic, too.

She wasn't concerned that they had been careful not to become intimate too soon in their relationship. Winston had never pushed her, had never made her feel pressured in any way. She was content with his warm kisses, with his affectionate attitude toward her, with the way he always seemed to be touching her—by holding her hand, resting his hand on her shoulder, hugging her, sitting with his arm around her.

He was the only man she'd ever dated more than three weeks who hadn't insisted that she owed it to herself to experience the delights of his expertise in bed. Of course, most of them weren't quite that blatant, but the bottom line was invariably the same.

But not Winston. How could she not love and appreciate him?

So they planned their wedding. They'd flown to Scottsdale over Easter to meet her parents. They'd flown to Chicago over Memorial Weekend to meet his parents.

It looked like they would be given promotions at work at the same time. Everything had been going so well in their lives, or so Melody had thought—until tonight.

"Where are we?"

She'd forgotten O'Roarke and let out a startled yelp at the sudden sound of a voice directly behind her.

"What's wrong with you?"

"You scared me. I'd forgotten you were back there."

"Wishful thinking, I'm sure. So, where are we?"

"Just north of Austin."

"You want me to drive?"

"I thought you were exhausted."

"I was, but I've slept for over three hours. That's a good night's sleep for me."

Now that he'd brought it to her attention, Melody realized that she *was* tired, not only tired of driving but tired of her mind's chattering. "I'll pull over at the next—"

"Find a truck stop or something. I need some coffee and we probably could use some gas for the car. I'll stay outside and you go in and get the coffee."

"Look, O'Roarke. I'm not your flunky and I don't take orders well."

"You never did."

"I didn't think you'd ever noticed. If you want us to get along at the most minimum level of polite behavior, I recommend that you start suggesting or requesting or asking—I'm not taking orders from you."

"Jeez, you've got to be the most contrary, inflexible, irritating, aggravating woman I have ever known in my life. Of all the people I could have found a ride with, you've got to be the absolute—"

"I'll be glad to let you off at the next truck stop, where I'm sure you'll find the perfect person to hit up for a ride to wherever it is you think you need to go."

When there was silence in the back seat, she smiled to herself. Good. She was going to get rid of him. She didn't care why he was in Dallas, hiding in his parents' home. She didn't care if he got to where he needed to go. Most particularly, she didn't care if she ever saw him again.

Sheba stepped onto the console between the front seats and pushed her head against Melody's arm. Melody reached down and stroked her just behind her ear, receiving immediate approval. What did Melody care about Ryan O'Roarke's opinion of her? She had her cat, she had her job, and she had—

She almost groaned out loud. How was she going to face everybody at the office? How was she going to hold up her head, to pretend that everything was all right, when her world had crumbled into pieces?

"There's a truck stop at the next exit."

"Thank you. The fact that there's been billboards advertising this particular stop for the past five miles somehow managed to escape me. Only your eagle eye saved me from the horror of missing the opportunity to get you immediately out of my life."

"Oh, shut up," he drawled wearily.

As soon as they pulled up in front of one of the pumps, Melody got out of the car and circled around to where her gas tank was located.

"I'll fill it. You go on inside." Ryan was stiffly unfolding himself from her car.

She glanced around at him in surprise. "I thought you were leaving."

"What I'd like to do and what I have to do are not always the same thing. I need to get to the coast as soon as possible and you're my fastest ticket there. Whether either of us likes it or not—and we've never once had trouble expressing our feelings on the subject—we're going to have to put up with each other for the next few hours." He walked over and flipped on the pump, grabbed the hose and inserted the nozzle into the gas tank. "I suggest—and remember, this is only a suggestion—that you go inside and find us something to eat, something to drink, and think of some pleasant subject or two that might occupy us for the next few hours."

"Forget the conversation. I'm going to sleep."

"Well, of course you have that option. But at this time of night and with only three hours of sleep—not to mention my injured condition and lightheadedness—I can't be totally certain that I won't fall into sleep or unconsciousness without your keeping me alert by talking to me."

She couldn't believe the audacity of the man. "You know, O'Roarke, I'd really hate to have your nerve in a tooth." She spun on her heel and stomped into the truck stop. What infuriated her the most was that she knew that she was going to do exactly what he said. She was going to find them food to snack on in the car, buy plenty of coffee to keep them both awake, and then return to the car and pretend there was nothing she wanted more in life than to be running from a horrible situation that she would have to come to terms with in a very short time. All this while chatting up the man who had done his best to ruin her childhood and make her adolescence a miserable experience.

By the time she returned to the car, Ryan was behind the steering wheel adjusting the seat and the mirrors, as well as playing with the dials and switches.

She moved the kitty litter, then got into the passenger side in silence and handed him a large insulated mug of coffee and a sack containing a sandwich, potato chips, a candy bar and a package of cupcakes. "How much do I owe you?" He took a sip on the cup, wincing at the heat.

"More than you will ever be able to repay."

"Oh, that's cute. What's it supposed to mean?"

"I thought you wanted a pleasant topic of conversation."

He started the car. "With you? Even I don't expect miracles. Come on, Tiny-Toon. What exactly is your beef with me?"

He'd already pulled back onto the interstate before she could find her voice. "Are you telling me that you contracted amnesia in the ten years I haven't seen you? You don't remember?"

"I have all kinds of memories, but I have a hunch they're nothing like yours. You obviously have been hoarding a whole bagful of the suckers. So—we've got a few miles to cover before dawn—fill 'em with whatever's been eating at you. You'll feel better for it."

Chapter Three

"You're right," she replied slowly. "I don't need to carry around any excess baggage where you're concerned. Maybe you've come back into my life for a reason. Maybe I can get it all said and forget about it. After all, I'm an adult now. I can take care of myself."

"You make it sound like you've only recently learned that skill."

"Meaning?"

"You've always been able to take care of yourself, Tiny-Toon. You have a real knack for carving up a person with your tongue with the speed of Zorro. Your tongue should be listed as a lethal weapon."

"Cute, O'Roarke. Really cute."

"But we aren't talking about you, are we? Go ahead, tell me what I've done to cause such animosity."

"You may have found it amusing to terrorize me when you were a kid, but it did nothing for my own sense of safety and security. You used to give me nightmares!"

He jerked his head around to look at her before hastily returning his gaze to the road. In the brief glimpse of his expression, she could see real shock on his face.

"What in hell are you talking about?"

"Don't you remember the number of times you used to scare me with a frog or a snake or a mouse? And what about the time you found that horrible tarantula down by the creek?"

"Ah, c'mon, Tiny-Toon. That's what little boys do, after all. Are you saying that you've been holding stuff against me that I did before I was ten years old?"

"You were an obnoxious, insensitive, hateful bully who seemed to seek out ways to make my life miserable, and you know it."

Instead of denying his behavior, she saw a smug grin appear on his face, the same smug grin that she used to find infuriating on the boy. On the man, however, the lopsided smile called attention to the flash of white teeth in his darkly tanned face. For the first time in a long while Melody saw Ryan objectively, and with a flash of ingrained honesty admitted to herself that Ryan O'Roarke was devilishly good-looking. The flash startled her, revealing a long-standing bias on her part that had viewed him through the eyes of the child she had once been. Ryan interrupted her introspection. "All right, so maybe it wasn't particularly nice of me to tease you when I knew you were afraid of creepy crawlies, but you were so much fun to tease, Tiny-Toon. You had a screech that could be heard all over the neighborhood."

Dryly she responded, "I never particularly wanted my screech, as you call it, to be my single claim to fame in the neighborhood."

They drove through the night in silence for a while before Ryan said, "All right. I guess I'm twenty years late in apologizing, but if it makes any difference in your opinion of me—I want you to know that I'm sorry I was a typical boy with the need to impress the girl next door."

Melody eyed him suspiciously but he didn't look around at her. In fact, he seemed to be watching the road with unusual attention considering the late hour and almost nonexistent traffic.

"You were trying to impress me?" she finally repeated.

"Mmm," was his noncommittal response.

Now there was a provocative thought. She had honestly thought he'd hated her the way he'd continually tormented her. She reminded herself that her conclusion was based on a child's point of view, after all. She'd never considered another reason for him to go to so much effort to get her attention, since it was all negative attention.

"What else?"

She blinked at his words, trying to recall their immediate conversation. When she didn't say anything, he asked again, "What other behaviorial defects are you holding against me?"

She was quiet for several minutes, then stiffened as other memories flooded into her head. "I will never forgive you for telling Jamie Forester I had a crush on him."

He threw his head back and laughed wholeheartedly. "Yeah, I remember you were pretty hot under the collar over that one."

"I was totally devastated and humiliated beyond belief."

"It was the truth!"

"Which was exactly why I was so humiliated. I was all of thirteen years old, naive beyond belief, thinking my secret was safe. How did you know about it, anyway?"

"Oh, I heard your mom say something about it to my mom."

"Great. Add eavesdropping to all the rest."

"It isn't eavesdropping when I was right there in the kitchen getting a drink while they were talking over coffee."

"Well, it was a terrible thing to do. Poor Jamie. He avoided me for weeks after that, which was tough since we had three classes together. As soon as he would see me, his ears would go bright pink."

"And since his ears were the most noticeable thing about him, you didn't have any trouble witnessing the phenomenon."

"And that's another thing. You were always saying insulting things about my friends."

"Not all your friends."

"Oh? Which ones missed your critique?"

"I liked Susie, and Kay, and Coranne, and Janice—and Mavis had a great sense of humor."

"Oh, sure. All my girlfriends."

"Yep. You had great taste in female friends. I used to enjoy hanging over the back fence talking to them."

"Flirting with them."

"Whatever."

"But you were horrible about Kurt and Lance, and Haywood."

"Hey, hey, cut me a little slack, babe. Nobody, absolutely nobody, liked Haywood Harrison."

"Because he was a genius."

"Because he was a jerk."

"He was brilliant."

"Jerks can come in all forms."

A sudden vision of Winston flashed into her mind and she muttered, "Yeah, I'm finally figuring that one out, myself."

"From the sound of your voice, I'd say the lesson has been a little painful. Wanna tell me about it?"

"No."

"We have a long night ahead of us. I'm really good at listening and I have a nice broad shoulder in case you need to shed a tear or two."

The trouble was that he was right. She hadn't seen him in years. During those years the tall lanky young man she'd known had broadened and toughened into a person that seemed in many ways a stranger to her. She looked out at the black night and the occasional light off in the distance, wondering how everything could have changed so quickly for her. How was it possible for her to be dashing off in the night to the island, hiding away from the shambles of her per-

sonal and professional life, when only yesterday she'd
been looking for a good caterer for her wedding?

She shifted in her seat, wishing she could blot the
past few hours out of existence. She wanted to rewrite
the evening, she wanted to—

"All right. If you don't want to talk about yourself, then I'll tell you the story of my life," he said into
the silence.

She crossed her arms. "Don't bother. I've already
heard it too many times."

"What is that supposed to mean?"

"Your mother has kept first my mother then me up
to date on all your exploits."

She could hear the amusement in his voice. "I doubt
if she's been able to fill you in on *all* of them."

"Let's just say that my imagination is healthy
enough to fill in the blanks."

"Well, I'm very sorry to say that I don't know
what's been happening to you. You graduated from
SMU when I did, as I recall, then planned to take some
graduate classes. What happened after that?"

"I went to work for a CPA firm."

He made a face. "Do you like that kind of work?"

"Absolutely. I enjoy working within a stable environment. Working with figures is very soothing. They
don't lie, they don't wake you up in the middle of
night, they have a consistency and conformity that is
reassuring."

"That's one way of looking at them, I suppose. I
never could sit still long enough to have the patience
for paperwork."

"I'm aware of that. I'll admit I was surprised to hear you'd taken a desk job with the government."

"Is that what my mother told you?"

"Yes. Isn't it true?"

"I still don't get anywhere near a desk if I can help it."

"But you do work for the government, right?"

"In a manner of speaking."

"What particular manner is that?"

"Only a handful of my associates know that I work with the government. As a matter of fact, several law enforcement agencies have me on their wanted-for-questioning lists. I'm rapidly gaining popularity, it seems."

She stared at him in horror. "Are you serious?"

"Absolutely."

"You're wanted by the police?"

"In some places."

"Can't you just tell them you work for the government?"

"Nope. The government would deny any connection to me."

"How horrible."

"Only if I get caught."

"From the looks of things, you had a close call tonight."

"Closer than I like. Somebody betrayed me, and I don't know who in order to figure out what camp they're in. I've spent too long getting into this position to bail out unless my cover is totally blown. For the moment, I can't do anything until I get some answers.''

"You're in real danger then, aren't you?"

"Aren't you feeling guilty for giving me such a bad time," he asked, "when I'm one of the unsung heroes in the war against drugs?"

"You and I both know that the only reason you're doing this kind of job is because you love the danger. You're an adrenaline junkie. You always have been."

"Yeah, I forgot how well you know me. And if there's one thing that does not impress you, it's a high-energy, restless character like me."

"You've never been particularly stable, that's for sure."

"Hey, I resent that. I'm really a very steady fellow—reliable, thoughtful, trustworthy, dependable . . ."

"I suppose all of that's on your governmental resumé."

"Of course."

She rolled her eyes.

"So tell me about your love life?" he asked without missing a beat in the conversation.

She tensed, wishing she wouldn't react every time she thought about Winston. "There's nothing to tell," she replied.

"Ha. Since when?"

"Since earlier tonight."

"Really? What happened?"

"I had a falling out with my fiancé and—"

His hands tightened on the steering wheel. "Your fiancé! I didn't know you were engaged!"

She stared at him, puzzled by his reaction. "Why should you? I'm sure your mother probably figured you wouldn't be interested."

"Do you have the wedding date set?"

Still puzzled by his peculiar interest, she replied, "Winston and I picked September 12. Why?"

"I mean, it wasn't just something you decided to do—to get engaged because it was the next step in your carefully planned-out life, was it? You're actually going through with— I mean, you're getting married, just like that?"

She decided to ignore his dig about her carefully planned life. With dignity, she replied, "Actually, it isn't just like that after all. I broke the engagement tonight."

"No kidding?"

"No kidding."

"Why?"

"Has it ever occurred to you, O'Roarke, that my personal life is none of your business?"

"Yep, but it never stops me from wanting to know more. So tell me, what happened?"

"I don't want to talk about it."

"You don't seem too broken up over it."

"Whatever I'm feeling is none of your business and I certainly have no intention of discussing the matter with you."

Once again, silence reigned supreme in the car. Melody closed her eyes, trying not to think about

Winston. It was like being told not to think about a black horse. Her mind went immediately to the forbidden subject.

"Let me guess," Ryan said into the silence. "You found the steady, reliable, intelligent, literate male of your dreams, only to discover that he bored you out of your mind for more than a few hours at a time. That's it, isn't it? You discovered that boredom isn't a sure choice for marital bliss, after all, right?"

"I can see that your obnoxious quotient is holding at a steady level."

"Aw, c'mon, Tiny-Toon. Indulge me. Here I am, taking over the driving chores for you, keeping you company on the long drive south, being my usual charming, adorable self. How can you possibly resist me?"

"Believe me, O'Roarke, it isn't difficult."

"Admit it. You've always had a secret crush on me."

"Let's put it this way. If I have, it's been a deeply guarded secret from me, as well."

He sighed with obviously feigned dismay. "I can see that my work is going to be cut out for me on this little jaunt. Somehow, in the next few hours—possibly days—I've got to convince you that I've been the one constant in your life, the one person you could depend on. You'll never find any real happiness or contentment with anyone else but me."

Melody burst into laughter. Maybe it was the lateness of the hour, the fact that she was overtired and stressed out. Whatever it was, Melody found his remarks hilarious. When she looked over at him and saw his grim profile, she fought to control her response. There was a slim possibility her laughter might have hurt his feelings.

O'Roarke? With sensitive feelings? Wasn't that a contradiction in terms?

"It wasn't all that funny, was it?"

She gulped down a chuckle, cleared her throat, and said, "Sorry. It's been a long day. I may have overreacted a little." She peered at him through the shadowy interior of the car. "You *were* kidding, weren't you?"

"And if I wasn't?"

"Are you trying to tell me . . . that I'm supposed to believe . . . you've been pining for me for all these years?" She smothered another chuckle. "Not in this lifetime, O'Roarke."

"So what's this fiancé character got that I haven't got?"

What a ridiculous question. The men were polar opposites. Or so she had always thought. However, she would never have guessed that Winston would have behaved so shabbily toward her. O'Roarke, maybe. But not Winston. If she could have been so wrong about Winston, wasn't it possible that she could be wrong about O'Roarke, as well?

"Give it a rest, O'Roarke, okay? It's almost four in the morning, not my best time of day for presenting intelligible, comprehensive character comparisons."

"I'll make it easier for you. Tell me what first drew you to Winston?"

"He treated me with respect, listened to my opinions, acknowledged me as an equal—"

"Sounds like a business associate."

"He *is* a business associate."

"Good grief, Tiny-Toon, why would you want to get so wrapped up in your professional life that you have to take it home and sleep with it?"

"Don't be crude."

"I'm being honest. Don't you want more out of life than an all-engrossing balance sheet or a rip-roaring P and L statement? What do you do for fun?"

"The idea of going to the beach was my idea of fun. Having company to harass me along the way wasn't exactly a preference of mine."

He smiled, ignoring the part he didn't want to hear. "I've always enjoyed the beach, myself. Remember the summer your folks took me to the island with you on your family vacation?"

"How could I forget waking up to find sand crabs scampering all over me!"

"Hey, that wasn't my fault. That's what they do."

"It was your idea to take our sleeping bags out on the beach and sleep out under the stars."

"What a celestial show that was. There have been times during these past ten years when the memory of lying there listening to the waves roll in and feeling the peace of that heavenly display kept me feeling sane in an insane world."

A sudden realization hit Melody. O'Roarke was much more sensitive than she'd ever noticed. The thought made her uneasy. The entire night had made her uneasy as she'd been forced to face some of her set-in-stone opinions.

"Would you like for me to drive for a while? I know you must be exhausted," she said quietly.

He glanced at her in surprise. "I'm okay."

"You must be in pain."

"I took some aspirin, which helped take the edge off. You can do the driving later."

"I don't think over-the-counter medication was intended to aid the pain of gunshot wounds."

He laughed. "The advertising people may be missing something, then. Just think of an ad campaign that would include all the miscellaneous side-benefits of pain relievers."

"I'd rather not, thank you. By the time the commercials run through the existing list, I'm already feeling some of the same symptoms. I have a highly suggestible mind."

"Don't I know it! I used to be able to make up the most impossible scenarios and convince you they were true with no real effort on my part."

"Don't be modest, O'Roarke. Admit it. You have a tremendous talent for making outrageous lies appear to be the truth."

His smile faded and he was quiet for a moment before he muttered, "I know."

"You make a living lying, don't you?" she asked, as another realization hit her.

He shrugged, feigning nonchalance. "As you say, it's always been one of my major talents."

She shook her head. "It's difficult to understand how a person can go about living a lie." Once again her mind flashed to a brief picture of Winston, looking winsome and earnestly sincere.

"The unfortunate truth is that living a lie becomes easier with practice. Eventually, the lie becomes so real that any other life takes on a dreamlike quality."

Melody hadn't understood at the time, but her careful plans to find a suitable mate and marry had set into motion her present predicament. Unknowingly, she had been living a lie. The truth had brought her to this moment ... shared with this man.

With no more plans in the making, her future seemed as dark as the night around her.

Chapter Four

The night sky was gradually lightening over the Gulf by the time Melody turned into her grandparents' driveway. The beach house was built on stilts, leaving room beneath the house to park. The home faced the water, its wide veranda wrapping around the structure like a flounce on a matron's skirt.

She glanced at Ryan who had not awakened when the car finally stopped. There wasn't enough light to see his face, but she knew that his sleep was filled with pain by the way he held his body so stiffly, despite his obvious exhaustion.

Sheba leapt from the back seat and crawled into Melody's lap, peering out the side window with cat-like curiosity.

"Ryan?"

He lifted his head from its rest and looked at her. "We're here?" His voice sounded gravelly with sleep.

"Yes. I wasn't certain whether you intended to come to the beach house or not, but since you didn't seem to be on a particular schedule, I thought you might want to come inside, maybe get a shower and rest a while before you have to go."

He moved gingerly and got out of the car. She did the same, keeping a firm hold on Sheba. She found the key to the back door on her key chain and walked up the steps to the porch. She heard Ryan's steps behind her.

Once inside, she let Sheba loose, then went around to each window and opened it, allowing the soft night air to waft inside and dispel the mustiness of the empty house.

When she turned away from one of the bedroom windows she saw Ryan watching her from the hall-way.

"Help yourself to the towels and whatever else you might need," she said, walking toward him. She paused at the door. He didn't move and they stood facing each other a short distance apart. A very short distance. His nearness unnerved her, which was ridic-ulous considering the fact they'd just traveled several hundred miles in a car together.

She couldn't seem to pull her gaze away from his eyes. How could she have forgotten how blue his eyes were? She felt like she was drowning in them when he moved closer and brushed his lips against hers. Too stunned to step away, she simply stood there, giving him all the time in the world to slip his arms around her and pull her into his body.

What was wrong with her? Her brain had shut down and her body had betrayed her by turning into a quiv-ering mass of jelly.

He took his time, as though he was consciously sa-voring each action. He pressed his mouth to hers with a gentle pressure that coaxed her into opening to him. With leisurely disregard for the fact that she had vocally expressed her dislike of him, Ryan proceeded to kiss her until her knees gave way. Seemingly encouraged by her deplorable weakness, he lifted her up into his arms and carried her into the bedroom without halting his intense exploration of her mouth and face with his lips.

Melody felt the solid comfort of the bed supporting her at the same time that Ryan straightened away from her. He offered her his lopsided, cocksure smile while his eyes sparkled with hidden lights.

"A shower sounds good to me," he murmured in a husky voice... and walked away.

Melody continued to lie there even when she heard the bathroom door close and the shower come on. Her world had just been tilted on its side and given a whirl. All of her thoughts, beliefs and rules were skittering around in her head, bumping into each other hysterically.

No one had ever kissed her in that way before. More importantly, she had never reacted to a kiss so intensely before. She couldn't believe what had just happened to her... and with Ryan O'Roarke, of all people.

She had kissed Winston many times and had felt warm and content. Ryan's kiss left her in a state of turmoil and—all right, she could admit it—frustration. Her body was aching with unfamiliar sensations, wanting for him to continue what he had started.

How could he have kissed her so thoroughly, with so much passion and enthusiasm, then dropped her on the bed and walked away?

Okay, okay. He didn't exactly drop her, but she definitely felt deserted.

"Melody?"

She jackknifed into a sitting position as though Ryan's voice had touched a hidden spring. "Yes?" she finally said on her second attempt at answering. She couldn't see him but realized the shower had stopped.

"Do you think your granddad would mind if I borrowed a pair of shorts and a shirt?"

"Help yourself," she called. "The hall closet is full of things we've all left here at one time or another."

She eased off the bed, determined to get a grip on her wildly swinging emotions. She was being ridiculous. It wasn't Ryan she was responding to...not really. In her present frame of mind, she would have reacted to anyone who had shown her some warmth and caring.

Sure, jeered a small voice in her head. She ignored the voice and went into the kitchen. The small room was separated from the large living area by a kitchen bar. The other three walls of the living area were made up of floor-to-ceiling windows.

Early morning sunlight glinted and danced around the room, kissing each object with a golden glow ... which was exactly how Melody felt after Ryan's kiss.

She shook herself out of her totally inappropriate thoughts and began digging in the freezer and pantry for something for breakfast.

Coffee was made, a tidy mound of toast sat buttered, and crisp bacon decorated one of her grandmother's colorful plates when Melody heard Ryan say, "Hmm! You can't imagine how good everything smells to me. I can't remember the last time I had a chance to sit down and savor a meal."

She picked up the plates, saying, "I'll need to go to the store for milk and eggs, but at least we won't..." Her voice trailed off when she turned and saw Ryan.

She didn't know who the owner of his borrowed clothes was, but she was certain her grandfather had never owned a pair of biker shorts! They fit him like a sleek second skin, indecently hugging his hips and thighs and lovingly cupping his masculinity.

She jerked her gaze upward in embarrassment only to see a broad expanse of bare chest liberally covered with a thick mat of black curls. Only then did she see the angry, red gash in his side.

"Ryan! Your side!" She rushed over to him, then abruptly halted as his body heat seemed to scorch her. This close, she could see where the flesh had been torn. "You should have that looked at," she said faintly, swallowing.

"You're looking at it. As long as I keep it clean and bandaged, I'll be all right. I've had worse injuries playing football."

She knew that wasn't true. She had seen most of his ball games, both in high school and in college. They were classmates, after all.

This close to him she could smell the fresh after-shave he wore—the scent of Old Spice, which she'd always adored. She gave her grandfather a set of it every year.

"No," she absently replied. "Your concussion our junior year was the worst injury you ever had."

His eyes gleamed with humor. "You remember that, do you?"

"Remember it?! I thought you were dead! You lay there so still and showed no signs of recovering consciousness. It was horrible!" She continued to talk while staring at his wound.

He laughed. "Too bad I don't remember much about that day."

"I remember you were going with Sylvia Stanton at the time."

He lifted his brows slightly, then turned away in search of a cup of coffee. Melody watched him as he moved away from her, and swallowed convulsively. If she'd found his choice of apparel provocative from the front, the view of his tautly muscled buttocks took her breath away.

Dear God, the man was gorgeous—a perfect specimen of male fitness despite the awful-looking gash in his side. Her body seemed to be humming with an ancient tune that coaxed her to explore and memorize every silken inch of his well-hewned body.

Ryan filled a plate with toast and bacon, then sat down at the kitchen bar, wrapping his bare feet over the rungs of the bar stool.

He glanced up. "You going to eat?"

"Uh—yeah, yes, of course I'm going to eat." How could he be so nonchalant about his near nakedness? She busied herself filling a plate, then joined him at the bar. "What are your plans now that you're here?"

she asked him, congratulating herself on how relaxed and casual she sounded.

He rubbed the back of his neck. "I've been working out the details on the drive down here. Unfortunately, I don't have a foolproof plan mapped out. Too much depends on who I manage to contact. I know of three people who are working in this area, but at the moment I don't know exactly where they are. I'm going to need to make some very discreet phone calls, then wait for more information."

"Do you intend to wait here?"

He gave her a sharp glance. "Not if you don't want me here," he said in a flat voice. "You've done more than enough for me, getting me out of that mess in Dallas."

"Do you think anyone knows that I helped you?"

"I made damn sure no one knew where I was before I involved you in all of this. Don't worry."

She took a few bites and chewed, thinking about her options. "Then I don't see any reason why you can't stay here. You're probably safer keeping out of sight. Since nobody knows where I am, it should be—"

"What do you mean, nobody knows? Didn't you tell your parents, or your office, or your fiancé where you were going?"

"I only decided to come down here an hour before I left. I figured I'd call the office Monday morning and tell them I was taking a few days off. As for my family, I have a standing invitation to use the place whenever I want, so nobody thinks anything of my coming down here from time to time."

"What about this guy you plan to marry?"

"Since I don't consider what I do to be any of his business any longer, I saw no reason to inform him of my decision."

"Sounds like you had a doozy of a fight."

"I'd rather not discuss it."

Ryan yawned. "Sorry to be such lousy company, but I'm thinking of doing some serious sleeping. If you're sure you don't mind, I'd appreciate staying here. That way I can leave this number as a contact when they have any information for me."

Melody stacked their empty plates, poured the rest of the coffee in their cups, and busied herself with cleaning up the kitchen. "As soon as I finish here, I'll get a shower and maybe a quick nap before I head for the water. I intend to spend most of the day on the beach." She waved to the phone on the kitchen wall. "I'll be out of here in a few minutes so you can have the privacy you need."

By the time she was in the shower, Melody was seriously doubting her sanity. Why in the world would she invite Ryan O'Roarke, of all people, to stay with her at the beach house? Was she out of her mind? If one kiss could so totally unnerve her, what would being in his constant presence do to her peace of mind?

Her body still tingled at the thought of that kiss. What had happened to her? Why had she never responded to Winston in such an inflammable manner?

Drying off in front of the mirror, Melody shook her head, unable to come to grips with the sudden changes in her perception of herself and the people around her.

Maybe she'd stumbled into a parallel universe or something.

Now *there* was a rational explanation if she'd ever thought up one!

When she came out of the bathroom, she heard the low murmur of Ryan's voice in the kitchen. She slipped into the spare bedroom, leaving the larger one for Ryan. Feeling ridiculous, she actually locked her door before she dropped her towel and dug into her bag for a change of clothes. It was obvious that she didn't trust one of them, but she didn't want to dwell too closely on which one.

The sun was already setting by the time Melody left the jetties for the long walk back up the beach toward her grandparents' home. She'd had a wonderfully relaxing day. During the hottest part, she'd found shelter from the sun at one of the many hotel outdoor restaurants along the beach.

She'd chatted with several people she knew—locals she'd met on other visits—and caught up on what had been happening in their lives. When the sun was less intense she'd walked along the shallows, allowing the spent waves to wash across her ankles and feet.

The beach had a calming effect on her. In some way she couldn't explain, the atmosphere of fresh sea air, continuous flow of water and cheerful sunlight created a cleansing energy that chased away the turmoil of thoughts and feelings that had been churning within her.

The sky continued to darken into a deeper blue in the east as a counterpoint to the blaze of peach and gold filling the western sky. Despite the many hours and the miles she had walked, there was a spring to her step as she headed back to the beach house.

She wondered if Ryan was still at the house or whether he'd already left to meet his contacts. Now that she had taken the time to think about their night-long conversations, she felt much more mellow where he was concerned.

He wasn't the ogre she'd conjured in her mind over the years. As a matter of fact, several memories had popped into her head today, as though they'd been given permission to replace the less flattering ones....

She'd recalled the time in junior high school when Ryan had picked a fight with Billy Best because of something Billy had said about her. She no longer remembered what it was. What she remembered was Ryan defending and protecting her from Billy's callous remarks.

She'd also remembered the one and only time they had double-dated. Her date—Jeremy somebody—had come on a little strong and Ryan had pulled him aside and told him to cool it. She'd been so embarrassed that Ryan had witnessed her panic, she'd refused to go out with him in the group again.

She'd also refused to see Jeremy as well.

The sky was a black velvet backdrop for crystal-looking stars when she climbed the stairs at the front of the house. She was pushing the sliding-glass door open when Ryan loomed in front of her.

"Are you okay? I was beginning to worry about you."

He wore a pair of jeans and a T-shirt with splashes of color down the front proclaiming the joys of surfing.

"I'm fine. I was watching the dolphins frolic around the shrimp boats going out to sea, and the time slipped away from me." She edged past him warily, more aware of him than she'd ever been. Only then did she smell the aroma coming from the kitchen.

"Something smells delicious. I didn't realize how hungry I was until I got a whiff of it."

"I hope you don't mind. I borrowed the car and went to the grocery store, plus bought myself some clothes. I would have walked, but I didn't want to have to carry everything home in my arms."

She paused on her way to get cleaned up and changed and turned back toward him. She felt too mellow to be upset by anything. "I don't mind. Besides, having dinner waiting more than compensates for anything you might have done." She started toward the hallway, then paused once again. Sheba was rubbing against his leg and purring. "Did you make your necessary connections?"

"Not enough to get out of here, if that's what you mean." There was no emotion in his voice.

She smiled. "I didn't mean that. I was just curious, that's all. You're welcome to stay as long as you wish." She realized when she said it that she was sincere. She really didn't mind having Ryan O'Roarke back in her life. He'd always been a part of her existence, hovering on the edges. Even though she hadn't seen him in years, she'd continued to hear about him from his mother, although it was now obvious what Ryan had meant—his mother had no idea what he really did for the government.

"I'm going to get a quick shower," she added, then headed to the bathroom.

"Uh, Melody?" His voice sounded strange.

"Yes."

"I, uh, was expecting several calls today, so when the phone rang a few minutes ago, I, uh, answered it."

"Oh, that's okay. Did you tell them my grandparents were away?"

"It, uh, wasn't for them. It was for you."

"For me? But nobody knows I'm here."

He sighed, looking more and more uncomfortable. "I know. I mean, that's what he said... that he was trying to find you."

An ominous feeling seemed to fill her stomach.

"He?" she repeated faintly.

"He said he was your fiancé."

Oh, no. "You told him I was here?" She couldn't quite manage to sound casual.

"Yeah. He sounded worried so I thought I'd let him know you were all right."

She eyed him thoughtfully. "Did he ask who you were?"

She could almost swear that his cheeks turned a ruddy hue.

"Not exactly. I, uh, made it sound like I was a neighbor who'd popped by to repair something for your grandparents."

"It really doesn't matter. Our relationship is over. Winston knows that, but I guess he hasn't quite accepted it."

His eyes narrowed. "You're certain?"

"Oh, yes." She turned away. "I'm starved. I'll be back in a few minutes."

She retreated to the bathroom, quickly stripping and stepping into the shower. The high-level sunblock she'd continued to spread over her skin had done a great job protecting her. There was no redness or soreness as she sponged her body with soft lather and rinsed.

As soon as she got out of the tub, she towel-dried her hair and blew it dry with the hair-dryer. Her skin looked fresh and glowing. She peered into the mirror in surprise. She couldn't quite believe the change. Her eyes sparkled, her hair seemed to have acquired a healthy buoyancy and her face—why, her face seemed to shine like a woman in love, instead of a woman whose marriage plans had been terminated.

How could this be? Was she such a shallow person that her feelings were never truly engaged? Or was it possible that after seeing Winston without the virtues she had projected onto him, she had faced the fact that she hadn't known the man at all? How could she love a person who didn't exist?

She wrapped a towel around her body and darted down the hallway to her room. She found a floor-length, sleeveless beach cover to wear. She'd bought it because the blue-green swirls of color had reminded her of the ever-changing colors of the sea. When she slipped it on, it gently flowed down her body, a side slit to the thigh giving her room to walk comfortably.

She returned to the living room, saying, "I feel several pounds lighter without all the sand. I hope—" She came to an abrupt halt and stared at the transformation the room had undergone since she'd left.

Ryan had set a glass table in front of the windows. He'd arranged some flowers and candles around the two place mats and settings. In addition, he'd put on some background music that flowed into the room— the darkened room—creating an intimacy that was irresistibly compelling.

She heard the kitchen screen close just as she realized that Ryan wasn't in the room. He was only now emerging with a platter of charcoal-broiled steaks. "Ahh, there you are," he said cheerfully. "You couldn't have timed it better. Hope you're hungry. I got a little carried away at the grocery store. I must have been hungrier than I thought."

He paused by the table, set the platter down, and reached for a bottle of wine nearby. He poured a rich red wine into their glasses. The filled glasses glowed in the candlelight like lustrous rubies.

"You didn't need to go to so much trouble," she said, feeling uneasy.

"I didn't. The meal's very simple, really. Besides, I haven't had much chance to relax and enjoy an evening with a beautiful woman for longer than I can remember. I've been looking forward to it.''

Her uneasiness grew. "Uh, Ryan, I'm not sure—''

"Here,'' he said, taking her hand and leading her to the table. "I want you to try this wine and see what you think.'' He picked up both glasses and gave her one of them. He touched his glass to hers. "Here's to new beginnings for old and treasured friendships.'' The smile he gave her reflected a rakish tenderness that caused her to catch her breath.

The man was stunning when he put himself out to be charming. She felt her resistance receding and her uneasiness slipping away.

"Hmm, it's very good,'' she said.

"Good. Here—'' he pulled out her chair "—let's eat.''

Later, Melody couldn't remember what the meal tasted like or how much she had eaten. All she knew was that Ryan had captivated her with wry and humorous renderings of various events in his life.

She found herself gazing at him in fascination. How could such an obnoxious little boy, such a cocky teenager, turn into such an attractive, exciting man? She became mesmerized by the way the light from the candle seemed to be reflected in his clear gaze.

When they finished eating, they made short work of clearing the table and cleaning the kitchen. Afterward, they took the wine and their glasses out on the porch to enjoy the view of the ocean and starry sky.

Ryan led her to the glider that hung from the porch ceiling by strong chains. They sat side by side, facing the surf.

"This is so beautiful," she said softly. "I always seem to forget when I'm busy with work just how peaceful the beach is, and what a calming effect it has on me."

"I'm glad it worked its magic on you. You were pretty stressed last night."

She took a sip of her wine. "I know."

Time passed without Melody feeling the need to break the silence between them. It felt good to share the night with a friend. There. She'd said it. Ryan probably knew her as well, if not better, than anyone. She remembered what he said about wanting her to share what was bothering her.

She turned her head and contemplated his strong profile. She could see only hints of the boy he had been. "Ryan?"

"Mmm?"

"How do you know when a relationship is going to work out and become permanent and when it isn't?"

He glanced at her wineglass, then grinned disarmingly. "Well," he drawled, "the first thing I do is look into my crystal ball, then I have someone read my tarot cards, commission to have both of our astrological charts done, check out the tea leaves—"

She made a face at him and he laughed. "Be serious, O'Roarke. I want to have a serious, philosophical discussion about relationships. Indulge me."

"Oh, in that case we'll need another bottle of wine. Hold on, I'll be right back."

Melody couldn't understand why he felt the need for more wine, considering the fact that she was feeling quite mellow and relaxed already. Maybe he was the kind of person who had trouble talking about his feelings. Usually, she did, too... but not tonight. Tonight she felt as though she could tell him everything—every little thing—about herself. She knew he would understand.

Good ol' Ryan. Her childhood friend.

"Here we go," he said, filling both their glasses before she could tell him that she wasn't the one who needed another glass of wine.

Oh, well, it didn't matter.

She turned in the swing so that she could see him without turning her head. "Does it embarrass you to talk about your love life?" she asked sympathetically.

He laughed; a sure sign she was right, she decided. "I wasn't aware we were. Actually, my life-style doesn't encourage much of a love life."

She patted his hand. "That's all right. I've recently discovered that forming a permanent relationship is really difficult. I had no idea how difficult."

He stared out at the water. "I'm not sure I'd know if a relationship could become something permanent, since I haven't run into that kind."

She nodded wisely. "You're lucky. I thought I'd found exactly what I wanted." She sighed. "Then I discovered that I'd made up most of it."

"Tell me," he said in a coaxing, sympathetic tone.

She looked at him thoughtfully. She knew that she truly wanted to tell him what had happened. He'd understand, she was sure of it.

"All right. A little over a year ago Winston Townsend came to work at our firm. He was everything I wanted to find in a man. By that, I mean he was a man who I found to be interesting, amusing, literate, intelligent—all the traits I knew would make me happy."

"So you let him know that—"

"No, of course I didn't let him know anything. I waited and I got to know him better. We worked together on a couple of matters, and then one day he asked me out for dinner. That's how it started."

He frowned. "It? Can you be a little more specific here? What is 'it'? An affair?"

"Not an affair, silly. You know me better than that!"

He leaned toward her and it was only then that Melody noticed his arm was resting on the back of the glider behind her head. "Do I?" he whispered, and placed a kiss on her earlobe.

She shivered. "I don't believe in getting carried away and having sex with someone just because I happen to find them attractive. We would have to be serious enough to be—"

"Engaged?"

"Well, I suppose that would be acceptable," she said slowly. "Except that in our case—I mean, Winston and me—well . . . I didn't feel comfortable about the idea."

His smile flashed. "Are you saying that you've never made love with Winston?"

"That's right," she nodded primly. "I mean, it isn't as though we ever sat down and discussed the matter, or anything. He just never pushed for more intimacy and I was comfortable with the level we had."

"Comfortable?"

"Yes. Why do you say it like that?"

"I don't generally think of engagements as a particularly comfortable period in life. Exciting, maybe, passionate, most likely, but comfortable?"

"Maybe that's what was wrong," she said, saddened. "Maybe if we'd—"

"Oh, no! You were absolutely right! Sex doesn't change anything and it can blind you to other areas where there might be problems."

"That's what I thought. I thought we needed the time to get to know each other. We were both so busy with our careers and we knew we'd have more time together once we were married." She sighed and rested her head against his shoulder. She rather liked the feeling of being curled up next to Ryan. Sometime during their conversation he'd taken her hand and was stroking it with his fingers.

She shivered.

He pulled her closer. "Are you getting cold?"

How could she be when his body radiated so much heat? She shook her head.

He kissed her brow, then allowed his lips to trail down to her cheek. "So what happened to make you decide to end the engagement?"

She was having trouble concentrating on the conversation. However, she knew this was very important. She needed to tell Ryan what had happened.

"The funniest thing. It's really so trite that it sounds like a cliché." She took another sip of her wine.

He brushed his lips across her cheek and whispered, "Tell me, love."

"He'd mentioned meeting his next door neighbor several months ago. I've seen her on a couple of occasions. She always seemed shy to me. Winston never mentioned her... until last night."

She took a deep breath before continuing. "It seems that she'd gotten into the habit of dropping by whenever he was home and talking with him. According to Winston, she'd been upset one particular evening and he'd let her share whatever had happened with him. He said that he'd attempted to console her, that one thing led to another and they ended up in bed together."

"Of course that's upsetting to you, I know. But at least he was honest enough to tell you—"

"That's just the point I tried to make with him. I might have better understood if he'd told me what had happened. I would have been hurt, but it wasn't as though they had planned it to happen."

"That's very mature of you."

She made a face. "Not really. But I think I could have dealt with it if he hadn't admitted that since that time they've continued to see each other. The only reason he told me now was because she had come by his condo a few minutes before he was to leave to pick me up and told him that she was pregnant. She suggested that he break off our engagement and marry her."

"I see."

"Only I discovered he didn't have any intention of breaking off our engagement. The only reason he told me was because he knew she would waste no time in informing me of their affair and he wanted to be the one to tell me. He said she didn't mean anything to him, that he wouldn't consider marrying her, but that if she was pregnant with his child, he'd take financial responsibility for it."

"What did you say?"

"Say?" She looked at him in surprise. "I didn't say anything. I just dumped my salad over his head and walked out of the restaurant."

Ryan threw back his head and laughed. "Would I have ever liked to have seen that!" he managed to say when he could get his breath. He gave her a quick kiss. "You haven't spoken to him since?"

"No. I assumed that he would understand that our engagement is over."

"Obviously he hopes to change your mind or he wouldn't have called."

"What is so galling is the fact that I never had a hint that he was seeing someone else. I knew he took a lot of work home, as I did, so we didn't see each other much during the week. He was, in effect, leading a double life. I guess he thought he could get away with it . . . and he did for several months."

"Oh, Tiny-Toon," he said, still chuckling. "I'm proud of you."

"You are?"

"I was afraid that all your natural impulses had been chased away by the prim little adult you've become." He kissed her again.

His kisses were very comforting. She slipped her hands up around his neck and returned his kisses. When he finally raised his head, both of them were breathing unevenly.

"You deserve better than that," he said.

"I couldn't agree with you more."

"You deserve so much love and devotion and loyalty. He was an idiot not to realize how much he had to lose."

"I'm just glad I found out now, before the wedding."

Ryan shifted, pulling her onto his thighs. "Me, too," he murmured, nuzzling her neck. "Me, too."

His next kiss was filled with purpose and passion. She gave a breathless moan and surrendered to the wonderful new feelings that seemed to be taking over her body. He slipped the top buttons on her beach cover open and cupped her breast through the filmy lace of her bra. His touch seemed to set her skin on fire. She arched into his hand.

With a twist of his fingers, he unfastened the front opening of her bra, freeing her to feel his heat against her bare skin. Suddenly she was on fire and couldn't seem to get close enough to him. She pushed at his shirt and he continued to unbutton her cover until it dropped away, pooling in her lap, leaving her upper body bare.

"Ah, Tiny-Toon," he whispered, "You are so damn beautiful you make me ache with it." He lowered his head and took the tip of her breast into his mouth. She felt the tug all the way through her body to a tingling spot at the apex of her thighs. She wriggled and he seemed to understand because he slipped his hand through the side slit of the skirt and placed his palm over the mound of soft hair covered in lace that seemed to be aching for his touch.

"Oh, Ryan," she whispered, shaking with need. "I need—I don't know—I want some . . . oo-oh, yes. Oh—" His kiss covered her soft cry as he slid her bikini panties off and began to stroke her in a rhythm that escalated to match the sharp movements of his tongue in her mouth.

She couldn't hold still. She rubbed her bare breasts against his hair-roughened chest, her sensitive nipples tingling with repeated pleasure. She was on fire and didn't know what to do to help. Once again his mouth found her breast and he tugged and suckled until she cried out. A sudden breath-grabbing moment and her body seemed to explode into an indescribable sensation as a convulsive rhythm from deep inside seemed to clench around his arousing fingers. She tightened her thighs and groaned as wave after wave of pleasure swept over her.

By the time she was conscious of her surroundings she discovered that Ryan had carried her as far as the front room of the cottage. He knelt, placing her on the rug. Drowsily she watched as he skinned out of his shirt and jeans. The faint light from outside gilded his body with a silvery sheen and she smiled up at him with pleased anticipation when he pulled the beach cover completely off her and lowered himself between her legs.

"I'm sorry, love. I know I'm rushing you, but—"

She gasped as she felt him pressing against her.

"Try to relax as much as possible," he whispered. He reached behind him and lifted one of her legs up around his waist. She moved the other one and heard him whisper "Good, sweetheart" as he began a steady pressure.

She could feel him now, much larger than his fingers—all sleek and primed—and she lifted her hips to receive him, suddenly impatient to have him buried deep inside her.

This was Ryan O'Roarke. Ryan, her love.

She clasped him to her as tightly as she could, reveling in the joy of his possession. He started to pull away, and she whispered "No!" fiercely before she realized that he wasn't really leaving her at all. Instead he was setting a tantalizing, teasing rhythm that brought her to another peak of sensation. She clamped her knees tightly against his sides while she found his mouth with hers and mimicked his actions with her tongue.

He stiffened before he hit a pounding rhythm of release that matched her convulsive movements, ending in one final surge that buried him deeply inside her.

He rolled so that his back was to the floor and she was sprawled on top of him. Her body still quivered in spasmodic jerks while she fought to regain her breath. "I'm too heavy," she managed to say.

Too winded to answer, Ryan just shook his head, holding her tightly against him, their bodies still coupled.

She must have dozed because the next thing she knew Ryan was carrying her once again, this time into the bathroom where he allowed her feet to rest on the floor while he adjusted the shower spray and stepped into the tub with her.

With a gentleness she'd never seen before in him, he bathed her, then rinsed her, kissing her everywhere he touched. He quickly soaped himself and she ran her hands lightly over his body as the sluicing water rinsed the soap away.

Her touch seemed magic, for he grew beneath her fingertips until he was hard and erect once again. This time she took the initiative, drying him off very carefully, paying close attention to detail and delighting in the way his flesh leapt with every touch.

As though he'd reached the limit of his endurance, he scooped her up and carried her into her bedroom. This time when he placed her on the bed, his mouth continued the exploration he'd begun in the shower.

When his tongue touched her in her most intimate place she quivered, jerking her knees as though to close them, but his body blocked her efforts. He took his time, teasing her, nibbling and stroking until she was clenching the sheet beneath her with both hands.

By the time he entered her, she was sobbing with need that he seemed to know how to assuage. She couldn't hold still. Her arms and legs restlessly caressed him as she kissed him everywhere she could—on his neck, his chest, the flat coins of his nipples. Something she'd never known existed had been activated inside her—demanding satisfaction while seeking to give satisfaction.

She cried out at her climax, feeling it surge through her body from her toes upward. Ryan's release seemed to be triggered by her explosive response and he rode the wave of his own climax while she took in gulping breaths of air.

She'd not known how it could be. She might never have known if Ryan hadn't come back to Dallas.

Melody fell asleep in his arms, her body sated, her mind at ease.

Chapter Five

She didn't want to move. The long walk on the beach yesterday and the unaccustomed swimming had exhausted her. Melody lay snuggled in bed, content to rest against the warm, muscled body curled around her.

Her eyes flicked open. Warm body?

No. Oh, no, it couldn't be. She couldn't possibly have—

A well-shaped hand lazily squeezed her breast, the fingers brushing over her nipple until it drew up into a tight bud of pebbled flesh.

A tingling between her legs reminded her of how easily she had been aroused...was still being aroused. She caught her breath in an attempt to muffle a moan.

Ryan trailed his hand lazily down her stomach and abdomen to her nest of curls where he began a circular massage. She squeezed her thighs together, trapping his hand.

"Are you sore, love?" he whispered drowsily in her ear. "Was I too rough with you last night?"

How could she think when he continued to touch her like that? Her body was already adjusting to his signals, heating up, throbbing with the familiar rhythm he'd begun—slow and sensuous.

Because she was tucked into the curl of his knees she knew he was as affected by what he was doing as she was. She squirmed, pressing against him.

"I don't want to hurt you," he murmured.

She reached down and touched him from between her own legs, guiding him into the position that gave so much pleasure.

He needed no more coaxing. From this angle he seemed to go higher and deeper than ever. He set a lazy rhythm that she matched, while he continued to stroke her breasts and stomach. Each time he made love to her seemed better than the time before. Each new movement, each position, managed to arouse her to higher and higher peaks until she was sure she'd soon explode into a million tiny pieces of pleasure.

The lazy stroking got to them both and Melody cried out when he pulled away from her and turned her to face him. His face was taut with passion, his eyes fierce with his need for control. He lifted her so that she was sitting on top of him, facing him, before he rejoined the two of them. He placed his hands on each side of her hips and showed her how to control their pace.

With a grin, she began to move over him. He gave her an answering grin as he pulled her forward and pressed her breasts together, his mouth and tongue caressing their pink plumpness. Once again he'd shown her yet another way to take and give pleasure. This one caught her on fire quickly. She delighted in her freedom of movement and she rode him to a rapid, explosive finish that left her sprawled limply across his muscled frame.

"Oh, Tiny-Toon . . . you've done . . . me in, love . . . I don't think . . . I'll be able to . . . move for at least . . . a week."

She rested her head on his chest, over his heart. It was thumping with great enthusiasm against her ear. "Who cares?" she murmured when she could get enough air in her lungs to speak. "Nobody knows—"

A loud knocking at the back door interrupted her and she groaned. "I bet it's one of the neighbors checking on the place." She sighed and slid off of him, shoving her hair out of her face. "I'll have to explain who I am so they won't think we broke in."

She grabbed her short terry-cloth robe and hastily pulled it around her, knotting the sash around her waist. She glanced down at Ryan who looked gorgeously wicked sprawled across her bed. "Hold that pose. I'll be right back," she said with a grin.

"You'll be the death of me, woman," he growled, but his grin encouraged her to believe he wasn't complaining, and the look he gave her made her cheeks flame.

The pounding at the door continued. She shut the door to the bedroom and hurried down the hallway. "I'm coming," she yelled, rushing to the door. She unlocked the door and swung it open, saying, "It's all right. I'm family and I—"

Her mouth continued to hang open but nothing came out. She was looking at Winston Townsend on the other side of the screen. "Winston?" she managed to whisper through lips that had suddenly gone numb.

"We need to talk, Melody. I can't believe how childish you've been—creating a scene in the restaurant, running off like a rebellious teenager." He opened the screen door and stepped inside. "We're both adults and I know that if we sit down and rationally discuss the matter you'll see that there's no reason for you to be so upset. We're to be married in less than two months—"

She ignored him and asked, "How did you get here?"

"I flew into Harlingen, then caught a shuttle bus to the island. I thought it would be a good idea to talk to you before you built some kind of ridiculous case against me. As soon as you get dressed, I'll drive you back to Dallas. What were you thinking of, dashing off like that? Where's your sense of responsibility—to me, to the firm, to our plans?"

"*My* sense of responsibility! Surely you don't think *your* behavior has been a model of responsible living!"

"I'll concede the point, of course. Yes, I've made mistakes. After all, I'm a human being and when that young, attractive woman made it clear that she found me attractive, as well, it became very difficult to ignore her. She never asked anything of me. She was content to see me whenever I was available. Of course, I didn't mean for it to go so far. I'm not convinced that she's actually pregnant, but whatever happens where she's concerned has nothing to do with us and shouldn't change our plans in the slightest."

He strode past her into the kitchen. "I need some coffee. I don't think I slept over a couple of hours last night. I spent all day yesterday looking for you, then trying to decide what to do. Once I made up my mind to follow you down here, I couldn't sleep at all. I ended up taking the first flight out this morning."

Efficient as always, Winston found the coffee and began to fill the pot with water while Melody continued to stand there watching him in disbelief.

"It was a good thing I happened to remember how much you like coming to the island. Otherwise I would still be calling your friends and family, looking for you."

"You called my family?"

"Well, no, not yet. At least, I decided to call here before I tried your parents' place. If your neighbor hadn't been here, I would have notified your parents that you seemed to be missing."

"That would have certainly endeared you to them."

"It was the truth."

"Why would you needlessly upset them?"

"I wouldn't have considered it needless." He reached in the cabinet for a cup. "Care for some coffee?"

"I have a hunch I'm going to need some."

"Really, Melody. There's no reason for you to be so dramatic about this. After all, sex is a part of life. It's a normal, natural function that can be enjoyed be-

tween adults without either party becoming emotionally involved."

"It sounds to me like your neighbor might argue the
point there."

"Yes. Well, I'll have to deal with that, of course.
But I think that..." He paused in the act of walking
into the front room to sit at the bar and stared.

Melody picked up her cup and followed him, her
gaze looking past him to whatever had caught his attention. Ryan's jeans, briefs and T-shirt lay in a
crumpled heap on the floor, right next to her abandoned shift.

She watched Winston turn to her as though in slow
motion, his mouth agape with astonishment. She
looked back at the incriminating pile of discarded
clothes before she walked over to the bar and sat
down, taking a sip of her coffee without meeting
Winston's accusing gaze.

"Would you mind explaining to me what in the hell
is going on here?"

She thought about that for a moment, then took
another sip of coffee before replying, "Yes, I would
mind."

His eyes narrowed and he sat down on the other bar
stool. "I believe you owe me some kind of explanation."

"Do you? Funny. That's not how I see it."

Melody couldn't believe how good she felt at the
moment. She couldn't remember a time when she'd
felt so wonderfully free and unencumbered... almost
uninhibited. Making love with Ryan had had a singu-

lar effect on her—freeing her from constraints and restrictions that had bound her for most of her life.

"Melody, I—"

"Do I smell coffee?" A baritone voice interrupted Winston, and Ryan sauntered into the room wearing a towel rather precariously draped around his hips. "Boy, could I use a cup!" He was almost to the bar before he stopped and ran his gaze over Winston. He flashed his cockiest grin and said, "You must be Winston Townsend. I've heard so much about you." He stuck out his hand. "Glad we had this opportunity to meet."

Winston's face filled with angry color as he stared at Ryan's hand like it were a snake ready to strike. When he made no move to accept the proffered hand, Ryan shrugged and went into the kitchen. He poured himself a cup of coffee and returned to the bar. Since there were no more bar stools, he contented himself with leaning against the bar, his chest lightly touching Melody's shoulder. He appeared totally unconcerned that his towel seemed to be losing its battle with gravity.

"Who are you?"

"Oh! I'm Ryan O'Roarke. I spoke to you on the phone yesterday."

Winston's jaw tightened. "You're the neighbor?" His tone reflected his disbelief.

"I used to be. Actually, Melody and I grew up together."

"Really? It seems strange she's never mentioned you."

Melody felt as though she were in the middle of a tennis match. With a man on each side of her, it was hard to keep up with their verbal volleys without getting whiplash.

Surprisingly enough, and she knew that given time to think about it she'd be shocked by her own behavior, she was enjoying the exchange. If anything, she felt a slight—a very slight—sense of pity for Winston. There was absolutely no doubt in her mind who was going to win this particular exchange.

She sipped her coffee and waited.

"Ah, Tiny-Toon. I'm crushed. How could you—"

"What did you call her?"

"Tiny-Toon. A little play of words on her name. Of course she's always hated the nickname," he said, nonchalantly placing his palm on the back of her neck and massaging the muscles there. "So I suppose I'll have to—"

She leaned into his hand. "Actually, I've grown to like the name in the past couple of days. Maybe it's because I haven't heard it in so long, and then again—"

"I don't give a damn what you call her or whether she likes it or not. What I want to know is what in the hell you think you're doing, staying here with her like this!"

Ryan grinned. "I don't have to think about it, I *know* what I'm doing here."

She bit her lip and concentrated on the steam rising from her cup.

"Are you aware that Melody is engaged to marry me in two months?"

"So?"

"I think that gives me a certain right to know exactly what has been going on between the two of you."

"Oh! Of course. I can see your point," Ryan said, then was distracted when his towel slipped another few inches. He casually caught it in front of him just as it would have fallen to the floor, exposing his naked hip and thigh, then hitched the towel around his waist and tied it more securely before he looked back at Winston. "Well, there's really nothing for you to get excited about. I mean, after all, sex is a part of life. It's a normal, natural function that can be enjoyed between adults without either party becoming emotionally involved. We all understand that."

He picked up his cup and drank the rest of the liquid.

Winston's face turned a very unhealthy, mottled color. "Melody! Did you and this man actually—? Is he saying that you and he—?" His mouth kept working, but he seemed to have run out of words.

"Do you have a problem with that?" she asked him.

She watched as all the evidence—the abandoned clothes, her hair-tousled condition, Ryan's battle with the elusive towel—coalesced into unmistakable and irrefutable proof in his mind. He paled, his face looking grim. Contempt seemed to fill his expression. He curled his lip and spat out the word "Slut!"

Only a blur of movement gave Melody any indication that Ryan had heard Winston's gutteral obscenity. By the time she blinked, Winston had been shoved against the wall, several inches off the floor. The only thing holding him there was the back of Ryan's forearm across Winston's throat. The poor towel never stood a chance. As she watched Winston's face turn an amazing puce color, she couldn't resist taking a peek at Ryan's bared bottom, the only part of his body not tanned. The muscles were taut and looked hard as stone.

Reluctantly she forced herself to return her gaze to Winston and to listen to what Ryan was saying between clenched teeth. "Listen, you worthless piece of cow dung, you are going to get the hell out of here right now, do you hear me? Or I'm going to chew you up and spit you out in so many pieces that your own mother won't recognize you. Do you understand me?"

Winston made a gurgling sound deep in his throat.

"I sincerely hope—for your sake—that means yes. I don't want to ever hear you using that word, or anything like it, when you speak of Melody. She has done nothing that you haven't been doing since you've been engaged to her. I've never believed in the old double standard myself." He eased his hold so that Winston could suck air into his lungs and allowed him to slide down the wall until his feet touched the floor.

"Now, then. When I remove my arm, I want you to walk out that door and keep on walking. You'll find a taxi service a few blocks down on Padre Boulevard. I'm certain you'll find they are eager to take you to the airport for the right price. Do you understand me?"

Winston nodded, audibly swallowing.

Ryan smiled. "Good. I've always had a real knack for communicating." He stepped away from Winston and walked over to the pile of clothing he'd left on the floor the night before. He pulled on his jeans for all the world as though he were alone in the room.

The instant he stepped away from Winston, Winston shot past Melody and was through the screen door and down the steps before the screen door swung closed again.

Melody went into the kitchen and brought the coffeepot out to refill their cups.

"I'm sorry, Tiny-Toon," Ryan said from close behind her.

She didn't look at him. "Why should you be sorry?"

He sank onto the bar stool next to her, previously occupied by Winston. "For manhandling him. It's just that—"

"I'm glad you did. He was being a jerk. If I'd known how, I would have enjoyed punching him in the face, myself. I thought you used real restraint. You didn't leave a mark on him."

He watched her closely. "You used to get furious whenever I picked a fight with anybody. You used to—"

"Be a child who didn't understand very much about anything."

He shook his head, as though bewildered by her calm expression. "He had no right to call you—"

"He can call me whatever he feels like, but calling me something doesn't make me one. I know who I am and what I am. Winston's opinion means absolutely nothing to me."

Ryan had never been so uncertain of her mood before. She didn't sound upset, nor did she look upset. He took her hand and gave a light tug that turned the bar stool until she was facing him. She watched him with amused expectancy and Ryan suddenly realized that he'd given himself away completely this time.

"You know, don't you?" he muttered.

If possible, her eyes brightened another notch. "I should have known long before this. The clues have all been there if I'd only known how to interpret them."

He took her other hand and placed both of them across his palm, marveling at how delicate they looked there. "Yeah, well—" he shrugged, without looking at her "—it wasn't anything I could control."

She reached up and cupped his face with her hands. "I feel like a blind person who was suddenly given sight. It's been there, all along, if I'd only understood. Why didn't you tell me?"

He could feel his ears tingling with heat. He forced himself to meet her gaze. "I didn't figure it was anything you'd want to hear."

"But you never tried! I mean, all those years, O'Roarke. We were almost the same age, we were in the same grade at school, we grew up together, and not once did you ever give a hint about your feelings for me."

Her face was filled with wonder and tenderness. Most crucial to him at the moment was the love that made her eyes sparkle and glisten as though they were filled with a skyful of stars.

"Actually," he drawled, "I gave you all kinds of hints. Unfortunately you called it terrorizing and humiliating you."

She laughed, a soft chuckle that seemed to fill his heart with joy. Such an intimate, private little sound to share. "You never asked me out on a date. Not once."

"And take a chance on being rejected? Are you kidding?"

"I guess it's all right to tell you that I was always jealous of Sylvia Stanton. I mean, there she was dating the campus jock, making a scene at the game when you were hurt—"

"How did you find that out?"

She eyed him uncertainly. "What do you mean?"

"The only hope I ever had that you cared anything at all about me was when I heard that when the officials carried me off the field unconscious you quietly fainted in the stands."

She looked at him, horrified. "Who told you that!"

"My mom."

"Your mom has a big mouth."

"She thought it was cute."

"She would."

"I meant to come back sooner, you know," he admitted. "I'm not certain where the years went. I wanted to get established. I knew you were taking graduate courses. I thought I'd give you some time on your own, then come back and tell you—" He couldn't seem to force out the rest of what he needed to say.

"Yes?"

Ryan scooped her off the bar stool and strode over to the sofa. He sat down with her on his lap. "I, uh, wouldn't want you to have to scrap all your plans for a September wedding. I mean, as long as you've got things moving toward that date, maybe we could..." Once again, he faltered.

"Yes?"

"Damn, I've been less nervous than this facing down drug lords," he muttered as though to himself. "Okay." He took a deep breath. "Will you allow me to substitute as the groom at your September wedding?"

"C'mon, O'Roarke, you're nobody's substitute. You never have been. You never will be."

"You're avoiding the question," he said gruffly.

"I'm not avoiding. I'm waiting...rather patiently, if you'll notice." She stretched her arms high over her head, then casually allowed them to drape around his neck. "I'm getting hungry. Would you like for me to make us some breakfast?"

He shook his head. "You're going to always keep me on my toes, aren't you? Never cut me any slack at all." He hugged her to him, holding her tightly against him. "Oh, Tiny-Toon, you have no idea what last night...and this morning...meant to me. Not even my wildest fantasies were so fulfilling. To finally be able to make love to you was a dream come true for me."

"It was very special for me, too. Now I understand why I never wanted to go any farther with another man, including Winston. On some level I must have known that it wouldn't be the same with anyone else. It had to be with you."

She was being so fearlessly honest. He owed her the same. "Oh, Melody, I...l-love you so damned much!"

"Picked up a stutter, have you, O'Roarke?"

He began to laugh. "At least I managed to get it out. I've never said it before. It felt very strange."

"Maybe it will come easier for you with practice."

"Maybe." He picked her up and started down the hallway. "I'm all for practice, Tiny-Toon. I may not get back to Dallas until time for the wedding. Will you wait for me?"

She smoothed his cheek with her thumb as he lowered her to the bed and stretched out beside her. "I've waited for you all my life. I just didn't know it until this weekend. I'll wait for you forever, if need be. I've suddenly discovered a fascination with one particular swaggering, macho male."

He untied the sash of her robe and bared her body to his gaze. "Me? Macho?" He leaned over and kissed her stomach. "Swaggering?" He nuzzled her breast. "You must have me confused with some other guy."

"Impossible. There's nobody else like you. Thank God I discovered that before it was too late." She tugged at his jeans, suddenly impatient for another practice lesson in loving.

Epilogue

"Have you heard anything from Ryan, dear?" Melody adjusted her wedding veil to hide her smile. Her mother's question couldn't have been more casual, but Melody knew better.

Assessing her image in the full-length mirror of the dressing room at the church, Melody said, "Ryan will be here, Mother. Don't worry."

"Oh, I'm not worried," her mother replied, ignoring the fact that her concern had slipped into her tone of voice. "I'm sure everything's going to be just fine. I mean, if there were any problem at all, he would have let you know... wouldn't he?"

"He'll be here," Melody repeated the soothing litany for her mother.

Gladys Young sighed. "Well, of course you're right. It's just that all of this is rather confusing. I mean, here you were just a few months ago—"

"Two months ago."

"Two months ago planning your wedding to Winston and pushing yourself to the limits to make partner of your firm by the time you were thirty. Now, here you are—leaving the firm, marrying Ryan O'Roarke, and moving to Washington." Her worried blue eyes met Melody's in the mirror. "I suppose that's the biggest shock of all. Debra and Phil were as startled as your dad and I to learn that you and Ryan were getting married." She narrowed her eyes slightly in thought before asking fretfully, "This isn't some kind of practical joke, is it, pretending to marry Ryan?"

"If it was, Mother, I've spent a great deal of money on a wedding and reception just to play a prank, wouldn't you say?"

"Oh! Oh, my, yes..." Her voice trailed off. "It's just that you and Ryan never got along as children. Why, you were forever complaining about how much you hated him."

Melody met her own gaze in the mirror. This time she made no effort to hide her smile. "That should have been a clue to everybody that I had tremendous feelings for him, even if I didn't have enough experience to know what I was feeling."

"He used to make you cry a great deal."

"That's true."

"I just hope he won't treat you shabbily now. I know that Debra and I are great friends, but I was never very comfortable around Ryan, even when he was a child."

"It will all work out okay, Mother. Wait and see."

Her mother stepped back and looked at Melody. "There. You look absolutely beautiful, darling. Oh, I'm so proud of you." She dabbed her handkerchief at the corner of her eye. "No. I am not going to get all maudlin. I'm just so happy for you. If Ryan is the man you want, then I'll accept your choice."

"Thank you, Mother," Melody responded dryly.

"I mean, *you* have to live with him, not me."

"True."

"Do you think he still keeps collections of lizards and spiders and things?"

"He solemnly assured me that he gave up those particular treasures by the time he reached high school."

"Oh, good! What I mean is, I'm glad to know he's found other hobbies."

Melody chuckled. "So am I."

Gladys glanced around the room nervously. "Well . . . if you're all ready, I think I'll pop out and check with your father to see if Ryan's gotten here."

"We have another fifteen minutes, you know."

"I know. I just thought—"

"Go ahead. I'd like to see you a little more relaxed today. If talking to Dad will help, please go."

Gladys met Melody's gaze in the mirror once more. "I know I'm being ridiculous. It's the bride who's supposed to be nervous at a time like this. You've been the calmest one of all of us."

Melody smiled and squeezed her mother's hand. "This is the happiest day of my life, Mother. Never doubt it."

Gladys quickly dabbed at the corner of her eyes again and said, "Yes, well, I'll see you in a few minutes, dear."

As soon as her mother left the room, Melody allowed herself to relax. She'd waited as long as she dared to put on her dress because she knew she wouldn't sit down and take the chance of wrinkling the satin. Now she wandered over to the window that overlooked the parking lot and watched the line of cars turning in. The church was going to be full.

Her thoughts returned to the recent past—to her short time on the island with Ryan.

He'd received word by Sunday evening that a pickup point had been decided upon for midnight that night. She'd driven him up the island to a deserted part of the beach and they had sat out on the sand and watched the full moon climb into the sky while they'd waited.

"I'm still wondering if I'm dreaming," he said, his arms wrapped around her as she sat between his legs with her back leaning against his chest. "I've practiced so many roles in my career, but I've never pictured myself engaged or getting married."

"Is this going to be difficult for you, Ryan?"

"Difficult, maybe. Impossible, no. As soon as I get back to Washington I'll ask for the time off. I'll also talk to them about taking a different type of assignment, one that won't have me living all over this side of the world."

"You'd hate a desk job."

"There are others. Besides, I wouldn't be much good to them if all I wanted to do was get back home to you." He nuzzled her ear. "I wish I didn't have to leave you now."

"I'm just glad you're going to be safe. I can't tell you how scary it was to see your injuries."

"Don't worry about me. I'm tough."

"Oh, I know that. Remember, I know you very, very well."

He nibbled on her earlobe before whispering, "You know me even better after this weekend. Here I was with a woman determined to hang on to her virginity only to discover that once she's aroused, she's insatiable. How can I leave you after making that startling discovery?"

"Hopefully your memories will coax you to come back as soon as you can."

"Don't ever doubt that, I—"

Melody had her head resting on his shoulder. When he broke off speaking, she raised her head and looked out toward the waves where he was staring. Her heart bounded in her chest as two sleek, dark shapes rose out of the water and moved toward them.

"Wha—?" she started to say when Ryan lifted her to her feet as he stood up.

"My ride's here."

"Your ride? I thought you were to be picked up by boat."

He nodded toward the horizon. "Oh, it's out there, all right. They just don't want to come in close enough to be noticed."

He took her hand as he spoke and led her toward the surf.

One of the shadows spoke. "Is that you, Shadowboxer?"

"Yep," Ryan replied, continuing toward the speaker. "Did you bring me a wet suit?"

The man handed over a waterproof bag. Ryan shed his clothes down to his briefs and pulled on the suit. He turned back to Melody and she stared at the transformation. It was more than what he was wearing. His face looked different—hard, relentless and determined. He gave her a quick kiss, hugged her and said, "I'll call you." Then he turned away and the three dark-suited men disappeared into the water. It had all taken place in a matter of minutes. For a moment Melody felt as though she'd dreamed the whole thing.

Ryan scaring her half out of her wits in his parents' home.

Ryan making love to her in ways she could never have imagined.

Ryan offering to marry her.

Ryan admitting his love for her.

Ryan disappearing into the Gulf without giving her a clue as to when she would see or hear from him again.

Ryan—the man she loved....

Now as she stared out the window and watched friends and relatives walk toward the church, she knew that all of it was very real. She and Ryan were meant to be together. Nothing or no one could change that fact.

Ryan leapt out of the cab and dashed toward the back of the church where he knew he was supposed to meet his best man, a college buddy he'd contacted several weeks ago, and the pastor.

He'd been in meetings and more meetings for weeks, breaking away earlier today, insisting he had to get to Dallas. To save time, he'd caught a private flight with a friend. He'd dressed at a private hangar and caught a cab.

Ryan paused long enough to smooth his hair and straighten his tie before calmly opening the door. The pastor was the first to see him. Reverend Downly had known Ryan since he was twelve.

"Glad you could make it," Reverend Downly said with a big grin, holding out his hand in welcome.

Ryan grabbed his hand. "No more than I am, sir. Have you had to hold the service?"

He shook his head. "No. Another minute and we would have had to signal the organist for an extra song or two. Are you ready?"

Ryan rolled his shoulders to ease some of the tension there. "That I am."

His friend Bret patted him on the shoulder. "Good to see you, man. It's been a while."

"I know. I really appreciate your flying in from L.A. to help me out."

Bret grinned. "I wouldn't have missed this for the world. I happen to remember Melody from college. Never could get her to give me the time of day."

Ryan chuckled. "I know the feeling well. I still wonder at times if I'm dreaming. If I am, don't wake me up."

"When you get a load of all the people out there waiting for us, you may feel like you're in some kind of nightmare."

"Ready, gentlemen?" Reverend Downly asked.

They both nodded, their smiles replaced by the properly solemn demeanor presently needed.

Ryan walked to the altar of the church and turned, facing the center aisle. His arrival signaled the organist who stopped playing the soft background music that had filled the church and began the music to accompany the maid of honor to her place. Once she was in place, the traditional Mendelssohn music began, announcing the bride. The congregation stood and turned toward the back of the church.

That's when Ryan saw her for the first time since that midnight goodbye on the beach. A rush of feeling swept over him with so much intensity it almost brought him to his knees. His heart seemed to swell with a surge of love for this woman out of all others.

She stood beside her father, her fingers resting lightly on his sleeve, and slowly advanced toward Ryan. Their gazes locked and never wavered. He felt as though they had made the necessary link—as though their hearts, their very breaths, were synchronized.

When he took her hand in his, a bolt of energy shot through and around him, encircling them both. The entire service was a blur to him, vaguely making an impression on him while he was totally and consciously aware of Melody beside him. Her voice sounded sure and very calm. When it was time to kiss her—at long last—he gathered her into his arms as though she was fragile and priceless. He kissed her slowly, thoroughly, and with unmistakable intent.

He'd never been good with words, but he hoped to show her how much he'd missed her, how difficult it had been to go without seeing her, and how completely and totally he loved her.

When he finally raised his head, the congregation was laughing and applauding, while Melody looked adorably flushed and disconcerted.

Too many hours passed before he was alone with her and could kiss her in the way he wanted to. They were in one of the suites of the Crescent Court and the door had barely closed behind the bellman when Ryan reached for her.

"Come here, you," he growled, pulling her to him.

She showed no hesitation. Instead she wound her arms around his neck and responded with heart-stopping enthusiasm.

"God, but I've missed you," he whispered when he caught his breath. "I don't ever want to spend this much time apart again."

She grinned up at him. "Did everything arrive all right?"

He nodded. "Yes, but I had to put most of your furniture in storage for now. However, Sheba has trained me to her routine and has me leaping to obey her every whim." Unable to resist, he gave her another kiss before saying, "We'll go house-hunting when we get back to Washington."

"Did you get the appointment you wanted?"

"After a great deal of arm-twisting. I finally managed to convince the powers that be to use me as a trainer rather than out in the field." He gave her a cocky grin. "They finally saw it my way, especially when I'd managed to discover who betrayed me. The department owed me one."

"My hero," she said, giving him a lingering kiss. She turned away. "Will you please unbutton me? Mother did the honors earlier."

Playing his brand new role of dutiful husband, Ryan began to work the tiny buttons through the loops. "Your parents looked shell-shocked, didn't they?"

She glanced over her shoulder. "How about yours?"

"Oh, mine were delighted, but not all that surprised. Dad's known for years how I felt about you."

"Too bad he never shared the information."

"Where do you think I got my early training for my present job?"

The dress began to fall away from her shoulders. Ryan assisted the process with commendable speed. She stepped out of the billowing skirts and underskirts and turned to him.

He thought he'd remembered how she looked, but he'd forgotten that special glow in her face and that exceptionally bright shine in her eyes. He forced himself to concentrate on other things before he behaved like a caveman and dragged her into the other room to the giant bed awaiting them.

"How did everything go at the office?"

"I told you most of it over the phone earlier. Winston played his role quite well, seemingly happy that you and I had finally recognized and acknowledged how we felt about each other. Everyone else thought it terribly romantic how you swept me off my feet and convinced me to marry you."

"I still can't believe you protected that louse by not telling them the truth."

She stroked his cheek. "But I did tell the truth. You swept me off my feet and—"

"I wouldn't have gotten the time of day from you if Winston hadn't been such a jerk."

"Then we have a great deal to thank him for, don't we?"

Startled by the thought, he paused for a moment then grinned. "Come to think of it, you may have a point there."

"I hope that Winston finds as much happiness as we have."

To hell with it. He was probably a throwback to caveman logic, anyway, Ryan decided, and scooped her up into his arms. "I was going to show you how civilized I could be by indulging in polite conversation, but I'm not able to ignore what you look like in those minuscule scraps of lace you call underwear," he muttered.

His jacket and tie had been discarded and his shirt hung open. She rubbed her breasts against his chest, almost purring. "I'm *sooo* glad they have that effect on you. That's exactly why I'm wearing them!" They were both laughing when they landed on the bed. What better way to start a marriage than with love and laughter?

* * * * *

Dear Reader,

Isn't summer great? It's a time to slow down a little from our hectic schedules, a time to curl up with a good book and get lost in another world.

Of course I find a time to curl up with a good book all year-round. I'm a real addict when it comes to involving myself in imaginary people's lives and problems.

Maybe that's why I became a writer. People interest me. What makes them tick? Why do they act a certain way? And what causes a person to fall in love?

It's wonderful to know that there are as many stories to be told as there are people to live them, with all kinds of personalities and foibles and fantasies.

Hope you enjoy this summer's read from our *Sizzlers* line. They're guaranteed to heat you up and curl your toes. Would we want them any other way?

Best regards,

Annette Broadrick

STRANDED

Jackie Merritt

Chapter One

This was not one of Tyler Ruskin's happier undertakings. His sister Connie had caught him at a weak moment awhile back and coaxed him into a promise to attend her silly party this weekend. Ty knew it would be silly; Connie's parties always were.

Actually anybody's parties were silly, Ty felt. He didn't like get-togethers without a purpose. Making small talk with a bunch of people he hardly knew, or worse, didn't know at all, was the biggest waste of time he could think of. And he would bet anything that Connie had another one of her female friends just lying in wait to meet him. Even telling his sister point-blank that he detested that sort of introduction, Connie possessed some awful flaw that made her determined to find him a mate. Though she wasn't married herself, she thought Ty should be, which was an attitude he found thoroughly amazing. He was, after all, thirty-three years old, and didn't require looking after from his kid sister.

Driving along under the glaring Nevada sun, Ty gave his head an indulgent shake. He loved his fruitcake sister, and God knew she had hordes of friends because of her outgoing, bubbly personality. But sometimes it was hard to believe they both had the same mother and father when they were so different from each other. Seven years his junior, Connie doted on crowds and activity, while he preferred the peace and quiet of country living. Which was why Connie divided her time between Lake Tahoe and various cities, and he rarely left the Ruskin family ranch.

Connie was currently spending the summer in Tahoe which was within driving distance of the ranch. The Ruskin home on the lake was spacious and sprawling, with acres of front lawn that stopped just short of the shoreline. Ty's favorite time of year for visiting the place was midwinter, when everything was white with snow and wonderfully silent. As Connie wasn't a skier, she usually avoided the winter scene, so during January, especially, Ty would drive up, check the place over and spend a few solitary days, sometimes getting in a little skiing, sometimes just sitting by a crackling fire with a good book.

But it was July now, and as hot as Hades. Unusually hot for northern Nevada. Ty was driving with the windows up and the air conditioner running on high. He had taken a back road, one that only showed on rigidly detailed maps. Even then, the designation was a minute gray line, which pretty much discouraged strangers from using it. Since turning onto the gravel and dirt road, Ty hadn't seen one other car, and driving took little concentration.

Instead his mind wandered. The thirty-thousand-acre C-Bar Ranch was never far from his thoughts, certainly the most important factor of his life, and he gave a few minutes to the new barn presently under construction. The Ruskin money had all come from the ranch, which had been in the family for three generations. Connie used her income to travel and entertain; Ty barely used his at all, which was another subject on which Connie wasn't adverse to stating an opinion. *Why on earth don't you at least buy yourself a new pickup, Ty? That relic you're driving is a scandal!*

But Ty liked his "relic," and thus far in its many years of usage, the truck had never given him a moment's trouble. Maybe next year he would go shopping for a new pickup, though he wasn't even positive of that.

An inveterate adherent of the credo "Live and let live," Ty never judged his sister's life-style, and didn't particularly enjoy her judging his. Connie popped in at the ranch periodically, but after a few days she always became restless and bored. He, on the other hand, thrived on the smells of nature and animals, and never saw the silence and solitude as depressing, as Connie did.

Regardless of opposing and often conflicting attitudes, there was a strong bond between brother and sister, which was why Ty sometimes allowed himself to be talked into crossing the line into Connie's world. Certainly it was the reason he was driving to Tahoe today when he would much rather be at the ranch working on the barn.

Resigned to his fate, Ty appreciatively eyed the panorama of high desert and distant mountains. He loved Nevada with a passionate possession, privately considering himself as one with the land. With the population centered in two areas, the Reno area in the north and the Las Vegas area in the south, the vast central portion of the state was sparsely dotted with small towns and ranches, giving any free-spirited individual all of the freedom and space he or she might require.

Northern Nevada was, in a word, home, and he had no desire, ever, to live anywhere else.

Ty squinted at the glint of sunlight on metal far ahead. Dips in the road obliterated the reflection at intervals, but after a few miles he could make out a vehicle. A parked vehicle, he concluded after another mile or so. Actually the vehicle wasn't a car but a motor home, and it wasn't parked on the road but situated quite some distance into the desert.

Then, as he got closer, he saw a person, who, from the way he or she began running toward the road, must have seen him, also. "Hmm," he murmured, suspecting a problem ahead. Maybe the motor home had broken down. Maybe someone had taken ill. He would stop, of course. People didn't leave other people stranded in these parts.

The person became more distinct: a woman. Her white shorts stopped just above her knees, and a large, floppy straw hat concealed her hair. She was waving rather frantically, trying to draw his attention. Ty turned his pickup onto the barely visible trail that the motor home had obviously followed. He frowned: the roadway was soft.

In a minute he pulled up next to the woman and rolled down the window. "Got a problem?"

"Oh, thank you for stopping."

She was out of breath. Her face was flushed. But her features were pretty, and from behind his dark glasses Ty found himself taking a good look. She was tall and shapely and tanned, and he could see now that the hair beneath her straw hat was a deep, dark auburn. He certainly wasn't immune to pretty women; he just didn't want Connie setting him up.

The woman's breathing had calmed. "My motor home is stuck in sand, and no one's come along since it happened. I was very relieved to see your truck."

Ty looked ahead to the motor home. It wasn't one of the largest models, but neither was it small. "Are you driving that thing?"

Loren winced. How many times had she heard that same question? Posed in varying ways, of course, by gas station attendants, by neighbors in overnight parks. *You're driving this big motor home all by yourself? Traveling alone?* This guy sounded a little put out that a mere woman would attempt to drive anything larger than an ordinary car.

"Yes, I'm doing the driving," she said with a note of impatience she simply hadn't been able to hold back.

Ty's head came around sharply. She was standing in the hot sun and probably getting a little frazzled from the heat. "Get in. I'll take a look at your rig."

Loren didn't hesitate to climb in. She was in no position to judge her benefactor's morals or ethics, not when he was the only person to come along in hours. Settling herself on the seat, she said, "I've done everything I know how. The right rear tires are sunk in sand up to their hubcaps."

Ty got his pickup moving. "This roadbed is soft. In fact, it's not a road at all, just an old wagon trail. Where were you going?"

"To that red hill."

Ty peered at the distant red-toned hill. "Why?"

Loren sighed inwardly. She didn't have a reason, nothing logical, at any rate. "I'm on vacation and just sort of following the back roads. That hill looks interesting. Or, it did," she added gloomily.

Ty wasn't at all reluctant to offer advice. "You should stick to the better roads with that kind of vehicle."

Loren managed to stifle the sudden resentment she felt, but just barely. Men were always giving her advice, her father, her brothers, and during the last year, Marshall Roberts, the man with whom she was very close to being engaged. But Marsh was getting just a little too overbearing for her taste, and her procrastination on the subject of marriage had gradually been evolving into out-and-out repugnance.

Still, she could hardly start reciting her independence and personal capabilities when her motor home was bogged down in loose sand. It was a rented unit, and until today she'd been having a fabulous time exploring old roads. Granted, getting away by herself to think had seemed necessary. Marsh was pressing her for an answer, and she had, at least, made a final decision on that matter. Any love she had once felt for Marsh Roberts had long disappeared, and it was time to break off their relationship, which had, in all honesty, become no more than a habit.

Ty pulled up behind the motor home, which was blatantly listing to the right. The right side of the back bumper of the unit was almost on the ground, so it was buried pretty deep. Turning off the truck's engine, he got out.

Loren got out her side and walked up to where he was standing and studying the damage. "It's bad, isn't it?"

"Yeah, it's bad," Ty concurred. "I can try to jack it up and roll it out of there, but..." He thoughtfully rubbed his mouth. The soft sand wasn't in just one small tire-sized spot. Even using the jack could be a problem on this unstable ground. "I need a flat rock or a board to set the jack on. See if you can find something while I get my jack."

"I have a jack," Loren said as he headed for his pickup.

"I'll use mine, thanks."

Loren scurried around seeking something flat and solid on which to secure the jack. The ground was littered with small pebbles and bits of dried sage, but she couldn't find either a flat rock of any size or a board. Aware of him bringing out his jack and setting it next to the buried tires, she kept searching.

"Find anything?" Ty called.

"Afraid not." Loren registered him walking over the same ground she had inspected to see for himself, which was slightly irritating as she certainly hadn't overlooked a usable rock or board. Men in general had become irritating, she thought as she walked with her eyes cast hopefully down. Not that she didn't appreciate his assistance. Unquestionably she wouldn't get out of this fix on her own. But the superiority of the male attitude was becoming intolerable. As the only female in the Tanner family—her mother died six years before—Loren bore the brunt of three monumental male egos—four, counting Marsh's—and her patience with the opposite sex was beginning to wear thin.

She glanced at today's Good Samaritan and frowned. He was tall and rangy, extremely well built, wearing jeans, boots and a Western-cut white shirt. The dark glasses on his face concealed his eyes, but he was young and good-looking, with lots of nearly black hair and a strong chin and mouth. A *stubborn* chin and mouth, she amended. No woman told that sexy buckaroo what to do, she'd bet anything.

"There's nothing," Ty announced with some disgust.

Told you so! "Want me to keep looking?"

"Do you have a pail or something?"

"A pail?" she echoed.

"Yeah, something to carry gravel in."

"Oh. Yes, I'll get it." Loren hurried to the motor home and went inside. Then she called out the door. "I have one of those folding camp shovels. Do you want it?"

"Yes, bring it out."

The interior of the motor home was nearly suffocating. Baking in the sun for hours had turned it into an oven. Sweating, Loren located the pail and shovel, and gladly went outside again. "It must be a hundred and twenty degrees in there," she said.

"It's close to a hundred degrees out here," Ty told her, taking the pail and shovel from her hands, a comment that instantly loaded her with guilt.

"I'm terribly sorry about this," she said quietly. "I've interrupted your Saturday, and now you'll get dirty, too." His clothing was clean and neatly pressed, she realized. He had been on his way to some destination. If he wasn't married, he had probably been going to meet a girlfriend.

"Can't be helped," he said. "I can't leave you out here alone."

Loren clamped her mouth shut. She wasn't his responsibility, for Pete's sake, but if he hadn't come along she might have been stuck here for days. "That road isn't very well traveled, is it?"

Ty was leaning forward and shoveling loose stones into the pail. "It's not even on most maps." He glanced up at her. "How'd you find it?"

"Not from a map," Loren admitted. "Hey, why don't you let me do that? I hate the idea of your getting dirty because of me."

"I'll do it."

There was that stubborn male tone again. He was definitely one of those men who wouldn't allow a woman to do anything menial if he could do it for her.

"Don't you have a hat?" she questioned.

"In the pickup." Ty wiped the sweat off his forehead with the back of his hand. "Would you mind getting it for me?"

Ah, a job suited for a woman's frail strength. Loren smiled sweetly. "Not at all."

In the next hour she also served cold drinks, courtesy of the gas refrigerator in the motor home. Her benefactor had finally introduced himself. "Ty Ruskin."

She had followed suit. "Loren Tanner." He had sweated in spite of his hat, which, Loren discovered, was an expensive cream-colored Stetson, and the motor home was buried deeper than it had been before. He'd tried pulling it out with his pickup, but the unit was too heavy and mired too deeply for the smaller vehicle's limited power. He'd tried digging, bracing, jacking and cussing, and nothing had worked.

He loathed, Loren sensed, admitting defeat. In fact, his pride was turning this into a personal crusade. She had seen that same heels-dug-in expression on her father's and brothers' faces many times.

"I think we should drive your truck to the nearest telephone and call a wrecker," she finally suggested. One of his eyebrows twitched, and his jaw set into even more stubborn lines.

"As a last resort," he said brusquely. "This can't be impossible."

He gathered more gravel. He used both her jack and his on various portions of the motor home. He cussed under his breath and sweated buckets. His white shirt was damp and soiled. The crease was gone from his jeans. His boots were dusty and scuffed. She delivered huge glasses of water, which he gulped down in two swallows.

Finally she sat on the overturned pail on the shady side of the motor home and resigned herself to his determination. Time passed. The shadows on the desert floor were getting longer. The day was waning. In another few hours the sun would go down.

She got up and walked around the rear of the motor home. Ty was on his back, his top half under the unit. "Look, you've tried everything, and I'll never be able to thank you enough. But don't you think it's time to give up and get a wrecker out here? It's going to be dark soon."

For the first time Ty took a look at his watch. Muttering an oath, he slid from under the motor home. "I've missed..." Aw, hell, Connie would have a fit, he thought to himself. He stood up, then bent over to snag his hat from the ground. "Guess you're right."

Those words had been said as though they contained a lethal sting. Along with his hat, he had gotten rid of the sunglasses, and Loren curiously looked into his dark blue eyes and felt a most abnormal hot flash.

"Uh...you did everything you could," she stammered in an attempt to soothe his wounded pride, at the same time wondering about her unusual reaction to a man's eyes, however marvelous. "I'll gladly pay you for your time," she added.

He stared. "Pay me?"

Oh, God, now she had insulted him. "Please don't take offense. You've put in hours out here in the heat, and..."

Ty slapped his hat on his head and began gathering up his jack. "Forget it." Standing, holding the jack, he looked at her. "If you need something—like your purse—go and get it. We'll drive to..."

"I've been thinking," Loren interrupted. "If you wouldn't mind calling the wrecker, I'd like to stay here with my things."

"You're not worried about thieves, are you?"

Loren had to laugh. Other than him, she hadn't seen another human being all day. "That does seem far-fetched, I suppose. But if I go with you to make the call, you would have to drive me back, which seems unnecessary. I've already imposed on you enough."

Ty shook his head. "I don't want to leave you out here."

"I'm perfectly safe. Please...I've traveled over a thousand miles by myself."

"It'll be dark soon."

"I'm certainly not afraid of the dark, Ty." With the weakening sun, the temperature was dropping. Summer nights were glorious in this high country. "Even if the wrecker can't come until morning, I'll be fine. I've already ruined your day. Please don't let this ruin your evening, as well." She could tell he was mulling it over. "Really, I'll be just fine."

He took another look at his watch. Being hours late for Connie's party would be better than not showing up at all. He could shower and clean up when he got there, as he always left clothes at the Tahoe house.

"Well...if you're sure," he said reluctantly.

Loren breathed a sigh of relief. "I'm sure." She followed Ty to his vehicle. "I'll never be able to thank you enough."

"I didn't accomplish anything."

"Just your stopping is worth a great deal to me, Ty. And no one could have tried any harder to free the motor home than you did." Loren offered her hand. "Thank you."

Ty dropped the jack onto the bed of his pickup, wiped his hand on the leg of his jeans and took hers.

He'd noticed her pretty face and long legs during the hours, of course, but standing so close and shaking hands gave him a whole new perspective. Her eyes were a startling shade of gray-green and heavily fringed with dark lashes.

He held on to her hand. "Where are you from?"

"California. Waycliffe. It's a suburb of L.A."

"I noticed your California plates, but I also noticed the sign on the back of the motor home about it being a rental unit."

"Yes . . . it is." Why had her voice become husky? Why was her mouth dry? And why wasn't she pulling her hand away from his? He might have worked in the dirt for her for hours, but he was still a stranger.

"How long are you staying in Nevada?"

"Not long. Another day or so . . . in this area."

"Then where?"

"I'm not sure. I've been thinking about Utah. I have another eight days of vacation time."

Ty glanced down at their joined hands. Hers was much smaller and fit into his as though by design. He liked her touch, *more* than liked it.

"What do you do in L.A.?"

"I work at a movie studio."

He raised an eyebrow. "You're a star?"

Laughing, Loren finally broke their handclasp. "I work in an office, Ty. What do you do?"

"I have a ranch."

"A cattle ranch?"

"Cattle and sheep." And timber and horses and miles of land. "Cattle and sheep" was enough of an answer, however. "Well, this isn't getting a wrecker out here, is it?"

"No, but it's been very nice talking with you." *Are you married?* He wore no rings, but she was afraid to rely on that.

Besides, it didn't really matter. When he drove away, that would be the end of their association.

Ty opened the driver's door of his pickup. "I don't suppose you'd like to stop at the ranch before going to Utah, would you?"

"Stop at your ranch?" Loren's eyes widened. "I'd love to see your ranch. How do I find it?"

"I won't be there until tomorrow night, but it's not hard to find. I'll draw you a map." Reaching into the glove compartment, Ty came out with a piece of paper and a pen. Using the top of the pickup as a table, he sketched a map.

Loren took it when he offered it and looked it over. He had marked highway names, landmarks and approximate mileage. "I'll see you on Monday, okay?"

They smiled at each other. Ty looked off for a moment, absorbing the isolation and silence again. Loren Tanner was a city woman and had no business being out here by herself. He brought an uneasy gaze back to her. "You're sure about staying here alone?"

"Yes, thanks."

She was determined, and he certainly couldn't force her to change her mind. "Then I'd better get going," he said gruffly, and sat behind the wheel to turn the ignition key. The pickup started, ran for a second and died. He tried it again and the same thing happened. On the third try, it didn't start at all.

Loren peered in through the open window. "What's wrong with it?"

"I don't know. I've never had any trouble with it before."

Guilt was hitting Loren again. "I'll bet it got damaged when you were trying to tow the motor home."

"Anything's possible," Ty muttered, getting a little irate that the damned thing wouldn't start. Maybe he had damaged something, but what?

He got out and lifted the hood. Everything looked normal, but obviously something wasn't functioning. He fiddled with the spark plugs for a minute, then called, "Loren, try to start it while I test for spark."

She jumped into the pickup and turned the key. "Again," Ty called. This went on for several minutes.

Finally, disgusted, he slammed down the hood. "It's either the coil or the condenser, which means we're both stuck."

Loren got out with a crestfallen expression. "You can't fix it?"

"Not without some new parts." The damned truck *was* a relic and should have been replaced with a newer unit years ago.

"Oh, my God! There goes a truck by on the road!" Loren began running toward the road, but the truck vanished in a cloud of dust before she had covered twenty feet. She stopped and turned back, slowly. "It's gone."

"The driver probably thought we were camping out here for the night." Ty's expression became wry. "Guess he wasn't wrong." Laying his hands on his hips, he let his gaze sweep the area. The sage and bunchgrass were becoming golden from the setting sun. Casting his eyes toward Loren, he realized that he didn't object to spending the night in her company.

In fact, the whole episode seemed rather fateful, as though both he and Loren were caught within the intricate web of an unavoidable scheme. It was an appealing thought. This morning he hadn't known Loren Tanner; this evening she seemed important.

But she looked worried about the setup. "If you've got an extra blanket," he told her, speaking nonchalantly to reassure her, "I'll sleep just fine in the back of my truck."

"Oh, there must be a better arrangement than that," she murmured, stopping herself from pressing the point when she realized that the only other arrangement would be sharing the motor home with him. It wouldn't be impossible—not when the compact bedroom contained twin beds—just personally uncomfortable.

"Let's not worry about that yet," she hastened to add. "The least I can do is feed you a decent dinner. I have a small barbecue grill with me, and the refrigerator is full of food."

Ty nodded. He hadn't eaten since this morning and his stomach was growling. "Thanks. Let me know if I can help."

Chapter Two

Loren brought out the best food in the refrigerator, which included two nice steaks and crisp greens for a salad. The inside of the motor home was still hot, and she opened every window hoping for a cross-draft. Once the meat was trimmed of fat, seasoned and ready for the grill, she went outside and unlocked the door to one of the vehicle's many storage areas.

Ty, she saw, had his head under the hood of his pickup again. She felt about two inches high. Without her interference, he wouldn't be stranded in the desert till God knew when. Loren peered into the twilight at the ribbon of road, which was becoming impossible to see with any clarity. Regardless of vagueness of form, there weren't any vehicles coming or going.

Sighing, she pulled out the tiny grill, a bag of charcoal and a can of lighter fluid from the storage cavity. If ever a man deserved a good meal, it was Ty Ruskin. If his pickup was any measure, he didn't have a lot in the way of assets. She could almost picture his ranch, probably one of those scrubby little places she'd seen during her backroads travels. At any rate, he had worked hard today and would undoubtedly enjoy a steak.

When the fire was going Loren walked over to the pickup. "Any luck with the engine?"

Ty came out from under the hood. "I'm pretty sure it's the coil."

"Was it damaged when you tried to tow the motor home?"

Ty shook his head. "No. I should have bought a newer rig a long time ago. This one's wearing out." He grinned slightly. "It's not your fault."

The comment didn't completely eradicate Loren's guilt, but it helped. Being with Ty certainly wasn't a hardship. It had been a long time since a man had been so interesting. During the first stages of her and Marsh's relationship, she'd had some starry-eyed moments. But she should have broken that off months ago. When he'd first started pressuring her about marriage, in fact. Her father wasn't going to like her decision to do exactly that when she got home, and neither were her brothers. The three Tanner men thought Marsh Roberts fit perfectly into the family, and why wouldn't they when they were all so much alike?

Of course, Ty Ruskin could have the exact same tendencies. Hadn't she noticed his protectiveness several times today?

Still, he was an intriguing guy. Generous with his time and considerate of fellow members of the human race, good traits, admirable traits. Besides, he had to be the best-looking man she'd ever spent a hot, trying day with. Any woman would notice his remarkable blue eyes and thick dark hair.

"Uh...Ty...is there anyone at your ranch who might be worried about you?" There! That was a cleverly subtle way to unearth his marital status.

He suddenly seemed agitated, and Loren's heart sank. "Not at the ranch," he said, tight-lipped. Connie had probably called the C-Bar by now and learned from Gabe or Sissy or whoever had answered the phone that Ty had left for Tahoe as planned. It was Connie who worried him, not anyone at the ranch. His sister was excitable enough to do anything, from organizing a manhunt to notifying the FBI.

Not at the ranch. She'd been right, Loren thought with a touch of sadness. He'd been on his way to meet a woman, and of course the lady would be distressed by his prolonged absence.

Well, any guy who looked like he did wasn't apt to be running around unattached, so she may as well stop eyeing his lean build and handsome face.

She put on a smile. "How would you like to take a shower before dinner?"

Ty blinked. "I'd love a shower. In the motor home?"

"The bathroom is almost too small to turn around in, but the water tanks are full. Have you ever showered in an RV?"

"Can't say I have."

"Then let me give you a few pointers. The waste water is also stored in tanks, so what you do is wet yourself down and turn off the water while you soap. Then you turn it back on and rinse off." Loren felt a blush creeping into her cheeks. Giving a man instructions on how to take a shower was darned forward, however necessary.

She cleared her throat. "There's a button on the shower head to turn it off and on."

"You're sure you don't mind?" The thought of a shower was exhilarating. He had perspired all day and the sweat had dried on his body.

"Of course I don't mind." She managed a teasing smile. "Just don't use all the water."

Loren led the way to the motor home's door. "Come on in. I'll get you some clean towels."

Inside, Ty looked around at the pale varnished wood and light blue fabrics. There were lots of cabinets, a dinette—a table and two padded bench seats—one upholstered chair, and a neat little kitchen, along with the two large captain's chairs within the driving area of the unit. "This is nice."

"It's a great way to travel," Loren told him.

Ty grinned. "It's going downhill in the back end, though."

The motor home was slanting to one side so that standing in the unit was a trifle dizzying, which suddenly seemed funny to Loren. "Just don't move too quickly," she said with a laugh, "or you might get seasick."

"I'll take it easy."

Loren was standing in the kitchen area. "Stay put until I get your towels." Two steps took her to the minuscule bathroom, and another two brought her into the bedroom. From a cabinet she pulled out fresh towels and a washcloth. "There's soap and shampoo in the shower," she called while laying the clean linen on the tiny sink counter.

She reappeared with a smile. "Now we have to change places. I'll wait outside while you shower, so don't worry about closing doors in here. That will give you more room."

Grinning, Ty waited near the dinette for Loren to go outside. She passed by him with mere inches to spare, and he experienced a pleasant jolt of electricity at their momentary nearness. Before she could close the outside door, he took hold of it. "Hey!" he said softly.

She turned. "Yes?" She'd felt the electricity, too, and was a bit confused about whether to enjoy or deny it. It had been a strange day, but the night could be a whole lot stranger if they didn't keep cool.

What Ty saw on her face was more denial than enjoyment, and he thought better of saying anything personal. "Just . . . thanks."

Loren knew he had changed his mind about something, which, of course, was only sensible. "You're welcome," she replied, then wondered if she weren't getting a mite odd here. Why else would she feel as if she had just missed something important?

Sighing, she closed the door. After checking the coals, she added a few more briquettes to extend the life of the cooking temperature. Thinking she might as well wait in comfort, she dug out her two folding chairs from a storage compartment and set them up near the grill.

Darkness was falling in earnest. It was a glorious night, warm and silky to the skin, utterly peaceful. The desert was much darker than the sky at this point of the evening, and Loren marveled at the lack of lights and people. Taking that ill-traveled road had been foolhardy, but leaving it for a drive on an old sandy trail to that red hill was worse. Look what she'd gotten herself into, and inadvertently drawn Ty into, as well. His lady friend was probably worried sick by now. Loren could only hope that his friend wasn't the type of woman to also get angry over something like this.

Loren sank into introspective speculation. What sort of woman was Ty's girlfriend? Pretty? Intelligent? A gal who jumped every time a man suggested she should?

If he preferred subservience in women, he would never like Loren Tanner.

The motor-home door swung open. "That was great," Ty exclaimed. He grinned. "And I didn't use all the water, either."

Loren got to her feet. "In that case, I think I'll take a quick shower myself."

Ty was eyeing the coals. "Want me to put on the steaks?"

He had apparently seen the meat on the counter. "Sure, that would be great. Thanks."

"It's clouding up," Ty remarked.

Loren raised her eyes to the sky. They had eaten, with relish, and were sitting outside in the dark. The clouds surprised her. "They came up awfully fast."

"It happens."

"Do you think it will rain tonight?" Loren was thinking, uneasily, of him sleeping in the back of his pickup.

"Hard to tell. Loren, I'm curious. I don't know any women who would take off in a motor home by themselves. Do you do this all the time?"

She laughed softly. "This is my first time, but it won't be my last, even with today's problems. Mom and Dad owned a motor home for quite a few years. After Mom died Dad sold the unit, but they traveled all over the U.S., Canada and Mexico before Mom became ill. I went with them on several trips, and I really liked this type of traveling. Anyway, I learned the ins and outs of RVs. There are all sorts of routines one has to know for maximum usage. Nothing difficult or physically strenuous, mind you, and certainly a woman can manage as well as a man." Loren was geared to ramble on about the positive aspects of motor-home travel, but Ty broke in.

"But you're traveling alone. I don't think it's safe."

"It's as safe as driving a car and stopping at strange motels, Ty. Safer, in my estimation. There are RV parks everywhere, and I have yet to meet anyone threatening in an overnight park. Mostly the people are friendly and unusually helpful." Loren smiled. "Of course, something like what happened today is always a possibility. But a male driver could have gotten stuck just as easily as I did."

"I suppose. Still, it doesn't seem very wise to me for a woman alone to be following old roads that aren't even on the map. What did your father say about your taking off alone?"

"He didn't like it," Loren admitted. "Neither did my brothers." She hesitated, wondering if she wanted to mention Marsh to Ty. Marsh had thrown a fit about this trip, using every argument in the book to prevent it, from roaming serial killers to mechanical problems. *I will not live my life in fear, Marsh,* she had told him. Being rescued, or semirescued, by Ty Ruskin, was an excellent example of the type of people she had met thus far in her travels.

But it didn't surprise her that Ty's attitude paralleled her family's and Marsh's. Regardless of so much publicity on the equality of the sexes, in her experience there seemed to be very few men who genuinely felt that a woman should boldly cross those invisible but remarkably durable lines between the traditional roles of males and females.

Of course, she thought with a sigh, that opinion could merely be a result of the company she'd been keeping in L.A.

She changed the focus of their conversation. "Do you have any family?"

"A sister. My parents have been gone for quite a few years now."

A comfortable silence ensued. Loren broke it with a long breath. "Gosh, it's nice out here. I love the quiet."

"You do? Not everyone does. My sister doesn't. Connie just naturally gravitates to crowds and commotion."

"And you?" Loren casually asked. The longer they talked—though their conversation was quite ordinary—the more interesting Ty became. She liked his voice in the dark, and the sense of him sitting within reaching distance. A long reach, granted, but his presence exuded strength and security and something subtly exciting.

"I don't like crowds and I don't like cities," Ty replied.

"Have you ever lived in a city?"

"No, and I never will."

"Did you grow up in rural Nevada?"

"Sure did." Ty chuckled softly. "But so did Connie."

"Point well taken," Loren said with a laugh. Her mind was swarming with curiosity about the Ruskins. More accurately, about Ty. Pinpointing the subject even finer, about Ty and his lady friend. Was theirs a serious relationship? If he had been driving on that old road to see her, she obviously didn't live on a neighboring ranch. But Loren couldn't picture him seriously involved with a city woman. Truthfully she had never met anyone who personified "country" any better than Ty. An image of him astride a big horse and directing a cattle drive might be a bit Hollywood, but it seemed to suit Ty perfectly.

Still, he was drinking iced tea rather than the beer she had offered him, and wouldn't one of those macho movie cattle drovers prefer beer?

Ty was noticing and battling an unusual restlessness. Some of it had to do with Connie, as she was perfectly capable of sounding an alarm over his disappearance that would be heard around the world.

But most of his aggravating urges to squirm were caused by the woman in the next chair. Loren had put on a gauzy skirt and a very feminine blouse after her shower. Her scent, whether it was from soap or the most expensive of perfumes, invaded his every breath of air. He didn't jump women just because they were alone, not even when the opportunity was as glaringly apparent as it was tonight. But he was only human, and the fabulously silken night, the quiet and isolation, and Loren herself all added up to a dynamite combination that would test the libido of the most passive of men. Something in the back of his mind kept devising erotic scenarios. He'd like to kiss her full sweet lips, and slide his hand under her skirt, and feel her long, long legs wrapped around him, and...

Adjusting his position on the chair again, he noisily cleared his throat. "Um...does it cost a lot to rent one of these units?"

"They're not cheap, Ty. As a matter of fact, one can travel by car and stay in motels for quite a bit less than what this trip will end up costing me. It's worth it to me, though. It's like taking your own home with you. The cabinets are full of books and journals and personal items I wanted with me. My clothes are hanging in a closet instead of getting wrinkled in suitcases. I can cook when I feel like it, or eat out when the mood strikes. And I can go where there *aren't* any motels."

"Like this spot," Ty said with some wryness.

There was disapproval in his voice, tempered by humor but still recognizable. Loren decided to set him straight about "this spot," and how she really viewed the day's events. "The only thing I regret about today is how badly I botched your Saturday, Ty. Other than that today was wonderful, and I will never be sorry for stumbling across this beautiful stretch of... of..."

"This is high desert," Ty said quietly. "You're different than..." He stopped. Comparing a woman, even favorably, to other women, usually turned out bad.

Positive that he was thinking of his special lady friend, Loren sighed inwardly. Her "difference" was probably a minus factor in Ty's opinion. Obviously *his* lady would never do anything so rash as to rent an RV and travel the back roads all by her lonesome.

Amazed that any woman would judge today as "wonderful," Ty peered at her in the dark. Her good humor had never flagged for one moment today, he realized, not even when the sun had been blistering hot and she couldn't possibly have been comfortable. She had hauled him water to drink instead of complaining, and she hadn't once pestered him with annoying questions when he'd been sweating over ways to free the motor home.

"You're an unusual woman," he said softly.

Loren hesitated. "That sounded suspiciously like a compliment." She'd spoken lightly, wondering why he would suddenly be handing out compliments. Besides, it was too dark to see his face. Comprehension of anything he said had to come solely from sound, and she wasn't all that certain of his intonation.

"It was the truth, not a compliment," Ty said. He let a few seconds go by, then said in that same soft voice, "I'd really like to know you better."

Her breath caught: His intonation in that statement had been abundantly clear. In one way she was disappointed. He had a girlfriend but wouldn't object to playing around with another woman. At the same time, her own reaction to what was suddenly a mind-dazzling idea was too influencing to ignore.

Loren didn't know what to say, although *I'd like to know you better, too* was certainly the highlight of her muddled thoughts.

"Did I offend you?" he asked.

His voice was quiet in the still night, little more than an extension of the silence surrounding them. They were engulfed in silence and darkness and warm, unmoving air. The motor home was a huge black shadow behind them. The desert landscape contained other black shadows, clumps of sage and Joshua trees. The road wasn't even partially visible, and only remained a fact in Loren's mind through memory. Even the moon and most of the stars were obliterated now, hiding on the other side of the expanding, voracious cloud cover. It was possible to envision herself and Ty as the only two people on the planet, and the sensation was like no other Loren had ever experienced, both achingly desirable and frightening.

"You didn't offend me," she said in a faint, slightly husky voice. "I'm sure you were only talking about friendship."

"That's how it begins for a man and woman, isn't it? With friendship?"

Loren swallowed hard. "I think our friendship is established, don't you? I mean, no other friend I have would have done any more today than you did." She attempted to lighten the mood. "Making new friends is one of the joys of this kind of travel, Ty."

His jaw tensed, though Loren couldn't see it. "You're deliberately evading the point. Maybe I should speak a little plainer. You're a beautiful woman. Do you find me unattractive?"

"Lord, no!" Loren took a breath and quickly tried to modify her hasty answer. "I mean, you're very good-looking and . . . all. But our paths crossed so accidentally, and . . ."

"You're getting nervous. Do you want to change the subject?"

He was right about her getting nervous, though she would rather he think differently on that score. "I'm not at all nervous, Ty. Should I be?"

"Not if you don't see something unique in our situation."

She managed to laugh, albeit briefly. "Oh, it's been a unique day, all right."

"You said you regretted nothing that happened, other than interrupting my Saturday. What if I don't mind the interruption? What if I'm glad you were out here stuck in the sand?"

"That would make you a saint, Ty. You had plans for the day, didn't you?" Loren held her breath.

"Yes, I had plans," Ty admitted. "I was on my way to Tahoe, which has nothing at all to do with what we were talking about."

"Oh, but it does," Loren said softly. A woman had waited all day for him. She was probably *still* waiting for him. Loren rose from her chair. "I'll get your blankets. I'm really very tired, and it's getting late."

Ty clamped his lips together. It wasn't like him to push a woman on any topic, let alone one with such personal ramifications. Obviously Loren wanted to keep their relationship exactly where it was, in the friends-only category. Given the diverse geographies of their homes, she was probably right.

A faint light came on inside the motor home. Ty could hear Loren moving around. He glanced up at the clouds and hoped it wouldn't rain during the night. He could always move from the bed of the pickup to the cab, but stretching out on any vehicle seat wasn't possible for a person of his height.

As frustrating as certain aspects of the day had been, Ty knew he would stop again if he ever saw a traveler in distress. Driving on by anyone in trouble was unthinkable for him.

Besides, he never would have met Loren Tanner if he hadn't stopped.

After a second Ty realized that conclusion wasn't particularly comforting. Once he managed to get a wrecker out here, she would drive away, and if she chose not to stop at the C-Bar before leaving Nevada, he would never see her again.

Unless he went to California. He frowned at the idea. She hadn't given him the kind of encouragement a man needed to pursue a woman to that extreme, so why had it even entered his mind?

Loren came out with an armful of bedding. Ty jumped to his feet. "Let me take that."

She transferred the load to his arms. "I brought you one of my pillows. There's a blanket to put under you and one to use for a cover."

"Thanks."

They made their way in the dark to the pickup. Ty dropped the blankets and pillow into the bed of the truck, then unlatched and pulled down the tailgate. Loren laid a hand on the flooring and suffered a pang. "This is going to be an awfully hard bed."

"No worse than the ground, which I've slept on plenty of times."

"You camp out?"

"During hunting season."

"Oh. Well . . ." She felt as if she should say something else. Maybe thank him again. After all, she was going to retire to an excellent bed, and he was going to spend the night on the back of a truck. The inequity was perturbing, especially when she was the cause of his upcoming discomfort. "I hope you get some sleep," she said uneasily.

"I will. Don't worry about it."

"Well . . . good night."

"G'night, Loren."

Returning to the motor home, Loren went inside. As she had told Ty, this mode of travel was like taking one's home along. She had a bathroom, hot and cold running water, a good bed, and even food, should she awaken with a sudden yen for something to eat.

Loren switched off the ceiling light and undressed in the dark. Her bed wasn't quite as comfortable as normal, not when it was going downhill from the peculiar angle of the unit. Still, it was familiar with her own sheets, and she settled down with a yawn.

But as far as falling immediately to sleep, forget it. She couldn't stop thinking of Ty out there on the back of his truck. Certainly her attitude was selfish when there was a perfectly good twin bed going to waste inside, but was it also prudish? She'd never considered herself prudish before, and the word was startling.

Still, envisioning Ty Ruskin sleeping across the narrow aisle was discomfiting. Good God, she thought in a burst of self-disgust. Did she think he was going to attack her? If he'd been so inclined, he could have behaved abominably at any given point of their long day together.

No, her discomfiture wasn't caused by fear. The man was just too damned sexy to share a bedroom with, and it was her own realization of that fact that prevented her from going to the door and inviting him inside for the night. He would survive one night on the back of a truck, and she would survive one night of worry and guilt.

It was better this way. *Much* better.

Chapter Three

Loren realized she must have gone to sleep when she awakened, rather dreamily, to the delicious sound of raindrops pattering against the outer skin of the motor home. At first she merely snuggled deeper into her blankets, but within seconds she leapt out of bed and ran to the door. "Ty!"

He was already up and moving around on the back of his truck, gathering his bedding and boots. "What?"

"It's raining!"

"No kidding," he muttered. Apparently it had been raining for some time because he felt damp clear through. "I'm fine," he yelled, jumping from the tailgate to the ground.

"But..." Loren saw him heading for the cab of his truck. Her priggishness over the sleeping arrangements had gone far enough. "Ty, come inside!"

He had the door of the pickup open. "Are you sure?"

It was raining harder. "Don't argue! You're getting soaked!"

He wasn't soaked yet, Ty realized. But he was getting chilled. Those clouds hadn't only brought rain, they had also brought a much lower temperature.

"Come on," Loren urged. "I've got to close the windows." Leaving the door hanging open, she switched on a ceiling light and began dashing around the motor home, slamming windows shut. The roof vents were also wide open, and she hurriedly cranked them closed.

Ty came in. Though dressed, he was in his stocking feet. Rain glistened in his hair. His boots were bunched with the bedding in his arms. Despite his own dank state, Loren in a short nightshirt was a compelling sight. Her long, disheveled hair and sleep-flushed face drew his gaze, as well as the arousing length of her tanned, bare legs below the shirt's hem. He was seeing more leg now than had been visible when she'd been wearing those knee-length shorts, and he definitely liked the view.

Concentrating on closing the window above the dinette, she didn't notice his approving appraisal. "Your clothes are wet," she remarked over her shoulder. "Maybe you'd better take them off."

"And put on what?"

"A blanket, or..." She turned to face him. "I'm sorry. I shouldn't be bossing you around. Look, I feel like a jerk for letting you bed down in your pickup in the first place. You can use the other twin bed. We aren't children, and these aren't exactly ordinary circumstances."

Indeed they weren't children, nor were the circumstances ordinary. Ty certainly wasn't inexperienced with the fairer sex, but spending a night in such close quarters with a luscious lady, who was creeping deeper under his skin with each additional twist of their startling acquaintanceship, had thus far eluded him.

He grinned, he couldn't help it. "I'm going to sleep in one twin bed, and you're going to sleep in the other?" His grin broadened. "What will people say?"

"Not as much as they would if we both used the *same* twin bed," Loren shot back. Immediately she rolled her eyes. "That was a stupid remark. I hope you don't take it wrong."

"Wouldn't dream of it," Ty drawled. He indicated the damp blankets in his arms. "Where should I put these?"

Until that "dream" comment, Ty Ruskin had not impressed Loren as a sassy or cocky man. She eyed him with a bit of suspicion. He could probably tease with the best of them. Trying so hard to free the motor home had taxed his strength and spirit, apparently, because he had shown more sobriety than levity during those hours.

After a moment she smiled, keeping it friendly but distant. "Just lay them next to that chair for tonight. I'll dry them outside in the morning. In the meantime, here's what we'll do. You go to bed first. I'll stay here until you're undressed and under the covers. Then I'll drape your clothes over the dinette to dry during the night."

"Sounds like a plan to me." Ty set his load down on the floor next to the chair, untangling his boots from the blankets and placing them upright by the door. He stood up. The only way to reach the bedroom was to slither past Loren. "Should I go to the left or the right of you?"

"Neither." Loren slid into the dinette and sat down. "You have plenty of traveling space now."

"So I do."

Loren's lips twitched in amusement. "You think this is funny, don't you?"

"Not funny, fun. I've never slept in one of these contraptions before."

"Motor home," she reminded. "And you just might discover that you like it."

He smiled beguilingly. "I already do."

Well, she thought when he disappeared into the bedroom, drawing a deep breath. Logically there was no earthly reason for him to shiver in the cab of his pickup for the rest of the night when there was an empty bed inside. She *was* a logical being, wasn't she?

But the rain on the roof made the small dimensions of the motor home feel very cozy. Intimate. Private. Ty's movements in the bedroom were all too audible. She even heard the zipper on his jeans, and she stirred on the seat and attempted nonchalance.

Then he called, "I'm in bed."

Loren cleared her throat. "I'm coming." Sliding from the dinette, she entered the tiny bedroom with a deliberately impersonal expression. His jeans, shirt and socks were on the foot of his bed. She gathered up the garments while trying not to notice how small the twin bed seemed with him in it.

His clothes weren't soaked, she realized during the short walk back to the dinette, but neither were they dry. Quickly she spread them out over the furniture. Snapping off the ceiling light, she made her way to the bedroom in the dark.

Ty's voice rumbled. "It'd be easy for a person to get in the wrong bed in this kind of darkness."

Loren crawled into her bed. "I don't have any trouble separating right from left, Ty. Good night." Turning her back to his side of the bedroom, she determinedly shut her eyes.

In two heartbeats they popped open again. Apparently she'd had enough sleep to take the edge off, because she didn't feel at all tired or sleepy now.

On the other hand, having a man in the same room—God, she could hear him breathing!—was disconcerting enough to totally destroy any chance of relaxing.

Ty yawned. "This bed feels great. Thanks. You're a sport."

Loren rolled to her back. A sport. Yes, she could be labeled a "sport" over this incident, but had there ever been another occasion when the word fit so well? She smiled in the dark, rather liking her own generosity. Certainly she never could have gone back to sleep knowing that the man who had done everything possible to help her today was huddling in the cab of his truck, chilled and damp.

"It's really coming down," Ty commented.

"As arid as this area is, heavy rain must be unusual," Loren said.

"Actually we've had quite a lot of rain this year. The locals are glad."

"Other ranchers, you mean?"

"Can't raise animals without water."

"Do you have a well on your ranch?"

"Several wells," Ty said. "Along with seven creeks and three springs."

Loren frowned. "Really?"

"You sound skeptical."

"I didn't mean to. Sorry." Seven creeks? Was this a line of blarney, or what? "You said that no one at the ranch would miss you, Ty. Isn't there anyone there?"

"Did I say that? There are people at the ranch, Loren, but they don't expect me back until tomorrow night."

Loren amended her thoughts with an inward sigh. What he'd said was that the person who would miss him wasn't at the ranch, meaning his lady friend, of course.

"You'll have to come and take a look at the place for yourself," Ty murmured. "I'd like to show you around. How do you feel about horses? Do you ride?"

"Never even been near a horse, Ty. I've always thought riding might be fun, though."

Talking in the pitch-black had a special quality of intimacy that Loren had never experienced with a man before. It was slightly reminiscent of girlhood sleep-overs, when one's most secret thoughts and yearnings were the cause of nearly hysterical fits of giggling.

But the person to whom she was talking was not a girl, and while this episode should be nothing but innocent, Loren's own imagination lifted it to the adult stage. After all, she was years away from childhood, and there was nothing wrong with her libido. As for what Ty might be feeling right now, hadn't he made it clear earlier tonight that he was interested in her as a woman?

"In that case, maybe I'll get you on a horse when you come to the ranch," Ty said.

"First I have to get this rig out of the sand," Loren reminded. "Ty, I drove in from the south. The last town I came through is at least thirty miles away. Is there anything closer going north?"

"Nothing within walking distance, if that's what you're thinking."

"What if no one comes along tomorrow?" Loren speculated uneasily.

"Then I guess we'll be stuck here until someone does." Ty grinned. "Don't worry. That road doesn't get much traffic, but someone'll be along. Sooner or later," he added on a devilish impulse. He was having fun. It was a different kind of fun than he was used to and there was no question about the woman he was with being at the heart of it. But lying in a too-short but otherwise comfortable bed, and listening to both the rain on the roof and Loren's husky voice was an exciting way to spend a Saturday night. A heck of a lot more exciting than Connie's party would have been.

"What if it's later, Ty," Loren said worriedly. "The tanks hold only so much water, and we used quite a lot of it today. Yesterday," she amended. "Last night."

He turned on his side to face her voice. Loren heard his adjustment in position, moved her head to look in his direction and swore she could make out the upper half of his body, obviously uncovered.

"Keep the faith, honey," he told her. "Someone will decide to take that old road. I did, didn't I? And so did you."

She told herself the endearment meant nothing, though it seemed to ripple through her in a tide of warmth. "Yes, but I was exploring. And you were on your way to Tahoe. Is this road the best route to Tahoe?" she questioned hopefully. Yes, she thought, straining her eyes in the dark. She could definitely make out Ty's upper torso. The blankets stopped at his waist.

"Depends on where you are when you start out," he said matter-of-factly. "Tell me what you do in that office you work in."

"Are you interested?"

"Seems kind of interesting to be working at a movie studio. Do you ever meet any of the actors?"

"Oh, sure." Loren recited some names that anyone even slightly abreast of current films would recognize.

Ty gave a low whistle. "No kidding? You've actually met those people? What are they like?"

"Like anyone else. Some stars are as common as apple pie. They come in and ask how you are, and how your family is. You know the stuff. Then there are others who wouldn't give you the time of day if their life depended on one act of simple kindness. Actually I spend most of my working hours at a computer—a word processor—typing contracts and correspondence. It's a good job. I've worked there for three years now. Before that I was one of many secretaries employed by a mammoth shoe manufacturer. And before that I was in college."

"Where did you go to school?"

"At UCLA." Loren wondered if he had gone to college, but she hesitated to ask in case he hadn't. "Have you always lived on a ranch?" she asked instead.

"Born and raised," he confirmed.

"Then your folks were ranchers."

"And their folks before them. Connie—my sister—and I lost our father about nine years ago, and Mom died two years later."

"I'm sorry," Loren murmured. "Do you get to see your sister very often?"

"We're close. Talk on the phone a lot."

"That's good. A family should keep in touch."

Ty crooked one arm beneath his head. "You mentioned having brothers. Are they older?"

"One is. Pete's married, but he doesn't have any kids. Joe, my younger brother, lives at home with Dad." Loren laughed softly. "Joe's still trying to figure out what he wants to be when he grows up." Quickly she added, "Not that Dad supports him, or anything. Joe's usually working at two jobs. He's not afraid of work, believe me, but he's perpetually enrolled in one class or another."

"Nothing wrong with continued education. So, you're a middle child."

Loren sighed. "And none of the men in my family let me forget it."

"Do I detect a note of resentment?"

"They're enormously protective, Ty."

"That's understandable."

"Are you protective of your sister?"

"When she's around, yes, I suppose I am."

"But it's so...smothering," Loren said. "Does Connie ever object?"

"Don't you think men should be protective of their womenfolk?"

"In a threatening situation, of course. But not in everyday life, Ty. Sometimes it seems more like a struggle for control." Loren frowned. "That's not precisely it, either. It's hard to explain without sounding like a complainer."

"Loren, your family would be worried if they knew you were stuck in the desert with a stranger. This is the sort of situation they were concerned about when you left by yourself, I'll bet."

"I suppose you're right," she concurred on a sigh. "But look who came to the rescue. Even they couldn't object to you, stranger or not."

"We're not strangers now, Loren. You want to hear something funny? I feel like I've known you for a long time. Why do you suppose that is?"

"I...don't know." It was strange to realize she felt the same about him. Less than twenty-four hours ago she hadn't known Ty Ruskin existed; tonight he seemed like an old friend.

He was a man she could fall very hard for, which wouldn't happen, of course. How could it when their lives were so far apart?

They fell silent. The rain on the roof was almost musical and hypnotizing. The coziness inside the unit, the warmth and comfort of bed and blankets, were making Loren drowsy. After a few minutes Ty decided she must be sleeping. He lay on his back again and thought of her lying so close to him, no more than two feet away. This was the craziest situation he'd ever been a part of. Any other time he'd spent in a woman's bedroom had been used in sexual games. He had enjoyed talking to Loren as much as he'd ever enjoyed anything, and if mere conversation with her was that pleasurable, what would making love with her be like?

Once his mind focused on that arousing picture, Ty found it impossible to think of anything else. She wasn't movie-star gorgeous, he told himself, then debated the point while mentally assessing her features. Unquestionably her eyes were spectacular. And her mouth. Her hair, too. He grinned. Maybe she *was* movie-star gorgeous. Certainly her body was the slender but curvy type that gave men erotic dreams at night.

But along with wanting her terrific body under his, he also liked her, which amazed him a lot more than his desire. Wanting a woman wasn't all that unusual, but liking her was when he could count on one hand the women in his lifetime that he had actually liked. Plus, the majority of them were in the distant past, when he was much younger and not so selective. These days his emotions were all poured into the ranch, and he'd been totally content with his way of life, never looking for a reason *not* to be content in spite of Connie's sometimes veiled, sometimes blatant comments to the contrary.

Liking a woman who was here today and gone tomorrow was a waste of time and emotion, however. What could come of it? Loren might decide to stop at the ranch for an hour or two before leaving the area,

but then she would drive away. Their time together
was too short for anything important to develop.

It was best to look on today as an enjoyable but
brief adventure and let it go at that. He had gained a
pleasant memory and met a nice woman....

"Damn," Ty whispered. Loren wasn't only nice,
she was the kind of excitement he may have been
seeking all of his adult life. Excitement with solidity.
Excitement with independence and intelligence and
generosity. And she was going to drive out of his life
tomorrow, nullifying any possibility of exploring
where their fledgling relationship might go. Could he
let that happen? Ty's eyes squinted in the dark, a re-
flexive action to his startling thoughts. Could he *stop*
that from happening?

He sucked in a long, slow breath. Someway, somehow, he was going to get Loren Tanner to come to the
C-Bar, and once there he would shamelessly flaunt
everything he owned. Possessions often impressed
women—he'd had that experience a few times—and if
that was a sneaky way to get through her reserve, he
didn't care. Right now she knew very little about him.
Showing her that he was a man of substance and roots
was bound to help his case.

He would, in short, do whatever it took to draw
Loren's notice.

With that decision made and irrevocable, Ty rolled
over on his stomach and went to sleep.

Loren opened her eyes to daylight. Instantly remembering Ty, she turned her head on the pillow to
see him. A smile twitched her lips. He was sprawled on

his belly, snoring lightly. The blankets looked as though a minitornado had sailed through the motor home during the night, tossing covers as it went. His feet were uncovered, as well as his back and shoulders. His skin was smooth and dark, as though he worked in the sun without a shirt. His face was partially buried in the pillow, but she could see the whisker stubble on one cheek and his jaw, and his hair was adorably mussed.

Her sigh contained intense admiration. Ty Ruskin could be the star of any woman's fantasies. That he was already taken seemed like an awfully low blow. If he were free would she let him know how interested she was? It wouldn't be difficult to do, she would just smile in the right way and say something like...

Frowning, Loren bit her lower lip. Say something like what? *Ty, I've been thinking about what you said last night, and I'd like to know you better, too.* Given the fact that he was already involved with someone, what had he meant by that remark? *Loren, I'd really like to take you to bed, but I can't come right out and say that, so I'm settling for getting to know you better.*

She sighed again. Never had she knowingly stepped on another woman's toes with a man, and she wasn't going to start now. Not that she had concrete evidence of Ty's involvement. But it had been obvious yesterday that he'd been driving to an important engagement, and who else would be important on a Saturday outing but a woman? And he himself had said a few things to lead her thinking in that direction. *Stop mooning over a man you cannot have,* she chided herself. All Ty Ruskin could possibly give you is heartache.

Quietly Loren reached for her watch on the minuscule nightstand and checked the time: 7:10 a.m. Setting the watch down, she stared at the ceiling and worried. What if no one came along today? There was enough water in the tanks for cooking and drinking, but any more showers were out. She should have been more conservative last night and limited their water usage to washing up at the bathroom sink.

For the first time ever Loren longed for some traffic noises. Other than Ty's and that one truck yesterday afternoon, she had not seen or heard another vehicle since the motor home got bogged down. What if—God forbid—no one else came along for days?

But in that case, wouldn't someone be looking for Ty? He said there were people at his ranch, and if he didn't return there tonight as planned, surely they would question his absence. As for the lady he'd been going to meet yesterday, she might have already become alarmed enough to call the police. Maybe a police car would cruise that old road and the officer would spot them.

It was all wishful thinking. Getting out of here seemed more crucial this morning than it had yesterday. Was that because of Ty? Because he was already in the next bed, and who knew which bed he might be using tonight, should this almost unbelievable situation persist?

Uneasy with that conjecture, Loren silently slipped out of bed. Nature called, and she used the bathroom facilities as quietly as possible. But the damned toilet flushed much too noisily, and she winced, knowing that Ty had probably been awakened by the disruptive sound.

Quickly she washed her hands and face, and brushed her hair and then her teeth. She had packed a spare toothbrush in her cosmetic case, and she laid it out on the sink counter for Ty to use, along with her razor. For a second she stopped to ponder Providence or whatever it was that had urged her to bring an extra toothbrush with her. This whole thing was beginning to feel like the Twilight Zone.

Shaking her head, she opened the bathroom door and stepped into the narrow hall.

"Morning." Ty was dressed and sitting in the upholstered chair.

Loren jumped. She had suspected he might be awake, but him being up and dressed hadn't entered her mind. "Good morning," she returned. He hadn't buttoned his shirt, and the visible portion of bare chest between the panels was highly suggestive.

Either that or she was unduly on edge this morning. Wasn't he looking at her nightshirt with a little too much interest?

"I'm going to get dressed," she told him. "Maybe you wouldn't mind waiting outside? Then I'll go out and you can have the bathroom. I laid out a new toothbrush and my razor for your use."

"Fine," Ty said agreeably, getting to his feet. He paused at the door. "These units aren't exactly designed for privacy, are they?"

"No," Loren agreed, avoiding his startlingly blue eyes. He *had* heard her in the bathroom! Bravely she looked at him. "They're not soundproof, at any rate."

"I'm referring to space, Loren, and to you and me, a man and a woman who can't get dressed and undressed in front of each other. It's probably great for a couple in love." He went through the door.

Loren stood there with wider eyes. She had never associated the compact living space with a couple in love, but this much togetherness with a man she loved would be fantastic. Her very skin tingled from an immediate barrage of intimate images. This could be a palace of sexuality. The tiny bedroom, herself aware of her lover's every movement, eating together, laughing together, sharing every small nuance of daily life.

The opportunity was at hand. From Ty's remark he was thinking of the same thing. A frisson of sexual excitement rippled up her spine and to the back of her neck. The sweetness of forbidden fruit had her grappling with her conscience. Making love with Ty Ruskin was suddenly the most desirable of pastimes. Would he really cheat on his lady friend? And if he would, didn't that make him the worst kind of heel, a man to steer clear of?

Realizing that she was standing as though frozen in place, Loren sprang into action and changed from her nightshirt to the skirt and blouse she'd worn last night with the speed of light. Without slowing down for makeup, she hurried outside. "Your turn!"

Ty had been walking around. The morning air was cool and fresh, but the storm had passed and the sky was clear. "It's going to be a nice day," he said as he approached Loren. "Not hot like yesterday."

"Good."

He stopped right in front of her. "Did you sleep okay?"

Her eyes darted to look into his. "I slept fine. Did you?"

He didn't answer immediately, but studied her with a concentration she found disconcerting. "I kept waking up and thinking about you in the next bed." Loren felt her face heating up. "Does that embarrass you?" he asked softly.

"Ty...please don't." She looked away from his face. "Let's keep this impersonal, okay?"

"Can we? Can you? I don't know if I can. I don't know if I want to."

"We hardly know each other."

"A condition easily remedied," he murmured, lifting a hand to brush a lock of auburn hair from her cheek.

She took a resistant backward step and changed the subject. "Have you seen any cars?"

He ignored the question. "I like being with you. Would you rather I pretended otherwise?"

"I...don't know." It was the God's truth. He was confusing her. "Ty, please go in and...and do whatever you usually do in the morning. I'd like to make some coffee and...and some breakfast." She paused for breath. "Then we had better decide how to deal with the situation," she added, referring to their two useless vehicles.

Smiling teasingly, he flicked the collar of her blouse. "I know how I'd *like* to deal with it."

Oh, God. How much plainer could he speak? What was just as bad, or worse, was Loren practically biting her tongue to keep from tossing the same remark back at him.

It took an enormous amount of willpower to turn and walk away from him. From a safe distance she heard him going into the motor home, and only then did she release the breath she'd been holding.

Her heart was beating crazily, feeling as though it were hopping around in her chest. She'd never been obsessed with sex before, so what in heaven's name was happening to her now?

Ty Ruskin was the most potent guy she'd ever met, that was the problem. Yesterday he hadn't made those suggestive remarks, but Loren had a gut feeling that he had only started his campaign today.

Anything could happen if they weren't rescued very soon. He hadn't even kissed her and had barely touched her, and her insides were already nearing the hot mush stage.

Her father and brothers were right. She never should have taken this trip!

Chapter Four

Breakfast was a strained event. Along with a pot of coffee, Loren set out cold cereal, milk and sugar. "Is this enough?"

"It's plenty." Ty took a swallow from his mug. "Good coffee."

With an acknowledging nod, Loren spooned a bite of cereal into her mouth. The dinette was much too cozy. Wherever she moved her knees beneath the table, Ty's seemed to follow. Dinner last night had been much more comfortable, probably because he hadn't played kneesies while wearing an innocent expression that stated each contact was pure accident.

"I strongly suggest we stay close to the road so we don't miss any car that might drive by," she said tautly.

"One could be driving by right now," Ty said with a teasing twinkle in his blue eyes.

"I can see the road through the window, and so could you if you turned your head," Loren said pointedly. "So far this morning there's been no traffic at all. But we have to be prepared. By the time a vehicle gets close enough to see, neither of us could run fast enough to catch the driver's attention."

"You did yesterday, with me."

"I was already halfway to the road when I saw your truck!" Loren exclaimed.

"Don't worry about it. I'll walk down to the road and be ready for anyone who comes by."

"We can take turns," Loren said, relieved that he was again being cooperative. Sometimes she swore he hoped no one would come along, which would mean another night together. Their relationship was changing by the minute. They were becoming more familiar with each other, losing the natural restraint people had with strangers. Ty's glances were getting bolder, of longer duration, and there were messages in his eyes that hadn't been there yesterday.

No, another night together wasn't what either of them needed, even though he was probably too cocksure to admit it. How many women did he want? Were two enough, or was he one of those guys who maintained a string of willing gals? Loren's opinion of Ty Ruskin was something else that kept changing. Yesterday she had thought him sweet, kind and considerate. Today he seemed like a predator.

True to his word, Ty left the motor home right after breakfast. Taking a mug of coffee with him, he hiked down to the road and stood there. Loren watched him from a window for a long time then, with an uneasy sensation seemingly bonded with the pit of her stomach, she washed the dishes and made the beds. Plumping the pillow on Ty's bed, she absolutely refused to acknowledge the faint aroma of after-shave rising from the linen.

Brushing her hair at the bathroom mirror and unable to stand the sight of her face without makeup, she applied her usual light coating of cosmetics and felt much better. If Ty thought the makeup was for his benefit, she would just have to set him straight.

But in the back of Loren's mind was a worry that setting Ty straight on anything, especially if he made a real pass, might not be so easy for her to do. In less than twenty-four hours and without one physical act between them, Ty Ruskin had gotten under her skin.

Grumpy about it, she went outside to call, "Ty, would you like me to relieve you for a while?"

Ty could hear her yelling and turned around to shout, "What did you say?"

"Would you like me to watch the road for a while?"

He waved his hand and shook his head. Frowning, Loren plopped down into a chair. Obviously he wasn't going to let her share the dull duty, which shouldn't surprise her after his macho attitude yesterday. She eyed the other chair. Ty should have it. At least he could be sitting instead of standing.

Carrying the folded chair, she trudged down to the road. Ty heard her coming. "What're you doing?"

"What does it look like? I'm bringing you a chair."

Her testy tone amused Ty. "What's the matter, Loren?"

"Nothing's the matter."

"Sounds like something's the matter," Ty insisted, taking the chair and setting it up. "This was thoughtful. Thanks." There was a furrow in Loren's forehead. "Maybe you're getting tired of Nevada."

"I . . ." She hesitated, then blurted out, "Ty, there must be something we can do, other than sit beside this road and pray for traffic!"

"Want me to set out walking?"

"No! Of course not. But..."

After looking at her for a moment, he put his hands on her shoulders. Her worry was genuine, and he shouldn't be making fun of her. "Take it easy, honey. Someone'll come along."

She was looking into his eyes, and his hands felt comforting. "You're not worried or scared at all, are you?"

He laughed softly. "This is my country, Loren. There's nothing to be afraid of out here." His smile disappeared. "Except maybe for what you're making me feel."

"Why..." She cleared her throat. "Why would I make you afraid?"

"Because I'm wading through unfamiliar territory with you."

"That's silly. You have women friends." She saw his gaze drop to her mouth. "Ty, I know you have female friends. Probably one who's very important..."

His face moved closer to hers until she could feel his breath on her lips. "No one but you is important right now, Loren," he murmured huskily. His mouth captured hers.

Her emotions went flying. Her first sensible reaction was to push him away, but when her hands rose to his chest to push, they just kept going till they had clasped together at the back of his neck.

He kissed her gently, then with urgency, and when she began kissing him in return, he drew her closer in a sweeping embrace. Her fingers twined into his hair; his roamed her back and hips.

She stood on tiptoe, leaned into him, kissed him with pleasure and passion and let him explore. He felt so male and solid, and kissing him was a delight. His tongue slipped between her lips to boldly plumb her mouth. That, too, felt marvelous, and she snuggled closer, enjoying the tingles and waves of warmth darting erratically within herself.

But then he pressed her hips forward, firmly uniting their lower bodies, and the strength and heat of his arousal startled Loren back to reality. Gasping, she exploded out of his arms. "Ty, stop!"

He looked dazed, as though coming out of a deep sleep. He'd been lost in that kiss, on an exciting plane of emotion and desire that had seemed like a whole other world, and had felt the same from her. "Loren . . . honey . . ."

Wild-eyed, she held up her hands. "I won't do this with you."

He stared, stunned. "Meaning you don't like *me?*" She'd kissed him as though she loved him, so the question seemed utterly inane. And yet he'd had to ask it. His disbelief, however, seeped into his voice, which hit Loren wrong.

"You're not irresistible, you know!"

Ty recoiled. His eyes became frosty. "Sorry. I must have misinterpreted the way you kissed back."

Several scathing retorts occurred to Loren, but fighting with Ty over a kiss seemed terribly ungrateful after all the trouble she'd caused him.

Spinning on her heel she strode away, heading for the pitiful collection of impotent vehicles. Her teeth gritted together as she walked, and when she passed by

Ty's pickup truck, she gave it an angry, resentful whack with her hand. Stalking into the motor home, she slammed the door shut.

But next she found herself at a window, furtively peeking out at the man sitting next to the road. Ty's back was to her, and she had ample time to remember his kiss and fume to her heart's content. What was he thinking right now?

Pacing in a motor home wasn't all that effective for letting off steam. Besides, Loren's steam seemed locked deep inside, scalding her most secret places, making the RV feel airless.

Angrily she jerked open windows, stopping after two to catch her breath. Why on earth couldn't she breathe normally? There had to be plenty of oxygen when there wasn't anyone within miles to use it up!

No one but Ty Ruskin. Gnawing a thumbnail, Loren moved to another window, this one providing the best view of Ty and the infamous road. Yesterday she had admired the isolation, the endless silence, the wide-open spaces. Had she lost her mind somewhere between L.A. and Nevada?

At noon she made a sandwich and a pitcher of iced tea, which she lugged down to Ty. "You can sit here while I take a little walk," he told her.

"Oh. Yes, go on. I'll wait here." Sipping tea directly from the pitcher, she stared up the vacant road and then down the vacant road. Her eyes played tricks on her, and the road seemed to go on forever, vanishing finally into wavering shimmers of light.

Blinking, she ran a hand through her hair, wishing she'd thought to put on her straw hat. The sun, though less powerful than yesterday, was high and hot. Ty couldn't sit out here for the rest of the day; how could she expect him to?

Regret for her own arrogant independence was strong and depressing, and by the time Ty returned ten minutes later she had descended into a self-accusing blue funk.

He seemed cheery, though. "You drank almost all of the tea. I thought you brought it for me."

Loren looked at the pitcher, which had been full and now was almost empty. Listlessly she stood up. "I'll make you some more."

"Hey." He caught her by the arm. "This is getting to you, isn't it?"

"Isn't it getting to you?"

"I'm used to the quiet, Loren."

Her eyes sparked. "Quiet is one thing! This is...it's positively primitive! Where are the people? Are you the only person living in Nevada?"

"Isn't this what you were looking for on America's backroads?"

"If you make fun of me one more time, I'll brain you!" she shrieked. Shaking her arm loose, she stormed off. Four steps away, she stopped and turned around. "I want you to quit."

He was laughing and trying not to let it show. "Quit what, honey?"

"Quit staring at that miserable road! No one's going to come along, not for the rest of our lives!"

That did it. Ty nearly doubled over with laughter. Loren stared as though he were demented, but then a smile nipped at her own lips, and finally a full-fledged laugh burst from her throat. She dropped the pitcher—which was plastic and merely spilled its contents in a tumble across the sand and gravel—to hold her sides and gasp, "Why are we laughing? What's so funny?"

"Nothing. Everything," Ty managed to get out between huge roars of laughter.

After a while they calmed down to occasional eruptions of mirth, until finally the compulsion passed. Loren bent over for the pitcher, then held it in front of her, raising her eyes to his almost shyly. "It felt good to laugh, but our situation really isn't funny."

"No, it isn't," Ty agreed. "But you've got to go with the flow out here, Loren. We can't conjure up a car just because we'd like to see one drive by."

"This whole thing is my fault."

"Do you hear me complaining?"

"You should be." She sighed and looked down the empty road. "You might as well give up and come back to the motor home. It's getting very hot out here."

"Just bring me another pitcher of tea, okay? I don't give up easily, Loren."

How well she understood that about him. Yesterday he hadn't given up on freeing the motor home until every possible method had been tried at least a dozen times.

"You're a stubborn man," she said quietly.

"I think that's a fair assessment." His eyes grew darker. "I'm especially stubborn when I see something I want."

She didn't pretend to misunderstand his meaning. "And you want me."

"In the worst way."

"Regardless of the consequences."

Curiously Ty peered at her. "What consequences?"

Loren opened her mouth to tell him, but the words wouldn't come. His special lady friend was his business, not hers. *If* there was a special friend, of course, which she couldn't believe there wasn't. That's who he'd been going to see yesterday, and him trying to convince her now that Loren Tanner was the only important woman in his life wasn't going to lure her into bed with him.

"Forget it." Loren walked away. "I'll bring you another pitcher of tea."

Puzzled, Ty watched her go. Her skirt had an intriguing sway from her walk, but her fascinating, totally female way of moving wasn't what held his interest; what she might have meant by "consequences" did. What consequences? Was she involved with someone in L.A.?

His eyes narrowed speculatively for a moment, but then, in a sudden surge of masculine self-pity, he wondered if a mere man could ever comprehend the workings of the female mind. All he knew for certain was that she'd kissed him back like a hungry woman, and if she had a man in her life, he wasn't taking very good care of her in bed. To Ty, that meant he had no reason to feel guilty about finally bringing Loren some pleasure. He plopped down in the chair and concentrated on that sensible opinion until he heard Loren coming back.

She delivered the pitcher of tea to his hands. "Did you eat your sandwich?"

"Not yet. I'll eat it now. Thanks."

"You're welcome." She didn't know whether to stay or go. "Are you bored sitting out here?"

He was swigging tea, as Loren had, directly from the pitcher. He wiped his mouth. "I'm never bored, Loren."

"I have some books in the motor home. Would you like to read while you're waiting?"

"What kind of books?"

She shrugged. "Several kinds. Reference material on the areas I've visited on this trip, some romance novels, some..."

"Romance novels?" he repeated with a grin. "Do you think I read romance novels?"

She looked at his incredibly handsome face. "No. I'm sure you get all the romance you want first-hand."

"And you don't?"

A flush crept up her neck. "I read murder mysteries, too, but that doesn't make me a frustrated killer."

"You're the one who suggested the parallel, Loren."

"All right, fine! I read romance novels and you don't. Let's leave it at that, okay?"

"It's okay with me, but I think it's mighty interesting that your first reaction to my question was that I wouldn't be reading romance novels because I experience all the romance I want firsthand." He took another swallow of tea. "Makes a man wonder, honey."

She rolled her eyes. "I'm sure you're completely capable of wondering about a woman's love life without one single remark from her, Ty Ruskin!" Whirling, Loren strode away muttering to herself.

Chuckling, Ty sat down and ate his sandwich.

By three Loren was on the verge of tearing out her own hair. She'd tried reading, writing in her current journal, sitting outside in the shade, walking in the desert and talking to herself. Nothing she attempted had the same lethal attraction as the man sitting down by the road. Sitting patiently. Sitting *stubbornly!* Did he never give up on anything?

One thing she hadn't done was figure out tonight's dinner menu. With that in mind she went to the refrigerator and opened the door to check her supplies. A distant sound jarred her senses: a car!

Giving the refrigerator door a hasty shove to close it, she dashed from the motor home, skipped the step altogether and leapt from the threshold to the ground in one bound. Ty was leaning over a car and talking through the driver's window with someone. Running at full speed, Loren realized that the old car was more rust than paint, and riddled with dents.

Its battered condition was immaterial; to her that old car seemed heaven-sent. Breathing noisily, she ran as hard as she could, and she was still running when the car drove away.

Shocked and incredulous, she came to an abrupt halt. Ty had turned around. Spotting her, he raised his hand in greeting and sent her a big grin.

Loren began walking. "Why did the car leave?" she called ahead, conveying the anxiety and concern she was feeling through the tension in her voice.

Deferring conversation until they could speak without shouting, Ty folded up the chair and started walking toward her. Approaching Loren, he began explaining. "It was a woman and three kids. She's going to call a wrecker when she gets home."

Loren switched directions and they started hiking toward the motor home. "She lives out here?"

"About twenty miles away. In the mountains."

Ty's explanation hadn't soothed Loren's concern. "Will she really do it? Do you trust her to do it?"

Ty gave her a peculiar look. "Of course I trust her to do it. She said she would call a wrecker the minute she got home, and I'm sure she will."

"I thought..." Loren's face was screwed up with doubt and apprehension. "I thought you'd go along. I mean, wouldn't it have been better to go and make that call yourself? If you didn't want to go, I would have. You should have kept her from leaving until I got here. Didn't you see me coming?"

A note of impatience flickered across Ty's face. "Loren, the woman will call. Why are you so mistrustful?"

"We waited so long for someone to drive by," Loren moaned. "And now she's gone." She sent him a probing look. "Did you know her?"

"No, I didn't know her."

"I can't believe she drives that rickety old car on this desolate road with three kids."

"Oh, really?" Loren's bad mood was starting to wear thin. "Maybe her husband prefers she stay at home. Maybe he tells her not to drive that old car on that desolate road and she does it anyway, regardless of his protective objections."

Loren stopped with blazing eyes. "You do enjoy pointing out the error of my ways, don't you? I suppose you think a male driver would never have gotten stuck in the sand, as I did. For your information, my own father got his motor home stuck in mud during a trip in the mountains." She took a quick breath. "But I suppose you've never been operating a vehicle that got bogged down, right?"

She was exciting to Ty even when she was angry, though he preferred pleasantness over anger. "Simmer down, honey. Neither one of us is on trial here. Sorry if I sounded patronizing." Walking again, he looked back. "Coming?"

It was either return to the motor home or stand out there by herself and stew. Loren opted for the motor home, but stayed behind Ty for the remainder of the trek.

He set the chair up again, placing it next to its mate. Then he stretched his back and wriggled his shoulders. "Got a little stiff sitting there for so long." When Loren didn't answer, he asked, "Mind if I go inside and wash up?"

"Help yourself." There was frost in Loren's voice and she didn't care, either. "How long do you think it will take for the wrecker to get here?"

Ty shrugged. "Probably two to three hours. Not long."

In Loren's estimation, "two to three hours" was a *very* long time. But she stifled the observation and sat down. Ty went into the motor home, and she dragged in a dramatically slow breath of air in a long-suffering sigh. If the wrecker arrived and pulled the RV out of the sand before dark, she could drive back to that little town she'd come through yesterday morning and park for the night. Ty would probably have his pickup towed somewhere, maybe to his ranch, and could ride with the tow-truck driver. By dark tonight, her and Ty Ruskin's association could, ostensibly, come to a screeching halt. Certainly there was no sensible reason for prolonging their feckless relationship by heeding his invitation to visit his ranch.

The strangest sensation of emptiness suddenly came to Loren. She had met numerous people on this trip and during other vacations, people she remembered fondly or humorously, men and women whose names became obscure long before their faces, and none of them, not one, had made the kind of lasting impression that Ty Ruskin had. Neither his name nor face would ever become obscure; she would bear his memory throughout eternity.

Loren's mouth literally dropped open. That was the silliest thought she'd ever had! Of course she would forget Ty, why wouldn't she? One little kiss meant nothing. So they had spent two days and a night together. Once she returned to her own routines and habits, Ty would fade away just like every other memory did.

He came to the door. "Mind if I have one of those sodas in the refrigerator?"

"Help yourself." This time she sounded more like her usual warmhearted self, which Ty didn't miss.

"Would you like one?" he asked, relieved that she no longer seemed angry.

"Yes, thanks."

Ty brought out two cans of diet cola and handed her one. Popping the top on his, he took the vacant chair. "This is nice."

They were sitting in the shade of the motor home, and Loren couldn't disagree with his comment. It *was* nice. With rescue imminent, the silent isolation no longer felt threatening.

"I'm sorry for sounding so grouchy before," she said quietly. "I felt ... trapped, I guess."

"You don't understand this country, Loren. You're accustomed to having everything at your fingertips. Want a pizza? Just pick up the phone and have one delivered. Need a tow truck? Look in the phone book for the nearest towing company." Ty gave her a quizzical glance. "And yet you prefer this kind of travel and deliberately look for little-used backroads. I'd say that deep down you're a nonconformist, but then, that's merely an old country boy's opinion."

"And I'd say you're rather astute," Loren countered. "Most people don't understand me that well."

Ty stretched his long legs out in front of him and crossed one boot over the other. "Well, I think the word *understanding* might be a bit strong, but then I wonder if men and women ever really understand each other."

"That's nonsense. I know some married couples who are so in tune they practically read each other's mind. You must know people like that."

Ty thought for a moment. "Yeah, I guess I do. Gabe and Sissy are like that." His gaze sought Loren's. "Gabe and Sissy live at the ranch. But they're not married."

"And yet they're in tune?"

He chuckled. "Been in tune for about thirty years."

"They live together, as man and wife?"

"Sure do."

"Well, different strokes for different folks," Loren murmured.

He grinned. "But you don't approve."

Loren gave a casual shrug. "Lots of people live together without marriage these days."

"Not Loren Tanner, though."

"I haven't, but I learned long ago to never say never, Ty."

"A remarkable attitude, ma'am. I admire your honesty."

Loren stirred in her chair. "Have you?"

"Lived with a woman?" Ty's grin flashed. "I believe I lived with you just last night."

She scoffed openly. "All we did was share the same bedroom for a few hours. That was hardly living together."

Ty threw back his head and laughed. "I do like your candor, Ms. Tanner."

She flicked a smidgen of dust from her skirt. "Not all the time, you don't." Her eyes lifted to his. "Isn't that true?"

"Let's say that I like your candor more often than not. Does that suit your picky penchant for precise phrasing?"

Loren laughed at his quick-witted alliteration. "That was clever. Are you a clever man, Ty? Yesterday I didn't think so. Today..." She let the implication dangle.

"Today you're wondering. Why? Because I kissed you and you liked it?"

Their amusement had vanished as quickly as a puff of smoke. Loren dampened her dry lips. "Does kissing well make a man clever?"

"Does kissing badly make him stupid? Or—" Ty's eyes narrowed slightly, "—does kissing inexpertly make him a Nevada cowboy? That's what you think I am, don't you, Loren Tanner?"

"Aren't you?"

Ty looked at her for a long time, then laughed. "That's precisely what I am."

Nervous suddenly, Loren got up from her chair. "I'm going in to see what I can scare up for dinner."

"Want some help?"

Ty's expression looked a tad too innocent to be genuine. "No, thanks." Bounding into the motor home, Loren stood away from the windows and door to ponder the last few minutes in privacy. Ty Ruskin had the most remarkable power to confuse her. He was as keen-witted as anyone she'd ever met. Brighter than most, actually. Getting down to hard facts, his good traits would make a long, long list.

She was becoming much too enamored of a cowboy she would never see again after today, which was something she hadn't planned along with her itinerary, haphazard as that was.

She should be extremely thankful that old car came along when it did. Much more "togetherness" with Ty Ruskin just might prove to be her undoing, and returning to L.A. "undone" would be the height of stupidity.

Chapter Five

To kill time, Loren cooked. She boiled potatoes and
eggs on the RV's gas stove and made a potato salad.
She popped a canned ham into the oven to heat
through, and prepared a butterscotch pudding mix for
dessert. Taking pains with the table settings was little
more than dawdling, though the result was gratifying
when she was through.

Finally the food and table were ready and Loren
couldn't come up with any more reasons for Ty to stay
outside and out of the way. She went to the door.
"Dinner is served."

Ty jumped up. "Great! I'm starved." Inside he admired the table. "Looks good enough to eat."

"Then, sit down and eat it," Loren said in a sac-
charin tone.

Ty's gaze snapped to her. "Are you mad about
something again?"

"Again? Thank you very much for that dig. I truly
appreciate it."

"You *are* mad."

"I am not!" Huffily Loren got the coffeepot from
the stove and filled the mugs on the table.

Ty sat at the dinette. After returning the pot to the
stove, Loren slid onto the opposite seat. Flipping her
paper napkin open, she laid it on her lap. "Help
yourself."

"After you."

"Fine." She scooped potato salad onto her plate and turned the handle of the serving spoon toward him. "Your turn."

They began eating. "This is great, Loren. You're a good cook. Make some lucky man a fine little wife someday."

Loren glared across the narrow table. "How do you have the ability to make a simple statement like that sound like a put-down? And where were you hiding that ability yesterday? While you were working on freeing the motor home, I thought butter wouldn't melt in your mouth."

"What got your tail in a knot, honey? The fact that I kissed you, or the fact that I kissed you only once?" They both laid down their forks. Ty's eyes were sparkling. "Wanna fight?"

"You're enjoying this!"

"Damned right I am. I've enjoyed every single minute of yesterday and today."

"Oh, please. Do you actually expect me to believe that you enjoyed sitting out by that road all day?"

"Well, maybe there were a few imperfect minutes."

They resumed eating. Loren saw the laugh lurking in Ty's eyes, and she was torn between laughing with him and keeping him at arm's length. But any encouragement from her would put them on dangerous ground. From Ty's estimate of the time it would take the wrecker to drive out here, she had an hour to get through. One hour.

Eating slowly did no earthly good, because Ty wolfed down two helpings while she fiddled with one and she had gained nothing. She served the pudding and refilled their coffee mugs. Forty-five minutes to go.

"I'll dry the dishes," Ty announced when Loren began stacking their empty plates.

"There isn't room for two people at the sink," she was happy to point out.

"Then since you did the cooking, let me do the cleaning up."

"You don't know where anything goes. I'll take care of it in two shakes."

She was right about the "two shakes," Ty saw. Loren's efficiency and speed in the tight unit already had the table cleared and the dishwater flowing into the sink!

"Listen!" Loren's head came up as she hastily turned off the faucet to hear the engine noise better. "That must be the wrecker. It's finally here!"

Ty slid off the dinette's bench seat and peered out the door. Loren had forgotten about maintaining their distance and peeked around him. "It's a police car!" she exclaimed.

"Highway Patrol," Ty murmured, pleasantly aware of Loren clutching his arm to see out the door. "He's driving in."

The patrol car slowly traversed the old trail from the road, and finally came to a stop behind Ty's pickup. The door of the motor home flew open as Ty and Loren exited the RV to greet the uniformed officer.

"Hey, Ruskin," the man called. "Wha'cha doing way out here?"

"Hey, Pat," Ty drawled. "What are *you* doing way out here? This isn't your usual territory."

Loren was smiling all over her face. "Hello," she said eagerly as the three of them met halfway between the motor home and the police car.

"Connie's been calling everyone she knows in the upper half of the state. Said you'd been missing since yesterday afternoon," Pat said with a grin and a glance at Loren. "Hello."

"Loren Tanner, Pat Wyatt," Ty said in introduction.

Loren offered her hand. "Very nice meeting you."

"I knew Connie would do something," Ty said with a laugh while Pat and Loren shook hands. "Loren's motor home got stuck in the sand. I stopped to help her, and my pickup conked out."

"Then you've been looking for Ty?" Loren said to Pat.

"Not officially," Pat replied. "But I remembered you using this old shortcut sometimes, Ruskin."

"Well, I'm very glad to see you," Loren stated brightly. Pat Wyatt's arrival guaranteed rescue. She glanced at Ty and felt some of her eagerness draining away. Would they ever see each other again after today?

Pat wandered away to take a look at the buried tires of the motor home. "Who was driving this rig?"

Loren and Ty had followed. "I was," she said quietly, her thoughts on their impending separation. Certainly she couldn't remain stuck in the sand, but why was rescue suddenly feeling like an enormous loss?

"She was heading for that red hill," Ty volunteered in the most nonchalant way possible.

Gathering her wits, Loren sent him a daggerlike glance. "It was a mistake in judgment, obviously."

Pat looked off to the distant red hill. When he returned an inquisitive gaze to Loren, she flushed three shades of red. "I know it was a dumb thing to do, so please don't give me a lecture."

Pat chuckled. "Well...do you want me to call a wrecker, or what?"

"Yes, call a wrecker," Loren said quickly, before Ty could answer. Unsettled about their separation or not, they couldn't stay here indefinitely.

"One's already been called," Ty reminded.

"But it wouldn't hurt to make sure," said Loren.

"What'll we do with two wreckers?" argued Ty.

"Are you really that positive of the first one?" argued Loren.

Pat was watching and listening with a straight face and a chuckle in his eyes. These two might have started out strangers, but they were arguing like a longtime couple now.

"How'd you call anyone?" he asked.

Ty explained about the woman with three kids stopping.

"Which company was she going to call?" Pat asked.

"Murphy's," Ty replied.

Loren looked at him. "You didn't tell me about a specific company."

Ty shrugged. "Didn't think it mattered."

"Of course it matters!" Just knowing that a specific towing company had been discussed gave the woman's promise credibility. Loren frowned for a moment. "I suppose calling a second wrecker would be..."

"Overkill?" Ty suggested with a grin.

Pat solved the problem. "How about me checking with Murphy's and making sure the lady contacted them?"

Loren visibly relaxed. "Wonderful!"

Pat started moving toward his vehicle. Ty walked with him and Loren stayed behind. "Thanks, Pat," she called.

"Glad to be of service, Loren. Good meeting you." Pat opened the door of his car and got in.

Ty leaned over the door to see in. "Give Connie a call, would you, Pat?"

"I'll do it right away." Pat's eyes twinkled. "Are you sure you want that wrecker? That's a mighty pretty lady you're stuck out here with."

"We've got to have a wrecker, but—" a spark of pure devilry entered Ty's eyes, "—it wouldn't hurt anything if it didn't show up until morning, would it?"

"You tell me."

With a completely masculine laugh, Ty rubbed his chin to think. "It would be a dirty trick to play on Loren, but..."

Pat supplied the rest of that idea. "But you like her, and the second that motor home is free, she's going to hightail it out of here."

"You saw the California plates."

"And the rental sign. She must be a gutsy lady to rent one of those units and hit the road alone."

"She's great, Pat."

Pat turned the ignition key and started the engine. "Leave it to me." He grinned. "Nothing I'd enjoy more than seeing Ty Ruskin hog-tied and branded like the rest of us mavericks."

"Don't try to convince me you're not nuts about your wife, Wyatt."

"Wouldn't have it any other way." Pat put the car in gear. "Look for that wrecker in the morning."

From a window in the motor home, Loren watched the patrol car turn around and head for the road. Ty was watching, also, she noted before deserting the window to return to the sink and the dinner dishes.

She had her hands in the soapy water when Ty came in. "I feel a lot better about that wrecker," she announced.

"I do, too," Ty said solemnly. "I definitely feel better about it."

When the kitchen was shipshape, Loren joined Ty outdoors. Working lotion into her hands, she occupied the second chair. The evening air was warm and pleasant. "No clouds tonight," she commented with a scrutiny of the clear sky.

"Nope, no rain tonight," Ty agreed.

Loren stirred in her chair. There wasn't any need to mention sleeping arrangements for tonight. The wrecker would arrive any minute now; Officer Pat Wyatt's visit had completely reassured her on that score. The silly thoughts she'd been entertaining about Ty, and any ideas he'd had about her, were no longer feasible. She felt relief about it . . . didn't she?

In truth, she was neither relieved nor comfortable. "This has been a real adventure," she said with a slightly brittle laugh.

"I'd say so," Ty murmured.

Seeking a neutral topic, Loren settled for "It'll be fun entering it in my journal."

"Oh?" One of his eyebrows shot up.

"Yes, I've kept personal journals since I was fourteen years old. I've got stacks of them."

Ty eyed her curiously. "You actually write down everything that happens to you?"

"Oh, I might go days and days without writing anything." At ease with the innocuous subject, Loren smiled. "Some days nothing very interesting happens. And sometimes," she added, "the entry isn't even about me." Her smile became slightly teasing. Not deliberately. That teasing note had appeared all on its own. "You'll be in it."

"You're going to write about me? What will you say?"

Loren drew a breath. Maybe the topic wasn't so innocuous, after all, and teasing Ty, even humorously, probably wasn't wise. Her answer was cautious, impersonal. "Well . . . that you came to my rescue, of course. And that you were kind. I'll probably mention your sister . . . and Pat . . . and the woman who stopped today. Things like that."

"Will you write about our kiss?"

Loren's confidence took a nosedive. If a man was determined to keep reminding a woman of a particular incident, anything she said could be related to it. "Um...I'm not sure."

"Want to hear what I would put in a journal about these two days, if I kept one?"

By telling him about her journals, she had opened a can of worms. But how could she elude the conversation now? Other than a flat refusal to participate further, she was stuck in a discussion of her own making.

Still, she was suddenly burning with curiosity. "What would you write?" came out of her mouth before she could stop it.

Ty became introspective. "I'd write that I'd met an unusual, vital woman with long beautiful legs and hair. I'd say that she kept surprising me, that the more time I spent with her, the more I wanted her."

He was going too far. Nervous about it, Loren broke in. "Ty...don't."

"Let me finish."

"I think you've said enough."

"Have I?" He got up, moved his chair next to hers and sat down again. But now he was within touching distance, and he reached for her hand. When he was holding it, he said softly, "Is this so terrible?"

Her heart had gone crazy in her chest. Her numerous objections compacted into a feebly stated "We barely know each other."

"I don't buy that. We know each other well enough." Ty slowly danced his fingertips up her arm. "I'm going to miss you when you're gone. Are you going to come to the ranch before you leave Nevada?''

The shivers in her body were distracting. "I...don't know." Never had the mere touch of a man's fingertips on such a public area as her arm caused so much internal fluttering. Easily she could break away. It would take practically no effort at all to get out of her chair and put some sensible distance between them.

But she sat there with a spellbound expression and let him toy with her arm, maybe because she had never seen bluer eyes on a man. Or maybe because she would be driving away yet tonight, and Ty Ruskin was the sexiest, best-looking man she'd ever met, and she herself had declared this an adventure no more than three minutes ago.

An adventure, yes. A fantasy, maybe. Her romantic side, which hadn't been truly nurtured for a long time now, not since Marsh had become so irritatingly possessive, was brimming with incautious urges. There was nothing permanent here with Ty, but they connected in the most sensual of ways. When one really got down to basics, was that so wrong?

"You're thinking awfully hard," Ty said softly.

Her eyes locked with his. "I'm looking for a reason for why I'm sitting here and allowing you to make a pass," she said in a near whisper.

"That's not so hard to figure out." His roaming hand lifted to her shoulder, where it slid upward to caress her hair. "It's chemistry, Loren. Yours and mine. We both noticed it right away. Don't deny it, please."

"You're asking me to forgo everything I live by."

Ty studied her eyes. "Is that what I'm doing?"

Loren looked away. "Maybe I'm taking this too seriously, but that's the way I am." She remembered something he'd said at dinner. "Why would you think I would be upset because you had kissed me only once? Wasn't I the one who broke things up out by the road? If I had wanted more, wouldn't I have stayed in your arms?"

"My arms are aching to hold you again," he whispered.

He hadn't answered her questions at all, and every traitorous cell in her body was responding to his nearness. An enormous weakness in her flesh made the tiniest movement seem like a great undertaking. "Ty..." she whispered helplessly.

He leaned forward, until his mouth was almost touching hers. "We're alone, but we won't be for very long. Let me kiss you."

It was true. The wrecker would be arriving. Everything would be over then. More than likely she would never see him again, and oh, he was special, so very special.

Her tongue flicked, moistening her lips. Ty's eyes glazed over. "Kiss me, Loren."

She moved her head a fraction, that's all it took, a mere fraction, and her lips were touching his. His hand went to cup the back of her head, and his mouth began moving on hers, slowly, deliciously. Closing her eyes, she let the sensual feelings flow through her body.

It was the headiest kiss of her life, rife with restrained passion, gentle, soft, mesmerizing, long-lasting. Her head began swimming with his scent. Her sense of unreality was heightened by the silent landscape. A thought filtered through the cotton fluff of her brain: Whatever she did or didn't do with Ty Ruskin, it must be her decision!

It would be, she realized in the next dizzying second. She sensed no inclination toward force or impatience from Ty. He was enjoying this sweet but sexy kiss and would drop it at that if she insisted.

She lifted a hand to his shirt and felt a strong rush of blood to her head, merely from laying her hand on his chest. Despite its harmless appearance, this was not an innocent kiss.

It wasn't for Ty, either. Loren's advancing hand felt like permission to him, and he deepened his kiss. Her lips parted beneath his, reinforcing his opinion, and then he stopped thinking at all and slid his tongue into her mouth.

Within the awkwardness of occupying two separate chairs, he tried to bring her closer and succeeded fairly well. His left hand began wandering, moving down her bare arm, then settling on her waist. He broke the kiss to catch a breath, but quickly claimed her mouth again. She was a potent, exciting lady, and he silently thanked God that delaying the wrecker's arrival till morning had come up for discussion between him and Pat.

Their kisses became urgent, their breathing ragged. Ty slowly worked his hand up to her breast, and his blood grew hotter at the whimper of response he heard in Loren's throat. Through her blouse and bra he caressed her breast. The quick peaking of her nipple in his palm conveyed her rising desire; his was straining the seams of his jeans.

"Loren," he whispered against her lips. "Tell me to take you inside. Say it, honey. You have to say it. If you leave it to me, I'll undress you right here."

Dazed, she buried her forehead in his shirt. Her breathing sounded like gasps. It was still daylight, she realized with a start. Behind her closed eyes everything had felt like velvet and darkness. "The wrecker," she hoarsely reminded. She was on fire, needing more of his kisses, more of his caresses.

"Give it time, honey," he whispered.

"It's been hours." Her own heartbeat filled her ears, wild and strong and fast. There was ordinary chemistry between two people and then there was this, which she never could have imagined herself as feeling. This was crazy, and wonderful.

"Give it time," Ty repeated huskily. Seeking her secret thoughts, he tipped her chin to look into her eyes. "Do you want me to stop?"

This was the moment of truth. They both knew it. His fingers left her chin to slither under her skirt. Her eyes widened at the invasion of his hand on her thighs. But it felt so damned good. Never had anything felt so good before. The intimacy of looking into his eyes while he caressed her thighs, higher and higher, was the most stunningly erotic moment of her life.

Groaning, she hid her face in his shirt again. "Don't look away," he whispered.

"I have to," she moaned.

Gently but firmly he pushed her legs apart on the chair. Her wispy panties were easily slid aside, and then he was exploring her creamy flesh. She couldn't stand it like this, not like this, with them sitting outside in the waning light.

"Let's go in," she whispered thickly.

Without a word he withdrew his hand and got to his feet. Drawing her up from her chair, he led her to the door of the motor home. She stopped to cast a troubled glance at the vacant road. "The wrecker..."

"We'll hear it, honey."

In the dim recesses of her passion-fogged brain, Loren knew she was being thoroughly and expertly seduced. What was surprising was that every part of herself was cooperating. Even her pragmatic side that wanted to watch for the wrecker was lulled by his opinion that they would hear it coming. They would, of course. The windows of the motor home were open and any small sound from outside was clearly audible inside.

Ty firmly closed the door behind them. "Lock it," Loren told him. Giving her an understanding smile, he obeyed. Then he turned at once and pulled her into his arms.

Their standing embrace made Loren see stars. Bonded from chests to thighs, the heat of Ty's body raised her own temperature. Her mouth was waiting and hungry for his. Eagerly she wrapped her arms around his waist, welding the two of them tightly together. His maleness saturated her senses. He was solid and big and overwhelming, and everything she was yearned, desperately, to be overwhelmed.

How they could be standing by the dinette one minute and in the bedroom the next without moving,

Loren would never know. But the table and such were suddenly replaced by the two twin beds. The narrow aisle provided barely enough space for two people to stand together; Ty's legs bumped against one bed, and Loren's the other.

Laughing for no reason other than happiness, they sank to the twin Loren used. "I care for you. Believe that," Ty whispered before kissing her lips. The words came from his heart. He cared so much for Loren Tanner, in fact, it wasn't possible to completely grasp his feelings.

She was on her back, her arms around his neck. Nowhere was there a thought of their impending separation. Over and over she kissed his beautiful mouth. Again and again he kissed hers. Undressing seemed as natural as breathing, and there was no awkwardness with buttons or zippers. Everything vanished smoothly, his shirt, her blouse, though they never stopped kissing.

"You're so beautiful," he whispered at the first sight of her naked breasts.

She thought the same about him, but the impulse to tell him so was lost in the overpowering pleasure of his mouth opening around her nipple. Her skirt disappeared, his jeans. She couldn't imagine how he'd gotten rid of his boots so cleverly that she hadn't noticed.

Down to panties and briefs, their ardor expanded. The small bed prevented much movement, and yet she felt his hands stroking her, sliding down to her knees then up to her hair. She was learning every delightful contour of his muscular form, and she loved that his hot skin was as smooth as satin.

Pressing into her was the proof of his desire, his manhood, contained superficially by his pale blue briefs. He was the most exciting man she'd ever been near, but what thrilled her most was that he wasn't in a hurry. If he was worried about the tow truck driving in at this sensually critical moment, Loren couldn't detect it, not when he lingered enticingly over each kiss and caress.

Her head moved restlessly on the pillow, back and forth. "Ty...oh, Ty." She didn't even recognize her own voice, so hoarse and breathless it sounded.

"Loren, baby," he breathed in her ear while sliding his hand into her panties.

"Do...do you have something with you?" she whispered. There was no turning back, not from this, the most exquisitely thrilling experience of her life. Right now she didn't care if the wrecker ever arrived.

"Yes, don't worry." Ty guided her panties down her hips. Loren kicked them away.

Her emotions exploded when he began touching her intimately. Of their own volition, her thighs moved apart. "You're wonderful," he whispered at her uninhibited response.

"I can't help it. You're...you're making me crazy."

His chuckle was deep in his throat and sensuous. "Crazy is best in lovemaking, sweetheart." Shedding his briefs, he got on his knees over her.

Her eyes darted to his arousal. Desire skyrocketed through her. She raised a wilder gaze to his face. "Protection," she reminded raggedly.

Ty leaned over the edge of his bed for his jeans. Without turning away, he put on a condom.

Her expression was rapt when he looked at her.
"Now," she whispered throatily. "Fill me. Love me."

"You're incredible," he mumbled thickly while
getting into position. "You're beautiful and special
and exciting. Where in hell have you been all my life?"

His penetration had Loren gasping in pleasure. She
wound her legs around his hips, and moaned with each
deep thrust. They kissed breathlessly, hungrily, and
rocked together for long, sizzling minutes.

The blood pounded in Ty's veins, fast and hot and
getting hotter. He wanted her pleasure before his own;
only her pleasure would make this perfect. But the first
time for a couple was always iffy. There would be
other times yet this night. By morning Loren wouldn't
be so eager to drive away. He had found her in the desert, stranded, and something startling and important
had happened with them. He hadn't expected it, he
hadn't been looking for it, but he'd be damned if he
would let her disappear before they both understood
it.

"Ty... Ty... Ty."

His name was a litany in his own ears, bearing a
rhythm that matched the movement of the little bed
beneath them. He couldn't hold back any longer.
"Loren! Stay with me!"

"Yes... yes... *yes!*" she cried.

The final flurry to a blinding release brought tears
to Loren's eyes. Weeping and clinging, she rode the
wave to its crest. Ty stiffened upon her. She saw his
face, its intensity, and her tears flowed harder.

He lay still then, his face in the pillow next to her
head. She felt his breath in her hair, warm and moist.

His heaving shoulders and back slowly calmed. Her tears turned to a languorous mist. The most delicious peace she'd ever experienced moved through her body.

"Ty?"

He raised his head and looked at her. "I think I'm in love with you."

She swallowed. Her own thoughts had come dangerously close to those same words. But commitment between them was impossible. "Please don't say that."

"I shouldn't say what I'm thinking? What I'm feeling?"

"You couldn't know that so soon."

Ty's eyes narrowed slightly. They could debate the point, in which case they might end up bickering, or he could make her eat her own negativity with the proof of his feelings.

He shaped a dazzling smile. "You won't stop me from saying that I love making love to you, will you?"

Something in Loren sighed soulfully, but she managed an almost normal smile. "You're entitled to your opinion on that." She couldn't prevent herself from searching his eyes. "You mean it?" So far in her life, she'd figured she was no great shakes in bed. Certainly she had never touched the stars so acutely with...

No, she wouldn't think about the two other men she had made love with. Marsh had been one, of course. The other had been while she'd been in college. Neither had been a quickie fling as this was with Ty, which was an unpleasant fact to attach to so much emotion as they had just shared.

"I mean it," Ty whispered, supporting himself on one elbow to tenderly touch her face.

His tenderness renewed Loren's tears. Embarrassed, she turned her face away. "We'd better get up. The tow truck should be here any minute."

Chapter Six

When Ty came out of the bathroom, Loren—wearing a robe—went in. Her first thought was of a shower. Using the remaining water in the tanks wasn't a problem now as certain rescue was imminent, and with discretionary usage, both she and Ty could have a shower.

Her robe was half off when something stopped her. Draining the water tanks was an irrevocable step, and until fresh water was available it would be a foolish move. Frowning at her reflection in the mirror above the sink, she wondered about the tow truck. Wasn't it taking an inordinate amount of time to arrive? Had some other fluke occurred to delay it? The past two days had been filled with unexpected twists and turns, and would one more even be surprising?

No, she dare not subject herself—and Ty, of course—to a waterless night. The bathroom didn't function without water, and using the great outdoors for the necessities wasn't at all appealing. One had to think pragmatically with an RV. These units didn't come equipped with a plumber and an electrician, and keeping an eye on the batteries, the potable water, the holding tanks and the propane gas level was solely the operator's responsibility. The pluses of this kind of travel were the freedom of movement and the comforts of self-containment, which, in Loren's estimation, far outweighed the caution one must exercise in usage.

The wrecker would be here soon, Loren assured herself while freshening up at the tiny sink. Brushing her tangled hair, she smiled at the mirror. Making love with Ty had created a whole new meaning for the word *relationship*. Their relationship was . . .

Feeling suddenly breathless, she settled for *incredible*. Indeed, what had just taken place on that narrow bed had been unbelievably erotic. That she could attain such heights of pleasure was deeply thrilling. Apparently the chemistry between two people wasn't to be demeaned or scoffed at. She had learned a crucially important lesson with Ty Ruskin: never again would she settle for less with a man.

The concept brought Loren to a complete stop. Staring at her face in the mirror, memory plagued her. Ty had talked about love, and dare she think that's what they were dealing with? Had he fallen in love? Had she? Could it happen this fast?

But their relationship was so superficial! Touching upon each other and nothing else, no other factor of their lives! This was only one small segment of her life, wasn't it? Of Ty's? He already had a girlfriend! What about that woman?

Burying the disturbing questions in the back of her mind, Loren stepped out of the bathroom. Ty was immediately visible. He had stacked the pillows from both beds and looked at ease lying against them with a blanket over his lap.

Surprised at his procrastination, Loren opened a cabinet for fresh clothing. "We have to get dressed,

Ty." Daylight was almost gone, she realized, and snapped on a light to better see into the cabinet.

"Com'ere," he said softly.

Loren glanced over her shoulder. "Please, Ty. We have to be dressed when that wrecker arrives."

"Please come here and sit down," he persisted. "I have something to tell you."

She turned to face him with a quizzical expression. "What is it?"

He patted the bed. "Sit down and I'll tell you."

Reluctant to further risk getting caught in their obvious state of undress, even by a total stranger, which the tow-truck driver would most certainly be, to her, at least, Loren hesitated.

"Loren," Ty said with a plea in his voice.

"All right, but just for a minute," she finally conceded, and took the very few steps needed to reach the bed. Seated, the warmth of his body penetrated her robe and skin where she connected with his hip, though she tried, unsuccessfully, to maintain some space between them.

Ty took her hand. "The tow truck won't be here until morning."

She stared into his electric blue eyes and tried to grasp his message. "I don't understand. Why won't it be here till morning? How do you know? Pat said..."

"I told Pat to delay it."

"To *delay* it! Why?"

"Why do you suppose?"

Comprehension built in Loren. "So you could... And you did!" A flush seared her face. "You and Pat discussed this? How could you?" Jerking her hand from his, she started to get up from the bed.

Ty caught her from behind and brought her tumbling down on top of him. Sputtering and flailing her arms, Loren fought for escape. The rat! The snake! And she'd thought he was an especially nice guy. All he'd wanted was a sexual tussle from her, and she'd been stupid enough to cooperate. She'd give him a tussle, all right!

Her determination flagged when his arms clamped around hers in a grip she couldn't break. "Damn you! Let go of me!" she shrieked.

"Calm down and I will."

She was flat on her back on top of him, held by arms that felt like steel bands. His strength was so much greater than hers it was laughable.

But she wasn't laughing, she was hurt. Too hurt to even be angry. She felt like bawling, and would, she knew. But not where he could see it. She would do her crying when she was alone.

"Loren..."

"Don't talk to me. I thought better of you than this," she said bitterly.

"Don't take it like this. Please let me explain."

"Do you think I want to hear how you and Pat Wyatt plotted so you could have your fun? Think again."

"Loren, it wasn't like that." Ty could feel every curve of her body. Her shapely bottom hit him precisely where it counted, and his arms were crossed over her breasts, unignorable reminders of her femaleness. Her hair was in his face and smelled like soap and sun.

Becoming aroused again wasn't his intention, but it was happening, all the same.

His voice became softer. "I wanted tonight with you, but you were not discussed in any way you could find offensive. I don't talk about women like that, in the first place, and secondly, you mean too much to me to put you on that level with anyone."

"Yeah, right," she sneered. "I'm sure Pat Wyatt is much too dense to figure out what you had in mind, right?"

"Pat's a happily married man, Loren."

"Which doesn't make him ignorant of the facts of life! Let go of me!" Struggling again, Loren managed to free one arm.

But only for a second. Ty had her subdued again so fast, her mind spun. "If you think these caveman tactics are going to get you anywhere, think again!"

"I'm going to hold you here until you forgive me," Ty stated calmly.

"I'll never forgive you."

"Then we'll still be right here in the morning when the tow truck arrives."

Staring at the ceiling, Loren realized the bulb in the light fixture was getting dim. "The batteries are running down," she said furiously. "I've got to turn out that light."

"Nothing doing. You're staying right where you are."

"You dunce! The batteries are getting low!"

"Let 'em die. You're not moving."

But he was moving, Loren realized. Subtly, sensually, his lap against her bottom. The breath whooshed out of her as a wave of intense heat struck her. Responding to Ty again would be a final blow. She couldn't lie here and let him draw her into making love again, she just couldn't!

"All right, I forgive you," she lied. Ty's eyes narrowed. "Did you hear me?"

"I heard, but you didn't sound very convincing."

"Do you want it in writing!" she screeched.

"I knew it. You were trying to pull a fast one."

"How dare you have the bloody gall to talk about 'fast ones,' you...you jerk!"

Ty chuckled into her hair. "Damn, you smell good. Why don't you just relax and enjoy this, honey? That's what I'm doing."

"As if I didn't know," she fumed.

He laughed again. "Guess you can tell, hmm?"

"It's completely obvious."

"Guess it is," he agreed with another chuckle that sounded annoyingly like masculine pride to Loren.

Regardless, "it" was driving her crazy, pressing into her backside, making her remember his remarkable potency, and how she had begged him to "fill" her.

Humiliated, she went limp. Ty's arms gentled. "Honey?"

"Please don't 'honey' me," she whispered brokenly.

"You're making too much of this, Loren," he said softly. "I would never knowingly do anything to hurt you. Pat said you were a very pretty woman, and I said, 'She's great.' That's as personal as it got, honey. What's so terrible about a man wanting a little more time with a woman?"

"You could have asked."

"Something told me you'd say no. I didn't want you driving away tonight, and you would have, wouldn't you? You weren't planning to come to the ranch, either, were you?"

"Ty, this can't go any farther than right now, don't you see that?"

"No, I don't see that at all." He was silent for a moment. "Loren, is there a man in L.A.?"

She hesitated. "There was."

Ty's heart skipped a beat. "Was?"

"It's over."

"For how long?"

"I...haven't told him yet. But I've known it for a long time. I plan to tell him when I get home." She wasn't thinking about Marsh, though. "I'm sure you have someone."

"Why would you think that?"

"Don't you?" It was said with hordes of doubt.

"Absolutely not."

Loren dampened her lips, which had suddenly lost all trace of moisture. Who had he been going to meet in Tahoe? She was afraid to ask, which was silly. But catching him in a lie right now would be horribly painful, and she let the moment pass.

"Honey, if I let go of you, will you stay here and talk to me?" Ty wanted to know a little more about that guy in L.A.

"Yes." But she pictured talking to him from some sort of distance and Ty had other plans. He scooted to the edge of the bed and brought her down beside him, putting her in between himself and the wall. His face was inches from hers. "This isn't fair," she said huskily. "*You're* not fair."

His arm lay across her waist, his other arm beneath her head. In their scuffle the blanket had gotten lost, and he was nude and sexy and so handsome she couldn't risk looking at him.

Instead she looked at the failing ceiling light, which didn't seem to matter anymore.

"I love you," he whispered. Her startled eyes jerked to his. "Don't you love me, even a little?"

"How can you say that? How can you know? Ty, we've spent two days together!"

"And two nights." He nestled his face into the curve of her throat. "I don't know how I know. It's never happened to me before."

She moved her head to look into his eyes. "And you really don't have a girlfriend?"

He smiled indulgently. "And I really don't have a girlfriend. Except for you. Are you my girlfriend, Loren?"

She expelled a long breath and returned her gaze to the dim light bulb. "I am for tonight, apparently."

"You're awfully hung up on time, honey."

"My attitude is normal, Ty. You're the one who's a little weird about time. People don't fall in love in two days." They didn't, did they? Behind their conversation, Loren was envisioning a scene. *Dad, this is Ty Ruskin. We met in Nevada, spent two days together and fell in love.* No matter how cheerily one dispatched such news, friends and family were not apt to think a whole lot of it.

However, what did *she* think of it? Looking at Ty made the idea seem plausible. Lying next to him, feeling his heat and life, seeing the admiration and desire in his eyes ... Yes, one's imagination could get very carried away in these circumstances.

Especially when *his* imagination was working at full throttle!

"Ty ... we shouldn't," she denied huskily when his free hand began roaming.

"You're so sweet," he whispered, ignoring her plea. "We have all night, Loren. Don't put me in that other bed." His lips nibbled at her ear, while his hand smoothed downward to her thigh.

Her own body was betraying her by aching in a most suggestive way. Denying him was only sensible; denying herself was another matter entirely. She'd never been tested like this before, Loren realized weakly, pitying any poor woman who was this affected by men in general. Was this how some women earned a reputation for looseness? For being an easy mark?

Flip that coin over, she thought uneasily, and what should a woman think when she had finally met the one man who could turn her inside out with a touch? Was this kind of sexuality a basis for love? The lasting, permanent sort of love that created good and durable marriages?

"You're confusing me," she whispered. "You've been confusing me since we met."

"Ditto, sweetheart."

Loren wriggled around to see his face. "Meaning that I've been confusing you?" she asked with obvious disbelief. "What have I done to confuse you?"

"Smelled like wildflowers, looked like a sex goddess, smiled like a saint and presented arguments for female independence that made me consider campaigning for women's rights," Ty recited with a straight face.

"That's the most preposterous thing I've ever heard." But she lay back with a faint smile. Did she really smell like wildflowers and smile like a saint? As for that sex goddess business, wouldn't he be surprised to hear that she'd never, ever responded to a man so uninhibitedly?

Ty had found where her robe lapped shut, an exciting discovery. Casually he dipped a hand inside to caress her bare belly and was delighted to hear a soft sigh erupt from her lips. "I love touching you," he whispered.

She sighed again. "I think I love it, too."

He laughed softly. "At least we're single-minded on one point, honey." He raised to kiss her lips. She didn't turn away, but accepted his mouth on hers with a welling of gladness. They lived in two different worlds. For some crazy reason those worlds had collided for two days and nights. Facts were facts and couldn't be ignored, but she had only so much willpower and Ty Ruskin was an incredibly persuasive man.

Besides, she'd already given him her scruples, her morality, her standards. Maybe those traits weren't hers to reclaim until she told him goodbye.

However complex Loren's private explanations for responding to Ty, she was too honest to overlook the simple truth: he made her feel like no one else ever had. He made her feel sexy and beautiful, and like a wanton. Oh, yes, exactly like she imagined a wanton to feel—free, lustful, carnal, even a little lewd.

Especially when he did what he was doing now. Having most expertly located her most sensitive spot, he was lavishing it with gentle, caring attention and bringing her hips clear off the bed in promiscuous pleasure.

"Go with it, honey," he whispered between hot, hungry kisses.

She could do nothing else. Conversation was forgotten. Objections had vanished. Her robe was wide open, and so were her legs. Her mouth clung to his, taking his tongue, giving him hers. Ty reached for protection, then turned her on the bed so her legs hung over the edge. He got on his knees on the floor. Dazed with desire, she leaned back on her elbows and watched him slide into her.

This was not sweet or even slightly innocent. This was raw sex and so exciting she couldn't think. Sensation was everything. The look in Ty's eyes had her emotions reeling. Facing each other this way while making love was mind-boggling.

She tried to quip, and it came out feebly. "I'll bet this motor home has never been used like this before."

"Bet it has," he said deep in his throat and without a smile.

She didn't answer, she couldn't. Speaking clearly was impossible when she couldn't even breathe normally.

"It's good," he said raggedly. "So good."

With her eyes closed, she nodded. To disagree would be a lie of monumental proportions. Nothing had ever been so good before, nothing.

He brought her hips closer to him. She wound her arms around his head. His mouth found her breasts, and still he moved within her. It could have been a second, it could have been an eternity, but the next event with any clarity for Loren was the spiraling pleasure in her body.

Again she wept. Ty wrung out her emotions, shredded them. With Ty she had no control at all. Weeping and gasping, she climbed to the peak and went over. His release was instantaneous, and they held each other to calm their own speeding heartbeats.

Loren's head had dropped to his shoulder. She lifted it slowly, as though it weighed a ton. He was smiling. Not broadly or smugly or with humor. Just smiling.

"Lie down, baby," he said softly as he broke away from her.

She fell to the pillow, weak and exhausted and so sated she wondered if she would ever feel anything again. Wearily, blindly, she searched for the loose blanket and pulled it up over herself when she found it.

Ty returned from the bathroom and sat next to her on the bed. "Are you okay?"

Her eyes fluttered open. "You're...unbelievable."

He stared into her eyes. "But you love me."

"I do right now," she whispered.

Leaning over her, he kissed her in a slow-burning mating of their mouths. Finding herself kissing him back with pleasure was astonishing. How could she feel anything after what had just happened? Not one minute ago she'd been too drained to move.

Looking into his eyes, she touched his cheek in amazement. "What magic do you possess?"

"The same magic you do. We're perfect for each other. Loren, have you ever found what we have with anyone else?"

"No."

His gaze traveled her features. "Tell me about your friend in L.A."

"My friend?"

"The man you mentioned."

"That's over, Ty. I told you that."

"But he meant something to you for a while?"

He looked so intense. "About a year ago, yes. It's been over for months, Ty."

"But he doesn't know it yet."

"He will when I get home."

"Is he going to accept your decision, just like that?" Ty was watching her closely.

"What else can he do?"

"I wouldn't accept it easily. Not with you, I wouldn't."

Sighing, Loren lay flatter on her back. "Ty, you and I..."

"I don't want you to leave Nevada."

Her eyes widened. "I have no choice."

"We love each other."

She swallowed. "Please don't do this. My life's in California, Ty. Yours is here. I would never ask you to give up everything familiar, and you shouldn't ask me to do it."

He sat up straighter. "You have six days left of your vacation. Will you spend them at the ranch with me? Loren, if you leave tomorrow, we'll never know what might have been."

Troubled, she laid the back of her hand on her forehead. "You argue very effectively."

"You already knew how stubborn I was." Ty spoke lightly, but the expression in his eyes wasn't at all lighthearted. Nothing had ever been so important before. Yes, he was rushing Loren, but if he let her leave without trying every possible method of detaining her, he knew he would rue his negligence for the rest of his days. Maybe they weren't destined to be together. Maybe the momentous feelings she aroused were nothing more than intense physical desire.

But never had he been so driven with a woman to find out, and that, alone, had to mean something.

"Will you think about it?"

Her gaze flicked to his. "About going to your ranch? Yes, I'll think about it."

The dimming light bulb flickered and went out. They were suddenly enveloped in pitch-blackness. "The batteries died," Loren announced almost sadly. She had believed herself so capable of operating a motor home, and she'd gotten herself stuck, come close to running out of water and now she'd let the batteries go dead.

Worse than any of those sins, though, she had fallen for a man she shouldn't even have met.

Ty gently nudged her. "Move over, honey."

Loren sat up. "Let me pull down the covers first."

Shedding her robe, which had merely been haphazardly attached to her forearms anyway, she crawled under the covers. Ty lay down and wrapped his arms around her.

"We have tonight, my love," he whispered into her hair.

"Yes, we have tonight." That note of sadness was still in her voice, she realized. Fiercely then, she hugged him to herself. "Whatever else happens, we have tonight. Oh, Ty." Her tears wet his chest.

"Don't cry, sweetheart. Things will work out. You'll see."

Ty awakened in the morning before Loren. He was in the other bed, and he sat up to look at her. He hadn't slept very much, and neither had she. At some point in the wee hours he'd moved to the second twin to at least try to get some sleep. Together, sleeping had been impossible.

He released a long, quiet breath and filled his eyes with the sight of his lady. Her hair, which he thought so beautiful, was tangled on the pillow beneath her head. One hand was flung upward, the other lay on top of the blankets. Dusky shadows heightened her facial structure. She breathed shallowly, barely moving the covers.

Pondering the mystique and power of love, Ty watched her sleep. Envisioning the future without her in it created a dull ache in his midsection. Two mornings ago he hadn't known Loren Tanner occupied the same planet; today she was the most important person he knew. His life was neither empty nor dissatisfying, but if she decided to return to California without further contact, nothing would ever be enough again.

Lying down again, he recalled the night and the many times they had made love. Surely she couldn't leave and forget last night. It was unforgettable for him. Loren was unforgettable. She would live with him for the rest of his days, her laugh, her voice, her quirky but sweet personality. And the sex, the lovemaking, the way they connected on that most personal of levels. No, he would never forget Loren.

Hearing the rustling of bedclothes, Ty raised up again. Loren came awake slowly, stretching languidly, drowsily. "Hi," he said softly when her eyes opened.

She looked at him. "Hi."

"Sleep well?"

She smiled. "I'm exhausted. What time is it?"

Ty reached for his watch on the nightstand. "Almost nine."

"We have to get up."

Slipping from his bed, Ty moved to hers. Willingly she scooted over to give him room. He stretched out beside her under the blankets and brought her warm body up against his. The instant electricity between made Loren's skin tingle, and she snuggled into his arms.

"We have to get up," she repeated huskily.

"I know," he whispered, pressing kisses into her hair.

Her mouth moved on his chest. "Your skin has the most remarkable scent," she murmured. "I'll bet you use a magic lotion designed to drive women wild."

He chuckled deep in his throat. "Ditto, sweetheart." His hands roamed her nudity and stopped on her hips to press her closer.

His arousal sent shivers up Loren's spine. "If we start this again, we'll never get up," she whispered. "The tow truck will arrive, and the driver will have to beat on the door. We'll be terribly embarrassed to—"

"Never," Ty cut in. "I could never be embarrassed over loving you, Loren, no matter who interrupted us."

Loren realized she was sinking into desire again. It was the most incredible sensation, that melting of bones and tissue, that urge to forget everything else, that need arising in all of her secret places. One last time, she thought dreamily. She already had so many memories that were bound to be painful later on that one more would hardly matter.

Her hands slid up around Ty's neck. "I'm putty in your hands," she whispered.

"Ditto, sweetheart," he growled while seeking her lips.

They were outside drinking coffee when the tow truck arrived. The poor motor home had hardly any life left at all—at least not in its living quarters—as the batteries were dead and the water tanks were empty. Another day out here would have been rustic, indeed.

But the sight of the wrecker driving in weakened Loren's knees. Her hand rose to her throat as she looked from it to Ty.

"It's here," he said quietly.

Their gazes locked. "Yes, it's here," she whispered.

The heavy-duty truck pulled up and stopped. The driver hopped out. "You folks in trouble out here?"

"In very deep trouble," Loren said under her breath as Ty walked away to greet the man. Maybe she'd never been in so much trouble in her entire life as she was right now. Possibly she would never be so shaken and torn again.

She could hear Ty introducing himself and explaining the situation. "So, what we need to do is pull the motor home out of the sand, then hook up the pickup and tow it to my ranch."

"No problem," the driver stated confidently.

He hadn't been boasting, Loren realized a few minutes later. In no time at all, it seemed, he and his tow truck had freed the motor home. Then he called, "Hey, Ty, get in and steer that rig, and I'll pull it to solid ground so it doesn't get stuck again."

"I'll do it," Loren volunteered, and received a quizzical look from the wrecker operator.

"It's her unit," Ty told him.

So Loren climbed into the motor home, started the engine, and steered it while the wrecker kept it steady clear to the road. The man got out then, disengaged the towing mechanism, and walked over to Loren's open window to settle payment. Then he returned to his truck and backtracked to Ty and his pickup.

Loren sat there in the driver's seat, rather stunned
that it was over so quickly. She hadn't really said
goodbye to Ty, and she couldn't just drive away without doing so. In a rush of emotion she deserted the
RV, leaving the engine idling, and ran back toward the
men and equipment.

Ty saw her coming and took off to meet her. They
stopped a few steps from each other.

"Do you have the map I drew?" he asked anx-
iously.

"I have it."

He wanted to ask if she was going to use it, but it hit
him suddenly that anything he said now would be
wasted breath. She had to make up her own mind. Either she loved him or she didn't. Either she believed
that falling in love in two days was possible, or she
didn't. It was all up to Loren.

Instead of belaboring that subject, he touched her
face and spoke tenderly. "I'll never forget you, Loren
Tanner."

Her eyes were misty with tears. "I'll never forget
you, either, Ty."

"Do you wish we hadn't met?"

"No...yes..." Miserable, she looked away. "I don't
know."

They heard the wrecker's winch raising the front of
the pickup. "He's almost through," Ty said. "Where
will you go from here?"

Loren vaguely waved her hand. "Back to that little
town. I have to fill up with water and gas."

"I won't pressure you, honey, but I'll be awfully
glad if you decide to..." Ty clamped his lips together

to keep from begging. Then, throwing caution to the wind, he grabbed Loren around the waist and hauled her to himself. His kiss was hard, passionate and possessive. Breaking it, he looked into her eyes. "I love you. Remember that."

Then he was gone, loping back to the wrecker and his pickup.

With tears dribbling down her cheeks, Loren walked to the motor home and got in. It took three tissues to clear her eyes and nose, but then she realized the tow truck was right behind the motor home and waiting for her to move it out of the way.

Sitting in the driver's seat, she put the transmission in Drive and pulled out onto the road. In less than a mile the wrecker passed her. Ty leaned out the window and waved. She waved back.

And then she slowed the motor home down to a crawl, because her eyes were too full of tears to see clearly.

Chapter Seven

After stopping at a filling station that provided potable water and a sanitation dump for recreational vehicles, Loren drove to a rest area along the highway and parked. She left the engine idling to recharge the living area's batteries, got out her atlas and itinerary, and sat at the dinette to check the regional state maps.

Seeing Utah on this trip was out, she thought after a few uneasy minutes of contemplating miles and time. She only had five days left of her vacation, and if she wasn't going to stop at Ty's ranch, she really should get started for home.

Flipping pages in the atlas, Ty's hand-sketched map appeared, seeming to stare right back at Loren. She picked it up and studied it. It was neatly done, concisely pinpointing his C-Bar Ranch.

Never seeing Ty again was a painful thought, but if that was the case, why was she so reluctant to visit his ranch? Was there something about seeing him in his natural surroundings that bothered her? What did she know about ranches, anyway, and would she even grasp the success potential of his place if she were standing in the middle of it?

Loren frowned. Ty's old pickup had been gnawing at the back of her mind. Her family certainly wasn't wealthy, but the Tanners had never gone without. Was she afraid of becoming seriously involved with a man

of little means? She earned an excellent salary from
her job in L.A. and considered herself financially independent. Visualizing herself living on a rundown
ranch in rural Nevada definitely created some pangs of
doubt and concern.

Yet, how could she return to her safe, comfortable
life after meeting and loving Ty? She did love him, she
realized with fresh tears blurring the lines of his map.
Maybe theirs was not a traditional relationship. Certainly there were hordes of missing information re-
garding his life, and hers, within their brief if passionate time together. But denying any chance of
learning about each other by totally cutting off com-
munication seemed to be a monstrous decision. And
she was the one making it, not Ty.

She was at a monumental fork in the highway of her
life, Loren thought unhappily, rather dramatically,
and for a woman determined to the point of open re-
bellion to make all her own decisions, she wasn't doing very well. Why was she so torn? If it had to do with
Ty's material possessions, or lack thereof, heaven help
her.

Yet she couldn't think so ruthlessly about herself.
She could have married Marsh months ago, and he
was an extremely successful lawyer in the dual worlds
of entertainment and sports. Marsh's client list was
studded with names that made headlines the world
over, and if money was so important to her, Marsh
was the man she should have said yes to long before
this trip.

The thought of returning to California and taking
up her usual routines as though nothing of any im-

port had happened in Nevada gave Loren a cold chill. Her indecisiveness began to level out. She had to see Ty again and in his own environment. Most definitely she would use his map.

But haste wasn't necessary. Before she began the drive—tomorrow morning felt right—there were a few long-distance telephone calls she must make. Then she would find a grocery store and restock the refrigerator, give the motor home a good cleaning, locate a laundromat and do her wash and last but far from least, spend some time on herself. When she saw Ty tomorrow, she would look her best.

Pulling the motor home to the side of the asphalt road, Loren checked Ty's map and then took another look at the impressive sign situated on top of rock stanchions on either side of what was apparently a private road. *C-Bar Ranch*. This had to be it, but off in the distance was a sprawling, unusually attractive house, numerous outbuildings, what appeared to be a new barn under construction and hundreds, possibly thousands, of animals grazing in endless green fields. Miles beyond lay a line of purple mountains, smoky in the distance, indistinct but adding beauty to the scene.

Loren absently worried her thumbnail with her teeth while absorbing the view through the windshield. Was this really the ranch that Ty said he owned? This place was gorgeous, orderly, a striking example of country living. Why hadn't he boasted a little, or at least told her his C-Bar Ranch was a big place? Based on his

choice of pickup trucks, one would think he didn't
have two quarters to rub together.

A moment of gratitude filtered through Loren's
dismay: She had decided in Ty's favor before seeing
his home. Her love was focused entirely on him and
not influenced by one other factor. That had to be a
special kind of love when it had developed solely because of a man's smile and touch.

Loren put both hands on the steering wheel. "Well,
here goes." During today's drive a lot of weird
thoughts had run through her mind. Ty might not be
nearly as glad to see her as he'd indicated before they
separated. Their crisis was over, and his ardor could
have resulted from the circumstances of isolation and
opportunity. She certainly hadn't put up much of a
battle against intimacy, and it was possible that he
might be looking at their two-day affair as an exciting
but trivial interlude.

If that proved to be the case, she would know the
second she saw him. Her defense then would be merely
an admission of curiosity to visit an honest-to-
goodness working ranch.

With excuses and reasons for coming lined up in her
mind, Loren drove the C-Bar's private road toward the
buildings. Men became visible, those working on the
barn and several others moving within the com-
pound. There were half a dozen vehicles parked together, cars and pickup trucks, and larger pieces of
equipment near a long shed.

Admittedly Loren's heart was in her throat and
beating hard. Her confidence, usually completely dependable, seemed to be deserting her at this most cru-

cial of moments. What if Ty wasn't here? It was conceivable, after all, that his duties took him away from the house during the day.

But Ty was there, and he just happened to be near a front window. The sight of that motor home driving in was an answer to his prayers. Last night had been the most restless of his life. He'd been sure that if Loren was coming at all, she would have arrived yesterday.

He began running toward the back of the house. "What in the world are you doing?" Connie called.

"Loren's here!"

"She is?" Excitedly Connie ran after her brother.

Loren stopped in an open area near the house. The back door burst open, Ty came running out, and before she could even get the ignition turned off, the side door of the motor home flew open and he bounded in.

She knew then. She knew he was thrilled to see her, and laughing, she leapt out of the driver's seat and into his arms.

"You came," he breathed into her hair. "Loren, you really came. I was beginning to lose hope."

She nestled closer to his body, saturating herself with his warmth and scent. "I had to come."

"Thank God."

"Hey, you two, how about an introduction?"

The voice was female and friendly. Loren peered around Ty to see a pretty, young woman standing at the door and looking in.

With his arm around Loren's shoulder, Ty turned. "Loren, this nosy-Nellie is my sister, Connie. Connie, this is Loren Tanner."

Connie came inside and offered her hand. "I can't tell you how glad I am to meet you. This guy has done nothing but walk the floor since he got home yesterday."

Loren's insides had the substance of oatmeal. Ty's stance was a declaration of his feelings for her, and hers for him were making the air vibrate around them.

But she managed to shake Connie's hands and speak almost normally. "I'm glad to meet you, too, Connie."

"Told you she was beautiful," Ty said to Connie while smiling down at Loren.

"And you really drove this thing clear from California?" Connie questioned while glancing around the motor home. "Well, I'm impressed." She smiled at Loren. "Maybe I'll rent one of these and take a trip sometime. Sounds like fun."

"It is," Loren concurred. Connie Ruskin was pretty, vivacious, dark-haired and blue-eyed like her handsome brother, and obviously as independent as they came. Loren liked her at once.

"Of course, I was terribly worried about Ty this weekend," Connie said.

"An understatement, Connie. You called everyone in the state, with the exception of the Governor," Ty said wryly.

"And I was about to call him, too," Connie quipped with a smile at Loren. "When Ty didn't show up for my party after he'd promised so faithfully, I became worried and called the ranch. Sissy told me he'd left for Tahoe as planned, so I'm sure you can see why I got so alarmed."

"Your party?" Loren echoed. "Ty was on his way to see you?"

"That he was," Connie exclaimed. "Well, I'm sure you two want to be alone. Show her around the place, Ty," she called over her shoulder as she exited the motor home. "See you later, Loren." The door closed behind her.

Ty looked at Loren, and pure magic passed between them. "You're even more beautiful than I remembered."

"I wanted to look nice for you." Her makeup and hair were as perfect as she could make them, but the gladness in her soul was what Ty was seeing on her face. He'd been going to meet Connie on that fateful Saturday. There was no other woman, and the image of a shattered woman somewhere in Ty's background had been bothering Loren. It felt wonderful to be rid of that disturbing thought.

"You succeeded." His gaze washed down her bright blue peasant blouse to the bold print of her skirt and back up again. Placing his hands on her cheeks, he pressed his lips to hers for a sensual, drugging kiss. He spoke hoarsely when he raised his head. "Would you like to see the ranch?"

"Whatever you say."

His eyes darkened. "You know what I want."

"It's what I want, too," she whispered.

Ty swallowed and took a look out the windows. "Too many people here." His mouth turned up at one corner in a sudden grin. "I'll show you one of my favorite spots. May I drive?"

"You may do anything you wish."

He hauled her into a bone-jarring embrace. "Damn, I love you." His eyes were glittering when he backed away and occupied the driver's seat. "First things first. Tell me how to drive this thing."

Laughing huskily, Loren sat in the passenger seat. "Just like you drive a car, darling. Only you have to use the side mirrors and remember that you've got nearly thirty feet of vehicle behind you."

She could barely sit still during the drive. Though she attempted interest in the fields and animals they passed, her mind kept rebelling and focusing on Ty. He was taking her someplace private to make love, and their last time together, only yesterday morning, seemed to have happened eons ago.

The motor home lumbered into a stand of trees and then up a hill, getting farther and farther from the buildings. Finally the trees broke, and Ty braked the unit to a stop on the edge of a sheer drop that overlooked the immense valley below. The buildings looked like miniatures in the midst of such vastness.

"Oh, it's beautiful," Loren said softly. "I was surprised to see your ranch, Ty. I didn't expect anything like this."

"It's half Connie's. Someday she'll get tired of traipsing around the world and want to live here again."

"I'm sure she will."

Ty got up and took her hand. "It seems like a year since I held you." Willingly Loren rose and moved into his arms. "When you didn't arrive yesterday, I was afraid you weren't coming."

"I thought about leaving Nevada," she admitted. "But you knew I was ambiguous about it, didn't you?"

"It had to be your decision."

"Thank you for understanding that," she whispered, wrapping her arms around his waist and laying her head on his chest. "Oh, you feel good. No one has ever felt so good."

"I want to make love to you," he whispered. "May we adjourn to the bedroom?"

Smiling, she led the way to the compact compartment. They undressed quickly. Loren folded back the clean bedding on her bed. They lay down together, instantly lost in the wonder of each other's body. His hands on her skin created raptures of emotion within Loren. "Oh, Ty."

His mouth traveled downward to capture a rosy nipple, while his fingers tantalized the ache between her legs. "I want you for always, Loren," he whispered, rising to take her mouth.

"I want you for always, too," she told him when they had come up for air. "It seems so unbelievable, doesn't it? How we met? How short a time it's been?"

"It's the most believable thing that's ever happened to me. The best thing, Loren."

"Yes, the best," she agreed with a sigh of supreme pleasure.

He was all through talking then. His mouth lavished hungry kisses on her face, her throat, her breasts, her belly. Their pleasure expanded. Together, on that narrow little bed, they touched the stars. It was fast and earthshaking and even a little rough, as though they'd been apart for a long time.

Replete, they curled together, one of Ty's arms beneath Loren's head, the other lying across her waist.

"You're incredible," she whispered with her eyes closed. "I respond to you every single time. All you have to do is touch me and I'm excited."

"That's because you love me."

"Yes, I do."

Ty raised his head to see her face. Loren's eyes opened. "Tell me. Say it," he urged.

"I love you. Time doesn't matter anymore. I love you."

"Will you marry me?"

"Yes, but when? Where?"

"Do you want your family there?"

She nodded. "Oh, yes."

"Then I'd better go back to California with you and meet your father and brothers."

Her eyes widened. "You'd do that?" He grinned, and the sudden infusion of wickedness in his expression made Loren laugh. "You're thinking about sleeping in this little bed every night during the trip, aren't you?" she teased.

"I'm thinking about this little bed, all right, but I'm not promising to sleep a whole lot, sweetheart."

"We'll have to leave tomorrow," she warned. "I have to be be back at work next Monday morning."

Pointedly, Ty cleared his throat. "Are you planning to commute between Nevada and California, honey?"

Loren stared at him, then burst out laughing. "I still haven't digested it all, Ty. I'll give notice right away, of course."

They stayed there for hours, talking, making love and talking some more. New ideas were fun to toss around. "We could get a motor home of our own," Ty said. "Would you like that?"

Loren's eyes shone. "I'd love it. They're expensive, though." Ty laughed.

At long last, Ty decided they had to return to the house. "I know Connie wants to spend some time with you."

They made plans while they dressed. "We'll leave for California in the morning," Ty said. He stopped with his shirt still unbuttoned and put his hands on Loren's shoulders. "About that other guy..."

"I called him yesterday, Ty."

"You did?"

"Yes. I explained how I felt, and he surprised me by agreeing completely that we were never meant to be together." Loren smiled serenely. "I think he met someone else while I was gone. I hope so. I also called my father and told him about you."

"How did he take it?"

"At first, not well, which I expected." Loren grinned impishly. "But I was ready for his every argument with one of my own. I didn't grow up in the Tanner household without learning how to hold my own in an argument." Chuckling, Ty brought her head to his chest. "He'll like you, once he meets you," Loren said with a wholly contented sigh. "As for my brothers, they will adjust or not. That's up to them."

"You're a rare woman," Ty murmured. "A rare person."

"Ditto, darling. Double-ditto."

The trip to southern California was wonderful. At moments Loren felt like pinching herself to make sure she wasn't dreaming. They took turns driving. They stopped when they felt like it, where they felt like it. They cooked together, ate, talked and laughed together.

And they made love at the merest hint that either of them was interested in doing so. Which was often. *Very* often. Unquestionably they were falling deeper in love by the hour. At night, after sating themselves physically, they would tell stories about themselves and their families. Not one time during the three-day journey did they have a single disagreement or a harsh word. Loren was floating on a pink cloud of happiness, and if Ty's ardor and many kindnesses were any measure, he, too, was walking with his feet off the ground.

Things changed slightly when they reached Waycliffe. Loren installed Ty in her apartment. She went to work on Monday morning and gave her employer a two-week notice. Getting her family and Ty together was of the utmost importance, and she started making plans for a dinner party at the apartment.

However hectic the days, at night she and Ty were alone and in love. Sharing her queen bed the first time resulted in a hilarious session of off-color jokes and some ribald lovemaking. He continued to amaze her, bringing her to unknown heights of bliss with his vivid imagination. No room of her apartment was left un-initiated. They made love in the bedroom, of course, and in the bathroom, the kitchen, the living room, and of all places, the laundry room.

And then the ax fell. Loren's father refused her invitation to come to the apartment for dinner and to meet Ty. For the first time ever, Loren couldn't come up with a plausible argument. Tearily she put down the phone.

"What's wrong, honey?" Ty asked gently.

"Dad refuses to meet you."

"And your brothers?"

"Dad said they won't come, either, but I haven't talked directly to them about it."

"Did he give you a reason?"

Loren sank to the sofa. "He called me a . . . fool," she whispered, raising anguished eyes to Ty's face.

His jaw set angrily as he sat beside her. "You're not a fool, Loren."

Miserably she stared down at her hands clasped so tightly in her lap. "I don't know how to deal with this, Ty. Our . . . relationship probably seems foolish to him."

"It's not foolish!"

"Please don't get angry."

"Does he know we're getting married?"

"I was going to tell him when he came to meet you."

"Then all he really knows is that you brought a strange man home with you."

"He knows you're a rancher. I told him that," she whispered brokenly.

Ty sat back, pondering the problem. Loren's family, particularly her father, was very important to her. Granted, she had related her struggle for familial independence in many different ways, but obviously she adored her dad. In all of her stories, however, Ty had never gotten the impression that Lou Tanner was an innately unfair person.

"I think your dad's afraid you might move to Nevada, Loren," he said quietly.

"Pardon?"

"You told him you were in love with a rancher from Nevada. Wouldn't his first thought be that should the relationship endure, you would be leaving California?"

"Does he think refusing to meet you will destroy what you and I have?"

"Possibly."

"Oh, this is awful," Loren groaned. "What should I do?"

"I don't think you should do anything." Ty stood up. "I think it's up to me to straighten this out. What's your father's address?"

Aghast, Loren jumped up. "Ty, you can't just go over there!"

"Why not?"

"Because . . . because . . ."

Ty kissed her. "Give me the address, honey."

Loren was in bed when Ty got back. He came into the bedroom. "Sleeping?"

"No. How did it go?"

"It went great. Your dad and I are old pals now."

Loren bolted upright. "You're what?" She snapped on the bedside lamp.

Ty started undressing. "Everything's fine. We had a long talk."

"But what did you say?"

Leaning over the bed, Ty gave her a quick, teasing kiss. "Don't you know what curiosity did to the cat?" Straightening, he continued undressing.

"Aren't you going to tell me?"

"Nope."

"Ty!"

"If that's a call for love, sweetheart, I'm nearly naked."

He was. Weakly Loren watched him sliding down his briefs. And leaving them on the floor, as he always did.

"You're not only annoyingly secretive, you're messy," she said peevishly.

Chuckling, Ty got into bed. "Turn off the light and come here, honey." His levity vanished the second she was in his arms. "You should be X-rated, baby," he whispered gruffly.

She snuggled closer. "You're to blame, cowboy. No one else ever thought I was so sexy."

"Then I'm the lucky one."

"Ditto, darling."

About an hour later, they were speaking in drowsy tones. "Does Dad want to see me?" Loren questioned.

"He wants to take everyone out to dinner tomorrow night."

A lovely peace spread through Loren. "You're a miracle worker, but how did you do it?"

"I invited him to come and live with us on the ranch."

"You what?" Sitting up, she turned on the lamp. "What's wrong?"

"You asked Dad to move to Nevada? And he agreed?"

"Not exactly, but he said he'd give it some thought. I could tell the idea appealed to him, though."

Before leaving the C-Bar, Loren had met Sissy, Gabe and about a dozen other people, all of whom lived at the ranch. "For a man who goes out of his way to avoid crowds, you sure do have some peculiar habits."

"Me?"

"Don't look so innocent, Mr. Ruskin. You know what I'm talking about. Are you sure you want my family living with us? If Dad comes, so will Joe, and then probably Pete and his wife will follow."

"Not with us, honey, near us. There are other houses on the ranch, and if we need more, we'll build them."

Loren suspiciously eyed her beloved. "You're very wealthy, aren't you?"

A big grin widened Ty's sexy mouth. "Very. The truth is, honey, Connie and I inherited a wad from our folks, and the ranch just keeps making money. Until now, I've never had any reason to spend my share."

"You realize I thought you were probably next to penniless, don't you?"

He kept grinning. "You fell in love with my body."

"You're a sassy man."

"I'm a hungry man. Com'ere."

"Perpetually!" Laughing with pure delight, Loren turned off the lamp.

Epilogue

The wedding was held at the C-Bar Ranch. Connie was there, and so were the Tanners and about two hundred other people. Everyone was dressed to the nines, there were mountains of food and drink, and the whole place reeked of laughter and merriment.

In Ty's memory this was the first party he had ever enjoyed. Connie was in her element, having engineered the affair, and loving every minute of it. The Tanner clan was mingling with the natives and, Ty saw, fitting in remarkably well.

Needing a few minutes alone with his wife, Ty drew Loren into an empty room and closed the door. He kissed her soundly then asked softly, "Happy?"

"Ecstatic. You?"

"I love being married."

She whacked him on the chest. "You've been married for less than an hour."

Chuckling he squeezed her to himself. "About the honeymoon."

Loren tilted her head to see his face. "Are you ready to tell me where we're going now?"

"I wanted it to be a surprise."

"Yes, I know. But I've been on pins and needles for weeks now. Please tell me."

Ty took a look at his watch. "In . . . ten minutes."

"Ten minutes! Ty Ruskin, what are you up to?"

"You'll know in ten minutes." His eyes became devilish. "What can we do to kill ten long minutes?"

"Well, it's not enough time for what you have in mind," Loren said dryly.

"No? Maybe we should find out." He began backing her up to a wall.

"Ty! Don't you dare!"

But he never had been able to ignore a dare, and he was under her skirt in the very next heartbeat.

"At our wedding," she moaned huskily as his body filled hers. "What will we tell our kids when they ask about our wedding day?"

"That their papa adored their mama," Ty whispered. "That Daddy never could keep his hands off of Mommy."

"A lot more than just his hands," Loren gasped.

"Tell me you like it."

"Oh, damn, you know I like it." Never would she be able to refuse her big, handsome, sexy husband, not even now when her dress was sure to end up wrinkled and her makeup smeared.

It didn't matter. Nothing mattered but the overwhelming love they shared. If their guests wondered where they were for ten minutes, that was okay, too.

It was fifteen minutes before they came out of the room. Loren was flushed but her dress was fine and so was her makeup. Ty was wearing a huge smile.

"I want you to come outside with me now," he told her.

"Outside? Darling, we really should stay in with the guests."

"Outside, honey," he said firmly, steering her toward the back door.

With a resigned smile, she allowed herself to be pulled through the crowd. Laughter and jokes followed them, and Loren was positive she could never be any happier than she was at that moment.

Ty stopped at the door. "Ready?"

She batted her lashes in exaggerated seductiveness. "I'm always ready for you, cowboy."

"Not this time, honey," he said with a low chuckle. "Close your eyes."

With mock impatience, she lowered her eyelids. "Keep them closed," Ty cautioned as he led her through the door.

"They're closed, they're closed," she drawled wryly. Behind her, suddenly, were suspicious rustles and whispers. Obviously everyone was following them outside and, obviously, Ty had some sort of surprise for her out here. She didn't even try to guess what it was. The whole thing felt delicious, and she was loving it all.

"Okay, you can look now."

Loren opened her eyes, and they just kept opening wider. "Ty!" Before them was a gorgeous new motor home, a luxury model, the sort of unit she had admired and sometimes envied from afar.

Everyone was beaming. "Oh, Ty, is it ours?"

"It's yours, sweetheart. It's my wedding gift to you. Think you can drive a unit that big?"

"You bet I can!" Eagerly Loren ran for the door. Ty followed her inside and the crowd gathered around the rig.

It was stunning inside, roomy and elegantly decorated. "Oh, there's a microwave! And an ice-maker! Oh, look at the huge refrigerator!" Loren opened cabinet doors, and touched the tiled counter, and ran her hands over the plush fabrics. "Ty, it's fabulous."

She threw her arms around his neck. "Thank you, darling. You couldn't have given me anything I would like more." Her eyes shining, she leaned back to look at his face. "Are we going to take this on our honeymoon?"

"Would you like that?"

"I would love it! Where will we go? Oh, we could go anywhere! How much time can you take away from the ranch?"

"We can plan our itinerary later, sweetheart, but anyplace you want to go is fine with me."

"Oh, you're wonderful, the most fantastic man who ever lived!" Completely forgetting the crowd outside, Loren snuggled closer, a decidedly aroused and arousing movement.

"Whoa, sweetheart," Ty whispered. "We're not alone."

"Oops." Loren backed slightly away.

"Take a look at the bedroom," Ty suggested.

Whirling, Loren dashed to the back of the unit. "Oh, it's gorgeous!" There was a queen-size bed, a built-in TV set, and…a mirror on the ceiling. She gave the mirror a long look, then turned to Ty. "Was that standard equipment?"

"What do you think?"

"You are a devil."

"A devil in love, sweetheart." Ty took her hand and brought it to his lips. "We'll sleep here tonight, okay?"

"I can hardly wait."

"Oh, Loren." He pulled her close for an emotional hug. "There's nothing like being in love, is there?"

"Nothing," she whispered.

"We're going to be happy, honey. For the rest of our lives." He laughed softly then. "And to think it all happened because you got stuck in some sand."

"No, darling. It happened because you're a nice guy. If you weren't, you might have driven right on by me that day." She grinned impishly. "On second thought, you might merely have been looking for a reason to avoid Connie's party."

They laughed and laughed, happy together, feeling joy because of each other.

And then, holding hands, they walked out of the motor home to join their guests.

It was a wonderful day.

* * * * *

Dear Reader,

Living in southern Nevada means that you never have to own a winter coat. The fall months delight the senses with the most perfect weather imaginable: cool nights and warm, sunny days. Winter rarely demands more protection than a sweater or a light jacket, and one knows that spring has arrived when even the sweaters and light jackets are too much. Then comes *summer*.

Ah, summer. Everyone—regardless of figure flaws—hauls out their shorts and sleeveless tops, and still the heat cooks and sears and takes one's breath. Indeed, summer "sizzles" in this part of the world.

The summer heat is why my story "Stranded" was set in slightly cooler northern Nevada. Even so, the motor home inhabited by the hero and heroine for a few memorable days definitely got hot.

This was a fun project for me. My husband and I have owned and traveled in various motor homes, and I feel that I understand the units quite well. However, my heroine, Loren Tanner, was much braver than I could ever be, as I would never even dream of taking one on a long trip all by myself.

I hope you enjoy reading the story as much as I enjoyed writing it. Many thanks to Silhouette Desire and my editor, Anne Canadeo, for the invitation to join this year's *Summer Sizzlers* anthology.

Jackie Merritt

THE RAIDER

Justine Davis

This one's for Rufus J. Beakbanger,
whose assistance was invaluable.
Oh, yeah, and to his assistants, Virgil and Lori, too.

Chapter One

"If you want it, you'd better do it now."

Uncle Marcus's words echoed in Jill Brown's ears, filling her with an almost painful sense of truth, a truth much deeper than his casual words had been meant to dig. He'd been referring only to a last summer spent on his boat; she was thinking about her entire life. Her entire routine, monotonous life.

She tightened her grip on her canvas tote as she looked down the long dock in front of her. Nothing much had changed, she thought, except for the presence of that gorgeous old cutter, her masts raked back at an angle that hinted at speed even while she sat docilely tied in the visitors' spot used by the temporary residents of the marina.

Quite a contrast to Marcus's precious *Black Sheep*, she thought with a tiny smile as she started down the gangway, moving her gaze two slips farther to the blunt, blocky, converted trawler. The evening breeze caught at the wide brim of her hat, and she had to stop and clap the straw crown tighter on her head. Standing there on the slanted ramp, halfway between land and sea, she had a sudden flash of realization, feeling oddly as if her whole life could be condensed into this one moment.

Ashore was her reality; her books, the plain, sensible, white sedan, the concealing hat, the pull of the severe bun she forced her thick, mouse-brown hair into every day before she left for her quiet job in the quieter library. And out there was her dreamworld, the world that wanted to sweep away the hat and all the rest, a world of the *Black Sheep,* of the tales Uncle Marcus told of foreign ports and wonders seen, and of boats like that classic cutter. A world she had never dared to live in, had only visited, then left behind, filled with a powerful yearning. But if the *Black Sheep* was sold...

Her parents would be ecstatic, Jill thought wryly. They would welcome the end of this particular connection between her and Marcus. They would, she admitted as she made her way down the dock, welcome the end of any connection between her and her father's black sheep brother.

She stopped at the head of the slip that held the racy cutter. About forty-five feet, she guessed, then looked closer. A wooden boat, she thought in awed recognition. Someone had a lot of energy, to do the kind of work it took to keep an all-wooden classic like this in shape. Energy and time. Whoever the owner was, obviously had both; the boat glistened even in the fading light.

She walked on toward the sturdy little ship her uncle had converted from fishing vessel to comfortable floating retreat. She'd helped him, all those years ago, picking the bright colors for the cushions, the cheerful print curtains, and providing the whimsical drawing of a slightly bewildered—and certainly nonexistent—sea creature that looked like a cross between a fierce sea monster and a teddy bear.

"It's good to be reminded that even the most fierce creatures have a tender side," he'd remarked as he'd hung it in a place of honor, where "Cap'n Marcus," as the child she'd been then had called him, could see it every day.

Dear Uncle Marcus. He was—

A sudden rush of water made her breath catch in her throat. A vision of something like her sea creature rising up out of the harbor flitted ridiculously through her mind as she spun around, her hand pressed to her lips to hold back a gasp. What she saw bore no resemblance to either sea monster or teddy bear, although she stared as if he were a creature just as wild, just as impossible.

He pulled himself up to stand on the dock in one smooth, powerful movement. Water streamed over him, rivulets tracing the long, taut lines of a leanly muscled body. He glistened golden in the last rays of the sun, looking like some pagan statue come to life, his long, dark hair streaming wetly down his back, well past a pair of broad, strong shoulders. His flat, ridged abdomen rippled as he leaned his head back and swept the lingering droplets from his face.

Jill's canvas bag, dropped from suddenly nerveless fingers, hit the dock with a heavy thud. The apparition froze, halting in the act of reaching to squeeze the water out of that mane of dark hair. Muscular arms came down, and he turned. Slowly. Giving Jill far too much time to wonder why a pair of modest nylon swimming trunks seemed almost indecent on this man. He was quite sufficiently covered, but ... the way the wet fabric clung, outlining every taut plane and curve of what it covered . . .

"Sorry, did I startle you?"

A shiver raced through Jill at the low, husky sound of his voice. Horribly embarrassed, and aware that only her fist pressed against her lips had kept her from gaping at him with her mouth hanging open, Jill yanked her gaze upward. It wasn't much help; the strong, wide jaw, straight nose and beautifully shaped mouth were as devastating as the rest of him. Desperately, she made herself meet his gaze.

And backed up a step. Quickly. She wasn't sure why, except that for an instant she'd been certain she was about to plunge into swirling green depths that were bottomless. His dark brows rose at her sudden movement.

Only then did Jill realize she was still, quite rudely, staring at him. It was purely aesthetic appreciation, she assured herself. She stared at pictures of Michelangelo's *David*, too. But *David* was cool, inanimate stone. This statue was all too alive and breathing, and the long, white scar that slashed across his tanned abdomen only emphasized that fact. And this statue was looking back at her, quizzically now, and Jill knew that if he asked her what she was staring at, she would want to jump into the water he'd just risen from. Terrified of humiliating herself further, she backed up another step. The man's brows lowered.

"Hey, it's okay," he said, lifting his hands, palms outward as he took a step toward her. Jill knew that he was indicating he meant her no harm, knew, even, that the age-old sign had originated in the days when men had done it to show they held no weapons. The only problem was, this man had a more powerful weapon than any man-made kind. Just the sheer power of his intensely masculine presence was enough to overwhelm her meager defenses. She backed up another step.

The dark brows lowered again as he looked at her intently. Jill stood still, barely able to suppress the need to take another step back under the intensity of that green gaze. At last it was he who moved, shaking his head slightly, as if he hadn't found the answer he'd been looking for and then shrugging as if he didn't care. Then he turned his back on her and walked away, back the way she had come.

It was rude, Jill thought, but no more rude than she had been, staring at him without saying a word. As she was staring now, watching his steady stride, watching the muscles of his legs and buttocks flex with each long, easily graceful step. She looked at the mane of hair, trailing halfway down his back, thick even when wet. She'd never known a man with hair that long, she mused, caught up in her staring. She'd never known a man with eyes like that, either. Or a body. Or—

What on earth are you doing, standing here gaping like a fool? she asked herself sharply. *What if he comes back? What if he turns around and catches you staring, and gets mad?* With a quick, nervous movement, she grabbed her bag and scrambled aboard the *Black Sheep*.

"Rise and shine."

"Shut up, Kidd." Muffled by pillows, the man's words were indistinct.

"Up and at 'em."

"Knock it off." Still muffled, but decidedly more threatening.

"Move yer lazy—awk!"

The outraged squawk moved Gunnar Royce not at all. He sat amid the tangled covers of his bunk, scowling at the gray bird who was glaring right back at him from its perch, twitching its head zealously to shake off the water it had just been doused with. When the parrot showed no sign of continuing its comments, Gunnar set down the spray bottle and rubbed at his eyes.

I suppose I should be glad, he thought groggily. *At least his vocabulary is down to words that, if one was charitable, could be called merely colorful.*

He kicked aside the tangle of sheets and blanket and slid out of the waist-high captain's bunk. He reached for the jeans that lay crumpled on the floor, remembered that he'd decided yesterday that the rip in the left inside seam had finally crossed the line into indecency, and dropped them again. He pulled open a drawer below the bunk, took out another pair and yanked them on, foregoing underwear in the knowledge that he'd be changing to his trunks for his daily swim as soon as he was coherently awake. Making the full distance would be a little rough, since he hadn't gotten to it until very late yesterday afternoon—

Yesterday afternoon. When he had come up out of the water to find that odd, quiet female—he hadn't been able to tell if it was girl or woman, she'd been so camouflaged by those baggy clothes and that hat— standing there on the dock. She had gaped at him as if he were an escapee from some marine wildlife show.

He hadn't even noticed her until he'd heard the thud of something hitting the dock. When he'd turned to look at her, she'd been staring at him in such shock, he'd almost glanced down to make sure he hadn't come up out of the water buck naked without realizing it. But when he saw the canvas bag sitting lopsidedly on the dock below a slender, trembling hand, he understood that he had merely startled her.

Or at least, he'd thought he had, until she had taken one look at his face and started to back away. And when he'd taken a step toward her, intending to pick up the bag she'd dropped, her reaction had been unmistakable; she was afraid.

It had been disconcerting, to say the least. It had been a long time since anyone had been so wary around him. The reminder wasn't pleasant, even if this had been a different kind of fear, the female-caught-alone-with-strange-man kind.

"Great world we live in, Kidd," he muttered as he dragged a brush through the tangled length of his hair, "when a woman has to be afraid of any man she doesn't know." He set the brush down and looked at the bird. "And some she does."

The parrot tilted his head, looking as if he were considering the words. A grin curved Gunnar's mouth; more likely the bird was still deciding whether to forgive him for the spray bath.

"Come on, featherbrain," he said, chuckling as he went to stand by the perch. "Let's go take a look at the morning while it's still morning. I'll even share my toast."

At the last word, the bird's head came straight up.

"Jelly?" he squawked.

Gunnar grimaced. "If you insist."

The parrot flapped its wings once, then hopped up to Gunnar's shoulder, flexing its feet, talons against bare skin, as if to remind Gunnar who was in charge here. "Hey, ease up, I already said I'll share my toast."

The minute he opened the main cabin hatch, Kidd deserted his shoulder for the teak handrail that ran along the roof opening. Absently rubbing his shoulder where the bird had dug in, Gunnar followed in a more conventional manner, yawning as he went up the steep, narrow steps to the cockpit.

It was one of those mornings that made you want to settle down in some part of the world like this, he thought as he stretched. The kind of Southern California morning that made people decide to pack up and move there the day after the New Year's Day Rose Parade. The sunlight poured down like liquid warmth, soothing on the skin of his back. It danced off the waters of the marina, reflecting in rippling waves on the sides of the boats tied up in the slips. It looked like a great day for just lolling around, relaxing, like the woman sunbathing over there on Marc's boat....

On Marc's boat? He stood there, staring. Not that Marc didn't occasionally indulge in feminine company, but he hadn't mentioned anyone coming when he'd been down last weekend. This one looked a bit young for the older man's taste, anyway, from what he could tell from this distance as she lay facedown, her back exposed to the morning sun.

Not that she was a girl, not by any means, he thought as he leaned forward, eyes narrowing. No, she was all woman, ripe and luscious. The one-piece bathing suit she wore was modestly cut, but the sleek gold fabric couldn't disguise the womanly curve of waist to hip, the gentle swell of her buttocks, the fuller swell of breasts hinted at beneath arms raised to cushion her head. She was all curves; not soft, just female.

Heat, sudden, unexpected and powerful, clawed through him the way Kidd's talons had dug into his shoulder. Gunnar straightened, brows furrowed. His hand went reflexively to his stomach, fingers pressing against the scar that arced across his abdomen. The feeling ebbed slightly, settling into an odd warmth somewhere low and deep. He pressed harder against the raised ridge of flesh, but it wasn't the old pain he was feeling. It wasn't even pain, not really, not like—

"Aawk! Sexy lady!"

Gunnar turned his head to stare at Kidd. Then his gaze shot back to the woman lying on the aft deck of the converted trawler. She wasn't asleep, as he'd thought, for she'd bent one leg at the knee, lifting a gracefully arched foot to flex as if pointing at the sun. The heat shot through him again.

Sexy lady. My God, Gunnar thought, finally recognizing the long-absent sensation and nearly reeling under the shock of it. He hadn't felt anything beyond a mild interest—far too temperate to be called desire, let alone lust—for so long....

He shook his head sharply, as if that would make the feeling go away. It didn't. He turned back toward the cabin, stopping halfway down the steps when he realized he was, quite literally, running away. The idea stunned him nearly as much as his sexual response had. Gunnar Royce had changed, but he still didn't run from anything. Except maybe the windward side of the Caymans when a hurricane was brewing.

He glanced back over his shoulder. Kidd was still perched on the handrail, head bobbing up and down as he inspected the shapely figure on the *Black Sheep*. That was it, Gunnar thought. It had to be. She was just so different from what he was used to, so different from the too often painfully thin, driven women of the world he used to live in. That's all it was, he thought.

If they saw her, those women of his old world would no doubt tell this luscious creature she could stand to lose a few pounds, even though the muscles of the leg she had raised showed no sign of fat. He hoped she never met any of them; he liked her womanly curves just the way they were. He even liked the soft, brown sheen of her hair, long hair, apparently, since she had it pulled into a rather severe knot at the back of her head for her morning's sunbathing.

Not that what he liked had anything to do with anything. But, he mused thoughtfully, one foot poised in midair while it waited for the decision to go on down into the cabin or back up on deck, he supposed he should make sure she belonged aboard Marc's boat. Marc had been the first friendly face he'd seen when he'd arrived three weeks ago, and he and the slightly eccentric older man had hit it off well from that moment. The least he could do was make sure this woman wasn't a stowaway or something. The very least.

Kidd squawked. Gunnar looked at the bird, who was now level with his shoulder. "You're the expert. Can you be a stowaway on a boat that isn't going anywhere?"

"Stow'way." Kidd stumbled over the tricky word. "Walk the plank."

Gunnar chuckled at the decisiveness of the parrot's verdict. "Seems a little extreme, buddy. Besides, who'd want to feed *that* to the fish?"

"Stow'way."

"Maybe. Maybe not. Let's go see." He shrugged, and Kidd took his cue and hopped back onto Gunnar's shoulder. He came back up the steps and headed for the gate in the cutter's lifelines, knowing full well that concern for Marc's boat had little to do with his decision.

Chapter Two

Jill knew she was going to have to move soon. She hadn't been out in the sun much lately, and her skin was fair, anyway. She'd be as red as her Overdue stamp pad before long. But the warmth felt so good on her back, soft and gentle, easing away the restlessness that had been plaguing her. But then, being aboard the *Black Sheep* had always eased her, as if the boat, or just being on the water, held the answer to that nameless longing. As if—

"Aawk! Sexy lady!"

Jill stifled a shriek. In one panicked motion she rolled over and sat up. With the sun at his back and her eyes dazzled, at first all she could see was the silhouette of the man who stood on the dock steps. It didn't matter; she knew. *Oh, God,* she thought, *it's him. He's come back.* Somehow he knew she'd stared at his body, and he didn't like it.

She scrambled backward, wincing as she whacked her elbow on the bulkhead. She looked down, momentarily distracted by the painful, tingling sensation, but her head snapped up again at a piercing wolf whistle. The rudeness of it tipped her from fear into anger.

Her eyes were adjusted now. She could see that his were just as deeply green as she remembered. They flicked over her, making her conscious of what little her conservative swimsuit revealed. And how much his low-slung jeans revealed.

His chest was as broad and strong as she remembered, his belly as flat—and as scarred. Her gaze lingered there for a moment, wondering what had caused the thin ridge of tissue, but then seemed to naturally trail down along the path of soft hair that began at his navel, then dove temptingly down below the waistband of the snug jeans. Realizing she was staring yet again, and avidly, she forced herself to look up.

His hair was dry now, thick and shiny and falling in waves past his shoulders. To her surprise she liked the untamed look of it, found herself wondering if it felt as silky as it looked. The silliness of that reaction angered her even more. He was far too exotic, too wild for her conservative taste. *Really, Jill,* she could almost hear her mother's shocked voice. *A man with hair halfway down his back? I suppose an earring will be next? Don't be absurd.*

Her mother had taught her well. Wolf whistle, indeed. Her chin came up, and she gave him her best stern glare, a look that had chastened more than one rowdy child into silence in her library.

Dark brows rose as if she'd startled him. Then, unexpectedly, he grinned. "I didn't do it," he said, throwing up his hands in the same gesture of innocence he'd used yesterday on the dock. "He did." The man turned, then shrugged one shoulder, and Jill saw what the sun had prevented her from noticing before: the parrot perched on his shoulder. As if to prove his master's words, the bird produced a loud, equally rude kissing noise.

Despite her wariness, Jill couldn't help but relax a little. How evil could a man who walked around with a parrot on his shoulder be? *As evil as any pirate,* she reminded herself sharply. But it was too late; she was already smiling at the creature balanced on that bare, muscular shoulder, its head bobbing as if the bird were immensely pleased with itself. It was about the size of a large pigeon, just over a foot or so long, almost white-faced, with darker, soft gray, scalloped feathers edged in pale gray over its body and a reddish tail that was striking in contrast.

That muscular shoulder moved again in an ingenuous shrug. "Can't blame him for having good taste."

Jill stiffened. She knew well enough what she looked like. Her plain brown hair and eyes and plump figure didn't inspire men—or birds, for that matter— to this kind of flirtation. Especially men like this one; men who turned heads themselves, men who moved with such easy, confident grace, men with that indefinable edge that set them apart. Men that made even the quietly shy woman Jill knew herself to be look…and wonder. So there was only one reason she could think of that he was here.

"If you're angry about yesterday, I apologize," she said stiltedly.

"Yesterday?" The dark brows furrowed, then suddenly rose. "Yesterday?" he repeated. "That was you? In those baggy clothes and that silly hat?"

He sounded astonished, and Jill was suddenly at a loss, the anger that had enabled her to speak at all fading. If he hadn't recognized her, if he wasn't here to taunt her about her unrefined gaping, why was he here?

"It's not a silly hat," she said inanely, then wished she'd kept her silence when he grinned.

"Matter of opinion." He gave her a speculative look. "*I'm* sorry if I startled you yesterday. What are *you* sorry about?"

Jill felt the color rise in her cheeks. God, she hated the way she blushed! She must be as red as that bird's tail. "Never mind," she said hastily.

His gaze was fastened on her, and Jill felt that same odd sensation of bottomless green depths. He persisted. "What did you think I'd be angry about?"

In her embarrassment, it came out in a rush. "The way I stared at you."

His mouth twitched. "You did, didn't you? Why?"

"It's just that I've never seen—" She broke off as she realized she'd been about to tell him exactly what she'd thought when she'd seen him. She felt the color rise again and smothered a groan.

"Never seen what?" He looked intently at her, waiting, and she knew he wasn't going to let it go.

"I'm just not used to..." Her voice trailed away helplessly. What could she say? That she wasn't used to half-naked, gleaming wet, pagan gods rising up in front of her like the answer to some silly half-formed dream? That she'd spent her life afraid of, yet longing for, the wild side, and he was the living, breathing personification of it?

For a long moment he said nothing, just looked at her, his eyes narrowed. She got the strangest feeling of being assessed in an entirely different way, by a mind whose sharpness belied the casual, untamed look of the man. A feeling of being added up and the sum studied, until at last he nodded.

"You're Jill, aren't you?"

She gaped at him. "How—?"

The parrot's piercing wolf whistle sounded again. Jill flushed and instinctively reached for the towel she'd been lying on.

"Don't mind him. It doesn't mean anything. He's an African Grey, and it's one of his natural cries."

His explanation didn't stop Jill from wrapping the towel around herself. She keep her eyes focused on the task, tucking in the end to hold it securely.

"You *are* Jill, aren't you? Marc's niece?"

Her head came up. "You know Marcus?"

"That's why I came over here, to find out who was on his boat. He didn't mention you were coming."

Jill's logical mind was relieved at the simple explanation of his presence. She didn't understand the odd sense of disappointment she felt, as if she'd hoped there was another reason he'd come.

"He didn't know. I mean, I didn't decide until yesterday, when I realized . . ." She stopped, realizing she was about to broadcast the possible loss of the *Black Sheep* to a total stranger. She, Jill Brown, usually the most reticent of people even among her acquaintances. Jill Brown, usually as meek as her quiet name suggested. Jill Brown, usually utterly and totally tongue-tied in front of any man, let alone one as dramatically attractive as this one.

"Realized what?"

Why wouldn't he let anything drop? Why the pretense of curiosity, now that he knew who she was and that she had every right to be here? Why didn't he just—

"Knock it off," the bird said. Jill gave a little start; not only had the parrot's words been uncannily in tune with her thoughts, he'd said it in a low, husky voice that was unmistakably that of her visitor's. Her gaze flicked from the bird to the man.

"He can imitate anybody—or anything," he explained with another shrug. "African Greys are the best at it." He smiled at her then, a bit ruefully. "I'm afraid he learned most of what he knows from Cal, the old salt I got him from. His manners leave a little to be desired."

Jill had recovered from the start the bird had given her, but she wasn't sure that the jolt she'd felt at the sight of that smile would be so easy to recoup from. Drawing on years of practice in putting up a facade of control in front of boisterous children, she steadied herself.

"Whose manners?" she asked. "Cal's, or the bird's?"

The smile flashed again, and Jill, again, nearly gave a start at the odd little leap her heart took.

"Both," he admitted. "Kidd has a knack for saying the right thing at the wrong time. And vice versa."

"Kidd? After Captain Kidd, I presume?"

"I suppose. I never got around to asking Cal." A flicker of something dark and sad stirred in those green eyes.

"And now you can't?" Jill asked softly, a little surprised at her own temerity in putting forth the personal question. He raised one hand and flipped the long strand of dark hair the parrot had been tugging at with its beak out of reach. For a moment Jill thought he wasn't going to answer, and regretted having dared to ask. Then, abruptly, he spoke.

"No. He's dead. I . . . inherited Kidd—and Cal's boat—when no one else wanted them."

"How sad," Jill said, meaning it as she looked at the bird. "They live a long time, don't they?"

"Yeah. Cal had him for twenty years. It took Kidd nearly a year to come out of mourning and even speak to me." The shadow faded from his eyes, and the slightly off-center smile came again. "Most of the time, he talks in Cal's voice. Or yells at me like Cal used to do. It's like the old man's still here. I keep expecting to turn around and see him."

Jill didn't miss the undertone of affection that belied the words as he spoke of the parrot's former owner. She tried to picture the owner of the voice the bird had reproduced, tried to picture anyone with the fortitude to yell at this man. This man, she realized with a little shock, that she'd been talking to for several minutes now without even knowing his name. She drew in a breath.

"And what did he call you when he . . . yelled at you?"

"Stupid landlubber, mostly."

Jill stifled a giggle. "I can't imagine that."

"Trust me," Gunnar said, his tone wry. "He did. And at the time, it was true."

"I meant, do you have a name he used?"

"Oh." He got the hint. "Sorry." He looked at her for a moment, and Jill got that odd feeling of being assessed by a razor-sharp mind once again, although what that had to do with a simple request for his name, she didn't know.

"Gunnar Royce," he said rather abruptly, then waited as if expecting . . . What? she wondered.

"Jill Brown," she said, unnecessarily she supposed, since he'd already guessed, but it seemed like the polite thing to do, as did holding out her hand. And Jill had been raised to be, if nothing else, polite.

Gunnar Royce looked at her outstretched hand a little bemusedly, but then took it in a firm grasp.

"Nice ta meetcha," Kidd said.

Jill giggled despite herself, wondering where on earth this silly woman had come from. She never giggled. It was the bird, she decided. He was a character. It had nothing to do with the rush of heat she felt emanating from where Gunnar's hand held hers. She'd been in the sun too long, that was all.

"You, too, Kidd," she said. The parrot bobbed his head once, a killingly accurate portrayal of a royal nod. Then the bird moved to nip emphatically at his human perch's ear.

"Ouch," Gunnar yelped, letting go of her hand.

"Toast Gunnar," the parrot said imperiously.

Yet again, Jill stifled a giggle. "Was that supposed to have a comma, or was it a threat?"

The off-center smile became a grin, then a laugh, hearty and as sunny as the morning itself. Jill felt that laugh as she'd been feeling the essence of that morning, warm and soothing yet at the same time exhilarating. Unexpectedly, it roused that oft-smothered yearning in her, a longing for faraway and exotic places. *No wonder,* she thought wryly. *He's certainly the most exotic man I've ever met.*

"Probably both," Gunnar said at last. "I promised him toast this morning."

"Jelly," the bird put in.

"I know, jelly, too." He sounded slightly harassed. Then he looked at Jill. "Is Marc coming down?"

She didn't know. She did know her uncle had little time for the boat he loved these days. It seemed all he did anymore was work, he who had always insisted there was so much more to life than just work.

"Something wrong?"

Her gaze shot back to Gunnar Royce's face. He was looking at her intently, and she wondered if she had betrayed her worry. Marcus continued to insist to her that things would be fine, but for him to even consider selling the *Black Sheep* meant things were grim indeed. But that was not something she was about to tell this man she barely knew.

"I don't know," she said hastily. "He may have to work."

"He's been doing a lot of that lately." He eyed her. "Your family finally get to him?"

Jill nearly gasped aloud.

Gunnar shrugged. "He told me they were an uptight, draconian bunch, just like mine. All work and no play."

"He...did?" She was stunned. Marcus, indeed, must have found a kindred soul here, to have revealed the battle that had been waging in their family for years.

"He also said you were the only member of the whole family who had the potential to be a real human being, if you could just break loose from them."

Despite the fact that Marcus had told her the same thing many times, Jill found herself blushing. She looked down, tightening the towel wrapped around her even though it hadn't loosened a fraction. In her embarrassment, her voice became a little flat. "You and Marcus seem to have become very close."

"We hit it off." The dark brows lifted again. "Jealous?"

"No!" Flustered, she blurted it out. "I'm glad . . . I mean, my family hassles him so much . . . and people don't understand him sometimes . . ." Her voice trailed off when she looked up to see him grinning and realized that he'd been baiting her.

"I don't think he lets it bother him much," Gunnar drawled. "He's used to it by now."

Some combination of his tone and her own disconcertment let the words slip out. "Are you?"

The drawl vanished, a cool, rigid undertone taking its place, telling her unmistakably of the accuracy of her shot in the dark. "No. But then, I haven't been at it as long as he has."

Jill recognized that undertone. She'd heard it often enough in Marcus's voice years ago. *An uptight, draconian bunch, just like mine,* he'd said. Did this man wage the same battle Marcus had for so long? No wonder they'd hit it off, she thought.

Driven by an urge to comfort she didn't understand—he hardly seemed to need it—she said quietly, "They used to call Uncle Marcus the disgrace of the conservative Browns. The family flake." She gestured toward the stern of the trawler. "The black sheep."

"So he threw it in their face by naming his boat that?"

"Yes."

He smiled, but it was a cold smile that matched the change that had taken place in his voice. "Perhaps I should do my family the same honor, and rename my boat, too."

A tiny shiver raced through her, as if the chill in his voice had brushed over her skin. Yet, amazed at her own temerity, she still asked softly, "Rename it what?"

"*The Waste,*" he said flatly.

Chapter Three

Gunnar couldn't believe he'd said it. Less than ten minutes in the company of this woman, and he'd opened the door on a part of him he kept buried so deep he could usually convince himself he'd forgotten it altogether.

"Why do families do that?" she asked softly.

It was the last thing he expected to hear. He'd expected questions, yes, but about that name, and what he'd done to make his family feel that way. Instead he'd gotten a quiet expression of empathy that went a long way toward soothing a pain he refused to admit he felt.

"Maybe," he said after a moment, "because they know they have more power to hurt us than anyone else."

"But that's what should make them never use it," she said, a bit mournfully.

"Yes. Too bad they can't resist when someone doesn't quite fit in the mold they build for them. Like Marc." *And you?* he wondered. Or had she already surrendered, forced herself to meet those parental expectations, as he had for so long? And why did the thought bother him so much?

"Toast Gunnar," Kidd repeated.

"Okay, okay," he grumbled at the bird.

"Does he really eat toast and jelly?"

"Jam, actually, but he likes the word 'jelly' better. Not much, it's not that good for him, but he won't even look at seeds or greens unless he gets his treat first."

Jill was looking at the parrot, a smile lighting her eyes. He thought of what Marc had told him, that her family hadn't quite smothered her spirit yet, although they kept trying. Just as Marc kept trying to keep it from happening. "If she ever breaks loose," Marc had said, raising his half-empty beer glass in the main cabin of Gunnar's boat, "she'll really be something."

It had been several beers later, and oddly, in the middle of a conversation about whether Gunnar should take time to overhaul the cutter's diesel while he was here, that Marc had said, rather morosely, "I'll pull out of this, you know. Jill will be taken care of. She won't have to depend on those... ironhanded, pigheaded Browns."

Gunnar hadn't been sure what Marc was going to pull out of, but he couldn't doubt the man's sincerity. Or his love for his niece. His eyes strayed to that niece; she was still watching Kidd, still smiling.

"You want to come watch the spoiled brat eat?"

He didn't know why he'd said it; it seemed to have just slipped out. But when he saw her turn that smile on him, he was glad it had.

"I'd love to," she said. Then the smile faded, and the light left her eyes, as if a shadow had passed overhead and blotted out the sun. "But...I don't think...I mean, it wouldn't be..."

Gunnar didn't miss the way she looked at him, at his bare chest and feet, at his hair. If what Marc had told him of her repressive family was true, someone like him wasn't exactly what she was used to. And judging from the way she'd stared at him yesterday, as if he belonged locked away for people's safety, it was all true.

"I won't hurt you, Jill," he said, his voice quiet. "If nothing else, I like Marc too much."

A scarlet wave of color rose in her face. "I never...I didn't mean..." Again she tightened the towel around her, until Gunnar thought she was in more danger of it cutting off her circulation than of it falling off. "I'm sorry," she said, her voice low as she continued to stare down at the towel. "It's just...I've never known anyone like you. I've never even seen anyone like you, not in person."

"Like me?"

He'd thought his voice had been fairly even, but her head came up as quickly as if he'd snapped the words out.

"I mean..." She gave a tiny shrug, looking away shyly. "You look like a...a pirate or something. Something wild."

Gunnar suppressed a wry grin. "Amazing what a little hair will do to people's perception."

"A lot of hair." He blinked. Had she actually made a joke? "You've got the parrot. All you need is an earring."

She had. He could see the faintest quirk at one corner of her mouth. That mouth that was as lusciously curved as the rest of her. He grinned.

"I've got one. But Kidd likes to yank on it."

She met his gaze then, and he saw a golden glint in the warm brown eyes, a flash of the spirit Marc had sworn hadn't yet died. And he knew Marc was right. If she ever unleashed that spirit, she would really be something.

"I'm sorry," she said again. "I sound like my parents talking about Marcus. The more unconventional he got, the more scandalized they got."

"And the closer you felt to him?"

It had been a guess, based on what little Marc had said, but he could see by her expression that he was right.

"I . . . yes. And the more guilty, because I always liked him better than—"

She broke off, looking as startled as he'd felt earlier, as if she, too, had let something slip she'd never meant to.

"Don't worry about it," he said wryly. "I've never even met them and I already like Marc better."

She smiled, a shy little curve of her mouth that tugged at something inside him, something he'd never known was there.

"He understands." She'd said the two words as if they explained everything. Which, in a way, they did, he supposed.

"I know. He doesn't expect anybody to live to suit him, and refuses to live to suit anyone else. He's living proof that you don't have to be like them to make it in the world."

"Like them?"

"Your parents. Mine. And all the sharks out there."

She nodded slowly, absorbing what he'd said. "I hope you're right. I couldn't stand it if my parents turned out to be right."

Gunnar's brow furrowed. "Right about what? Marc? Why—"

"Toast Gunnar!"

It was definitely a threat this time, and the exclamation was accompanied by a pointed flexing of Kidd's long feet, talons digging in.

"Come on," Gunnar said, not wanting the conversation to end. "I've got to feed him or I'll be bleeding in a minute."

He climbed off the *Black Sheep*, not looking back to see if she was following him, afraid that if he did, she'd be scared off. He thought she had been until, at the head of the slip, he saw the old trawler lift slightly and knew she had gotten off. He glanced back. She had abandoned the towel and pulled on a huge, loose shirt that was a twin in everything but color to the one she'd had on yesterday. Out of sight was the modest bathing suit she'd seemed so conscious of, and Gunnar couldn't say if he was glad or disappointed.

It didn't register until they were almost to his boat how strangely he was acting. Except for Cal, and Marc, there hadn't been many people he'd found himself wanting to talk to for any length of time in the past three years. But then, he told himself, it was only logical; she was related to Marc, so, in a way, it was like talking to him—

"Oh!"

He turned at Jill's smothered gasp. He was halfway to the steps of the slip; she still stood on the main dock, staring at his boat.

"She's yours?" Her gaze flicked to his face and he nodded, wondering why she was so wide-eyed. "She's beautiful," Jill breathed, her eyes going back to the sleek cutter. "I noticed her yesterday, and I wondered..." A rueful smile curved her lips, and at last her gaze shifted to his face. "I suppose I should have guessed. She's the perfect boat for a pirate. Even your name is perfect for a pirate."

She said it with a touch of wistful longing that made him ache a little, at the same time that it made him nervous. He was afraid she was building him up into something he wasn't, some swashbuckling buccaneer type, when in truth he was just one of hundreds of sea bums who sailed from port to port, staying in one just long enough to replenish supplies for the sail to the next.

"My name came from my grandfather. He was a truck driver, not a pirate." He hoped that would slow down her lively imagination. "I see you don't have any problem with the traditional boat as 'she' terminology," he added.

Jill gave him a glance before going back to her perusal of the cutter. "No," she said. "I know it bothers some women, but it's been that way since men have sailed. Depending on your point of view, it could be as much a compliment as an insult." She shrugged, leaning back to look to the top of the raked masts. "Besides, I can't help thinking there are more important battles to spend our energy on."

"Like glass ceilings? And women making less than three-quarters of what men do?"

She turned then, looking a little surprised at what he'd said. "Yes, as a matter of fact." Then her mouth twisted ruefully. "Just don't tell my parents I said that."

"I take it they have...definite ideas about a woman's role?"

"They have definite ideas about everything," she said with wry emphasis.

Especially for their daughter, he guessed. He watched her as she walked toward the open end of the slip and turned to see the stern. Her brows furrowed and she looked back at him doubtfully.

"The Toy Killer?"

Involuntarily his jaw tightened. "It's a long story." And one he wasn't about to tell—to her or anyone. He went up the steps, unfastened the lifelines so she wouldn't have to climb over them, and jumped down into the cockpit. Kidd vacated his shoulder with another shouted "Toast!" and flapped his way down into the cabin.

Maybe he should have cleaned up a little, he thought as he surveyed the main cabin, only now noticing the charts scattered on the navigation station, the books piled here and there, and the clothing strewn around. Quickly he grabbed the clothes—remembering he was down to his last pair of jeans and putting a trip to the closest Laundromat on his mental list of things to do—tossed them into the master stateroom and pulled the door closed.

The rest could stay, he decided, not that he had much choice; he heard her boarding now. Besides, the boat wasn't dirty—Cal had taught him too well for that—it was just cluttered. Still, he caught himself apologizing as she stepped inside. She merely shrugged.

"When you live aboard, things are bound to get cluttered up." She looked around with obvious interest. "It's beautiful . . . Mr. Royce. All this wood and brass."

"I quit being Mr. Royce three years ago."

She pinkened, but she met his gaze. "All right. Gunnar, then. But it is beautiful. Those hatches look like mahogany."

"They are. Honduran."

"Beautiful," she repeated. "And lots of room, really. I like the old-style glass skylights. They make it seem so open and bright. And you've kept her in wonderful shape."

"I worked too hard and long restoring her not to take care of her. I had to do some modifications for the new diesel, and for solo sailing, but everything else is original except for the navigation gear, the radio, and—" he grinned "—the microwave."

Jill laughed. "Even traditionalism has its limits. I imagine you've been grateful for it on occasion."

"Especially sailing solo. It's hard to work up the energy to fix anything hot when you've been battling a storm all day."

"But that's when you need it most," she said, with an understanding he hadn't expected. Marc had said that as much as she loved the *Black Sheep,* Jill had never been out on her beyond the local coast.

She was looking at him quizzically. "You sail her alone? In blue water?"

She used the traditional sailor's words for deepwater, open-sea sailing with a touch of longing. "Most of the time," he answered. "She's rigged for it."

And he preferred it that way, he added silently. Not that he hadn't had some interesting offers along the way. That woman in Micronesia . . . come to think of it, she'd been nearly as curvaceous as Jill was, although she'd had nothing like this effect on him. Neither had the woman in Hawaii, on his first run, although she'd been even more voluptuous than Jill. Funny, he'd forgotten that. Okay, so Jill wasn't the first nonskeletal woman he'd seen since he'd walked away from his old world and never looked back. It was just that he hadn't been interested in any of the others. At least, not enough to take them along on the solo sails he relished.

Not that Jill cared if he sailed with women or not, he assured himself. She'd asked, he was certain, only because she seemed to know enough about boats to know that sailing one this size across blue water would be a lot of work for one person.

"Where?" she asked.

There was a world of that wistful longing packed into that single word, and Gunnar knew with certainty that this woman had longed for the distant places, the far reaches, and often.

"I think I've stretched Kidd's patience to the limit here. Let me feed him, and then I'll give you the rundown on the Gunnar Royce world tour, so far."

The parrot flapped his way up to the counter, then hopped over to balance on the narrow divider between the two stainless-steel sinks.

"Don't you worry about him flying away?" she asked as she watched Gunnar fire up a burner on the gimballed alcohol stove.

"No toaster," he said at her odd look when he stuck a quarter-slice of bread on a fork and held it over the flame. Then he answered her question. "His wings are clipped. But I don't think he'd take off if he could. He's too spoiled. Hand me that, will you?"

He gestured with his free hand to a jar that sat on a railed shelf just behind her head. She picked it up, glancing at the label as she handed it to him.

"Elderberry jam? I don't think I've ever seen that before."

"I can pretty well guarantee you haven't, unless you haunt specialty stores," he said wryly. "I have to import the damn stuff from England. But it's the only kind he'll eat."

Jill looked at Kidd, then back at Gunnar, the smile that lit her eyes again curving her mouth. "He *is* spoiled," she said, but so teasingly that Gunnar couldn't take offense. Not that he could have, anyway, with her looking at him like that. He made himself concentrate on spreading the jam on the barely toasted bread.

He'd expected, if he ever met the niece Marc talked about, to like her for his friend's sake. Marc had told him she was a brown wren who was someday going to blossom into a quick, beautiful hummingbird, and Gunnar had merely nodded, thinking about people who looked through the eyes of love and saw what they wanted to see. As he had done, for so long.

Because of Marc's words, he had expected the simple, girl-next-door look of her. He had expected she would be a little sheltered, a little shy, all of which was clearly true. He hadn't expected the ridiculous effect she was having on him. And he didn't quite know what to do about it.

Oh, yes, he did, he told himself sternly. He knew exactly what to do about it.

Nothing.

Chapter Four

Jill watched silently as Gunnar cut the small piece of jam-coated toast into smaller pieces. Kidd was dancing, shifting his weight from one foot to the other, head bobbing up and down.

"Geez," Gunnar said as he held out the first piece and the bird snatched it, "you'd think I've been starving you."

The parrot had no answer as he gulped down the tiny piece of toast. Jill watched Gunnar repeat the procedure, holding the toast with gentle fingers so that Kidd could take it easily, and found herself absurdly moved by his care of the bird—the way he prepared the treat, then carefully cut it into pieces so small the bird could handle them easily. And imported jam, yet, she thought, smothering a smile.

She shouldn't have been afraid of him, she thought. Not once she found out he was Uncle Marcus's friend. But it was odd that Marcus had never mentioned him to her. He seemed to mention any single man he met and liked. Or course, Marcus probably had taken one look at Gunnar and known Jill would go running in the other direction. She might not want to, but she would.

But Marcus had obviously mentioned her to Gunnar. Enough so that he'd been able to guess her identity. Jill stifled a little sigh. *I can just imagine,* she thought. *"Hey, Gunnar, if some plain, quiet, all-brown little thing shows up, it's only my niece."*

No, that wasn't fair. Uncle Marcus had never thought of her that way. How many times had he told her she was like a very special kind of flower that bloomed only under conditions that were just right for it? And when she'd been a teenager, how many fights had he gotten into with his brother over her, with Marcus accusing her father of choking the life out of her, turning her into another stiff-necked, close-minded Brown?

"Okay, bud," Gunnar said, "you've had the fun stuff, now let's get to the meat and potatoes." He made a quick movement toward the bird with one arm, and the parrot hopped nimbly aboard. Gunnar walked into the main cabin, then looked back over his shoulder and grinned at Jill. "You thought before he was spoiled? He's got his own stateroom."

Jill blinked. "You're serious, aren't you?"

"Yep."

He pulled open a small door just past the main table. Jill couldn't resist going to look. What had once been a small cabin had been cleverly converted into a seagoing parrot paradise, with the space that had once been taken up by two bunks now a huge, metal-lined cage with the lower bunk as the sand-strewn floor. A large swing hung in one end of the cage, and a long, sturdy branch that looked oddly chewed was fastened securely in the other. Close to it were two porcelain bowls fastened firmly to one of the frequent horizontal cage bars.

Jill smiled; she couldn't help it. "This is great," she said, following him inside.

"Yeah. Too bad he refuses to sleep here."

"Where does he sleep?"

Gunnar's mouth quirked. "My cabin."

Lucky bird, Jill thought, a vision of intimately sharing the equivalent of some pirate captain's cabin with Gunnar flashing through her mind. She blushed furiously at her own uncharacteristic, rowdy thoughts. She stepped closer to the cage, as if to inspect it, thankful that Gunnar hadn't seemed to notice her sudden rise of color.

"I think he just likes to wake me up in the morning," he said. "And believe me, morning to a bird is the first sign that the sun's going to come up in an hour or so."

Jill smiled again, recovered now. "What happens if you leave him in here?"

Gunnar sighed. "He sings. Loud. All night. Out of tune."

Jill smothered a giggle. "Sings what?" she asked, wondering at herself. She'd never been able to talk like this to a man—she couldn't say a man like Gunnar, since she'd never met one. Her shyness usually took over, and she froze up until she was exactly what her parents were so proud of: a nice, quiet, reserved, traditional girl. Even at twenty-four, they still called her a girl.

"'The Star Spangled Banner.' Some particularly lewd sea chanteys. Old German beer-drinking songs—in German. I don't know where those came from."

Laughter overcame her, erasing her previous embarrassment at thoughts that could have held their own with those lewd sea chanteys he'd mentioned.

She watched as he pulled open a door in the cage and set Kidd inside. He pulled a bag of what appeared to be sunflower seeds from a neat row of bags below the cage, and filled one of the bowls. He checked the water in the other, then drew back, closed the door and fastened the rather complicated-looking latch.

"I had to have that made in Australia last year," he said, indicating the latch. "He figured out how to work all the rest of them."

Australia. He'd been to Australia. And who knows where else. She could just see him, the captain of this beautiful little ship, at the old-fashioned wood wheel that only added to the fantasy, bare-chested as he was now, his skin golden in the sun, his long hair tossed by a stiff trade wind.... Jill stifled a sigh.

"What are all those?" she asked, pointing to the oddly shaped blocks of wood hanging from the top of the cage by various lengths of chain.

"Chewing toys," he said, and she realized that they all had the same chewed-on look as the perch. "He loves to chew, and it keeps his beak healthy." He grinned. "And keeps him from gnawing through the side of the boat."

Jill laughed again, and this time her smile lingered. He loves that bird, she realized. Her qualms began to fade, never mind that the slightly wild, exotic Gunnar Royce would give her parents heart failure at first sight. Of course, Marcus would say that the reason she found him so intriguing was precisely *because* he would give her parents heart failure at first sight, and she wasn't quite a stiff-necked, close-minded Brown yet. Right now, she wasn't altogether sure he'd be wrong.

"I've still got some repairs to do," Gunnar said, then paused for a sip of ice water, grateful for it as they sat in the sun on his bow deck. "And she needs to be hauled and scraped, but in three or four weeks, I'll be ready to go."

"Where to this time?" Jill asked.

Gunnar considered his answer. For nearly a week he'd found her waiting when he finished his morning swim, waiting with another spate of eager questions. Sometimes helping him with whatever task he was doing, sometimes merely watching, she'd listened avidly while he spoke of his travels. Spoke of his first problem-plagued solo to Hawaii, then the trip to Tahiti that had, as if to make up for it, gone so perfectly that he'd spent half the time waiting for the major disaster he figured had to be just in the offing.

But the disaster had waited and caught him this last trip in the treacherous, shark-filled waters off of Australia. He'd hit the strongest knockdown he'd ever seen, a huge gust of wind that had sent *The Toy Killer* careening until the masts had hit the water. Only the precaution he always took of hooking himself to a lifeline when abovedecks kept him from being swept away by the swells that followed the gust, swells that had turned out to be a blessing in disguise, righting the staggering boat just when he'd thought she'd never get up. He'd never been so glad to hear Kidd's furious, angry cries.

He'd told Jill of this, and of limping onward to Australia for repairs, but it hadn't done the least to dampen her fascination. She seemed to thrill to the edge of danger in the tale, as only one who had never truly been in jeopardy could. He'd purposely exaggerated the risk, made it sound uglier than it had actually been, although it had been grim enough. But nothing seemed to curb the longing he saw in her eyes. He wondered what it would take. Just as he wondered what on earth she'd been thinking the other day that had turned her face the color of Kidd's tail when he'd said the bird slept in his cabin.

"Tahiti, this time," he answered at last. "Papeete first, I think. Then Moorea." He shrugged. "Or maybe the other way around."

Jill let out a little sigh. "What about Pitcairn Island?" she said, her eyes taking on an unfocused, dreamy look. "You'll be so close, it seems a shame to miss it."

"Miss a chance to drink a toast to the bones of Fletcher Christian? Not me. Although I think I'd rather drink to Captain Bligh." The distant look vanished, and she was looking at him with some surprise—whether it was because he'd known what she meant, or because he'd suggested drinking to the ill-fated *Bounty*'s captain, he wasn't sure. "He was a hell of a sailor," he explained with a shrug. "Almost four thousand miles in an open boat... More than I'd want to tackle."

"You think he was the true hero, then? Not Fletcher Christian?"

Uh-oh, Gunnar thought. He'd come to know a little about the imaginative Jill Brown in the past days, had grown wary of the way she looked at him on occasion, and this question clanged in his mind like the ship's clock marking the end of the dogwatch.

"I suppose," he said slowly, "you think that since Christian and his fellows mutinied for what was supposedly love, he has to be the hero of the tale?"

She colored again, lowering her eyes. "The question wasn't what *I* think."

"What I think is that every person has to decide for himself, and the most you can ask is to be left alone to do it."

It came out rather sharply, and Jill's brows furrowed. They were delicate arches that were a shade darker than the soft brown of her hair, he noticed as he wondered why he'd said what he'd said, and why so vehemently.

"Why do I get the feeling we're not talking about Fletcher Christian anymore?" she said.

Marc had told him there was a sharp, quick mind behind the unassuming exterior; he was finding out for himself that it was true. What he couldn't figure out was why she was getting to him. Twice now she had somehow pried things from him he'd never said to anyone else, things he never talked about. No, he amended with the honesty he fought for every day, not *pried*. She hadn't had to pry. Something about her just made the words come tumbling out.

"Why the hell can't I keep my mouth shut?" he muttered under his breath.

"It's me."

Gunnar blinked. "What?"

Jill shrugged. "People talk to me. Uncle Marcus says it's because I listen." She smiled, an oddly sad smile. "At least he likes one thing my parents taught me."

"They taught you to listen?"

She grimaced. "Well, not exactly. They just said if you don't have anything worthwhile to contribute to the conversation, you should be quiet. And, of course, a child could never have anything worthwhile to say."

Nice parents, Gunnar thought. At least his had taught him to ask questions. They just hadn't liked the answers he'd come up with when, as an adult, he'd asked them of himself.

"Anyway," she went on, "people always talk to me. I think it's kind of like being around a vacuum. It draws people out."

"You think," Gunnar said carefully, "you're a vacuum?"

"Not exactly," she said, frowning slightly as she tried to explain. "I mean, I know I'm not stupid, but...sometimes I feel kind of...empty, I guess. Like there's nothing inside, because I've never been anywhere, or done anything. It's like other people want to fill the void, so they talk to me. Like you. Uncle Marcus. The kids at school."

This harebrained theory was more than Gunnar was ready to deal with.

"Marc said you were a . . . teacher or something?" He didn't care if his change of subject was obvious. Or that he was a little embarrassed that he hadn't bothered to ask until now; she had left him little time amid her keen questioning to ask about her own life, and hadn't seemed inclined to volunteer.

"A librarian. At an elementary school in San Juan Capistrano, a few miles from here."

Of course, Gunnar thought. Where else would someone so quiet, whose questions were smothered at home, go but to books, looking for the answers? "Sounds, er, nice."

Unexpectedly, she laughed. "Come on," she said. "To someone like you, it must sound as boring as . . . as the doldrums."

So he'd been right, he mused. No sign of Marc's hummingbird here; she saw herself as that little brown wren, plain and simple. And boring.

"There's a lot to be said for the doldrums," he said seriously, "unless you're in a hurry."

She looked at him for a long moment, her eyes going over him in that way that made him feel oddly tense. "I can't imagine you in a hurry."

Gunnar felt all the old defensiveness flood him. Before he could stop them, the words were spilling out. "Is that another way of calling me lazy?"

She looked startled, and he realized he'd done it again, let slip something he'd thought buried beyond retrieval. God, maybe there was something to her silly theory.

"No," she said. "Not at all. No one who can keep a wooden boat in this kind of shape could be lazy. It's just . . . I mean, I can picture you moving quickly, but you're so graceful . . . it just wouldn't seem like you were hurrying."

It was Gunnar's turn to blush. Graceful? Him? Admittedly, he had a certain amount of coordination. He'd been an athlete of some success in high school before his father had decided that wasn't to be his way in life, and three years of solo sailing had given him a hard-won calm that seemed to mesh well with a fit body. But graceful?

She seemed determined to idealize him, he thought again. It was only natural, he supposed. She was young. Not so much in years—the twenty-four Marc had said she was made only ten years difference between them—but in experience it might as well have been millennia. And for someone with the longing she had for the far-off places, he supposed he must seem . . . romantic?

Damn.

Was that what this was all about, this eager questioning, the fascination with every place he'd ever been, and everything he'd done there? Was she building up some exaggerated image of him, sailing the world, doing what she longed to do? An image that would seem irresistible to a spirit that had been caged, as hers had been?

"So what does a librarian do?" he said hastily, hearing the inanity of the question only once it was out. "Besides check out books, I mean."

She looked at him warily. "I told you it was boring."

"All of it?"

"Well, no." She looked thoughtful. "Keeping records and doing inventory is. We just switched to computers to replace the old card catalog—that was interesting, I suppose. I learned about computers, a little at least."

"What else?"

She seemed doubtful that he really wanted to hear this. Gunnar wasn't quite sure why he did, except that he needed to know her whole life wasn't anathema to her.

"Well, I buy the books, with what little budget we have. And—" she wrinkled her nose expressively, and Gunnar smiled instinctively "—with the approval of the school board, which finds the most bizarre things to object to. Do you know one of them tried to ban *The Adventures of Huckleberry Finn?*"

A story of just the kind of life she longed for, he thought. "I'll bet you fought them tooth and nail."

A spark of pride gave her eyes that golden glint again. "Yes. And won."

"Good for you."

"Thank you. But the best part is when I see a kid who doesn't want to be there, whose teacher made him come to the library, because of trouble with reading. I love sitting down with those kids, talking, finding out what interests they have outside of school—and then showing them how to find books about those things. There's nothing like seeing a kid who a week ago hated the very thought of reading come back to find out if there are 'more of those horse books,' or another book of 'those baseball stories.'"

That golden glint had turned to a steady glow now. And for the first time Gunnar saw more than just a flash of the person beneath the quiet, modest exterior. *There's more than a spark of spirit here, Marc,* he said silently to his absent friend. *There's the potential for real fire, if she could only break free.*

"You love that part, don't you?" He'd said it quietly, half-afraid that light would go out.

"Yes. I do. It's why I stay." She sighed. "Partly, anyway. I really have no choice. It's all I know."

No choice. He'd thought himself in that position once. Until he'd made the biggest choice of all.

"Not like you," Jill said, her voice going soft as she looked at him with that distant, dreamy look he'd seen before. The warning bell clanged anew. And finally he realized what made him uneasy when she turned that look on him; it held the same yearning and hunger he saw in her eyes when he talked of the places he'd been and things he'd done. And, finally, he knew what had been behind that furious blush the other day when he'd mentioned his cabin.

He should put a stop to this, he told himself. It wasn't him, he thought. Not really. She might think she was attracted to him, but it was his life she longed for. He'd seen it before, the longing to sail away, usually quashed by the weight of ties, expectations and responsibilities. It was the freedom she wanted and, he supposed, even the risk. He'd wondered himself, before he'd sailed away the first time, how he would handle trouble when it happened.

But when she looked at him like that—with all the need and longing in her eyes—even though he knew

that in her mind it had somehow all gotten tangled up
with him, that in her mind he had become the taste of
danger, of freedom that she'd never known, he found
himself wishing that look was really for him. He
swiftly quashed the idea. She was Marc's niece, for
God's sake, and the man certainly wouldn't appreciate it if Gunnar took advantage of his niece's romantic fancies.

He needed a header, he thought. A sudden wind
shift to make her change course. But she was looking
at him as if he was every woman's fantasy come true,
and he wasn't sure what would do it.

Unless, of course, he just told her the truth about
why his boat was named *The Toy Killer*.

Chapter Five

Gunnar filed the idea of telling her that particular truth away in his mind, in the manner of a man who knows he has the big gun, but hopes he'll never have to use it. There had to be another way.

"So what do you do?" Jill asked. "When you're not off to the four corners of the earth, I mean?"

It was as if she'd read his mind and handed him the solution to his problem. "Nothing," he said with a shrug.

Her brow furrowed. "Nothing?"

He'd known that would bother her. Raised as she had been, he was sure the idea of being purposefully unemployed would go against every tenet she'd grown up with. Even Marc worked for a living; it was the idea behind his company, supporting odd and quirky inventions and products from all around the world, that so displeased his family.

"Not a thing," he emphasized.

"But...how do you buy food and fuel for the boat?"

"There are ways."

She stared at him, her thoughts obvious on her face. Gunnar relented. Having her think him a shiftless bum was one thing, having her suspect he might be a thief—

or worse—was something entirely different. He found it bothered him more than anything had in a long time.

"I...came into some money a few years ago." That was true enough, he thought. He gestured at the cutter. "Enough to cover Cal's loan. She's paid for."

"Oh." She looked so relieved he wondered if he'd made a mistake by not letting her go on thinking the worst. "What will you do when it runs out?"

His mouth quirked involuntarily. Sometimes he wished it would run out; it was too painful a reminder. "I'm careful," he said evenly. "I don't spend much."

She seemed to accept that so easily that he wondered if he'd been mistaken about her reaction to his lack of work.

"So, I'm just a sea tramp," he said with some force. "Nonproductive, no-account, and generally worthless."

She studied him for a moment before she spoke, her voice very quiet. "Is that a quote?"

"A quote?" he asked warily.

"From your family. The ones who made you feel you should name your boat *The Waste*."

He drew back a little. He wished he'd never started this. She was too damn quick, too damn smart.

"Yes," he muttered, staring at the nearest mooring line as if looking for wear and tear, despite the fact that he had just replaced it two weeks ago.

"I'm sorry, Gunnar," she said, still in that soft tone that felt like the brush of a South Pacific breeze over his skin. "Perhaps they're just envious. I sometimes wonder if that's why my family is always so nasty about Uncle Marcus."

He'd steadied himself now. "Are they? Always?"

She sighed. "It seems that way. And it would just be awful if New Endeavors went under. God, they'd gloat."

Gunnar went very still. She looked startled, much as he imagined he must have looked when he'd realized he'd told her something he had never meant to. It gave him a brief feeling of satisfaction to know he wasn't the only one whose mouth tended to be running too much lately. But the meaning of what she'd said, and the kicking in of old instincts he'd thought long dead, quickly overpowered the feeling.

"Is it going under?"

"I . . . don't know. I shouldn't have said that."

I'll pull out of this, you know. Marc's words, coming out of the blue—and one too many beers—suddenly made sense. Gunnar chose his next words carefully.

"I got the impression he was worried, but . . ."

It was an old tactic, that leading statement, and he regretted using it on her the moment the words were out. But it worked.

"You felt it, too? I mean, he never says much—he doesn't want me to worry—but when he told me if I wanted another vacation on the *Black Sheep* I'd better do it now, I knew it had to be serious. He'd never sell that boat unless things were . . ." She trailed off again.

"No, I don't suppose he would."

"I wish I could help. I offered to quit and work for him, to try and help, but he insisted everything was fine." Her lips tightened a little. "I think he just wanted to save me from the uproar. My father would probably do violence." She laughed halfheartedly. "I suppose that sounds silly."

"No. Mine did," Gunnar said flatly, involuntarily rubbing his jaw as his mind raced over everything Marc had ever told him, searching for any clues. Then, in the same instant, he realized both what he'd said and what he was thinking. He had once more let slip something he never spoke of to anyone, and he had instinctively slipped back into the old ways, analyzing the problem, looking for the answer.

Jill was staring, eyes fastened on his hand as his fingers rubbed over that place on his jaw.

"Your father . . . hit you?"

He jerked his hand away. He hadn't even realized he'd been doing it. For a long time after his father had delivered the blow that had sent him reeling in more ways than one, he had probed at the sore spot, pushed at it, as if the pain were the hammer to drive the lesson home. But he'd thought himself long over that, thought he'd learned to live with it. That she'd caught him making the revealing gesture, disconcerted him. That she'd immediately understood it, disturbed him.

"It was just a . . . clash of points of view," he said, denying the pang that still dug at him. "It's not like he was beating on a kid, after all. I was thirty-one at the time."

"Did you hit him back?"

"No," he said, startled. "He's my father."

"Exactly," Jill said.

His brows shot upward. He stared at her. She'd set him up, he thought in shock. She'd led him on with that casual-sounding question, and then shot him down in one word that said everything there was to say about the unjustness of his father's action. Quick. Sharp. Hummingbird, he thought.

"Lady," he muttered under his breath, "you're dangerous."

She looked at him, as if she'd heard what he'd said but couldn't quite believe she'd heard it right. He got abruptly to his feet.

"I've got to get to work," he said, barely managing to control the edge in his voice. "I've got an engine to overhaul."

That until this moment he'd pretty much decided the overhaul could wait until after the next voyage was a fact he tried to ignore. Just as he tried to ignore the fleeting thoughts he'd been having that staying in one port for this long didn't seem nearly so hard this time.

Gunnar finished wiping the grease from his hands as he stood in the small, belowdeck engine room looking down at the diesel motor. From above, Jill watched as he lifted a hand to wipe a trickle of sweat from his bare chest, and she smothered a little twinge of regret. She would rather have watched that droplet trace its way down his muscled chest and ridged belly to disappear beneath the waistband of the nylon shorts that gave her ample—too ample—an opportunity to appreciate long, well-muscled legs and the high, taut curve of his buttocks.

At first he'd seemed reluctant to let her come along on this test run of the newly overhauled diesel, but she'd been determined. She'd worked right alongside him, handing him tools, providing a third hand when he'd needed it, and keeping the cold drinks—always water or fruit juice, she noticed—coming; he'd needed them down in the small compartment driven to high temperatures by both the engine and the summer heat.

"I've earned it," she had told him, barely even thinking about the fact that two weeks ago she would no more have thought of standing up to a man like Gunnar Royce than she would have thought of flirting with a stranger. Or anyone else, for that matter.

Besides, she needed this. She needed a taste of the freedom he'd known; she needed to experience the feel of this graceful cutter as she sliced through the waves, to see the land and all its troubles fade into the distance.

But most of all, she had admitted in the dark hours of the morning of the test run, as she huddled in the bunk aboard the *Black Sheep,* she needed a memory to cling to, an image of Gunnar at the wheel of the cutter, the wind tossing his long, dark hair, the sun gilding his skin and lighting his vivid green eyes. She needed it for the time when he would leave and she would be left with nothing but her drab, brown world. She knew it was fantasy, but her entire time here had been fantasy; quiet, little Jill Brown, talking, laughing, even arguing with a man like Gunnar could be nothing less. Reality would intrude soon enough; she wanted to savor this, and him, while she could.

Kidd, who had been watching Gunnar work with apparent interest from his perch on the handrail Jill was leaning against, bobbed his head as his owner climbed up out of the engine room. Gunnar had tied his hair back with a bandanna, but strands still clung wetly to his neck and shoulders, attesting to the heat he'd been laboring in all morning and into the afternoon. He grabbed the towel Jill had brought and wiped the sweat from his face.

"Gunnar toast," Kidd said.

Jill blinked at the now familiar words, reversed into an order that made an uncanny kind of sense. Gunnar, however, took the bird's observation in stride.

"Yes, Gunnar is," he muttered as he wiped at his chest with the towel. After the heat of the engine room, his nipples were reacting to the cool afternoon breeze that was rising, and Jill flushed at the sudden image that formed so vividly in her mind of her fingers stroking him, causing that same puckering of the flat, brown circles of flesh. She looked away, then spoke hastily.

"What about Kidd?"

"Cap'n Kidd," the bird corrected.

"What about him?" Gunnar asked, wiping his belly with the towel now. Jill forced herself to look at his face, not that it was any easier to meet those eyes and keep her stupid imagination under control.

"Does he stay in his room when you're under way?"

"No. He likes it up here. He likes giving me orders."

She glanced at the parrot. "But isn't it dangerous? I mean, what if he slips or something?"

Gunnar grinned at her. He reached over and scooped the bird up with one hand. "He won't slip. He just kind of hangs around."

"Hang around," Kidd repeated agreeably. To Jill's astonishment, the parrot hooked one toe around Gunnar's index finger, then flopped down to dangle freely below his hand, his head twisted back at a severe angle as if to be sure she was watching his trick. The bird was totally relaxed and clearly quite pleased with himself as he dangled there, swaying slightly.

Jill giggled; she couldn't help herself. It seemed she couldn't help a lot of the things she'd been doing lately. Or feeling, she thought as Gunnar slid his left hand beneath the suspended bird and lifted, until the parrot lay on his back in Gunnar's palm, head resting against the heel of his hand, quiet and utterly trusting. What she felt then was a flooding warmth that seemed related to, yet different from, the heat that filled her when she watched him move, or saw that crooked smile curve his lips.

Gunnar looked at her, and something he saw in her face made him suddenly cautious. Carefully he righted Kidd and returned him to his perch on the handrail.

"I'm going to cool off." His words were abrupt, but no more than his sudden departure; he was over the rail executing a smooth, racing dive into the water before she had a chance to react. But the image of him and Kidd lingered.

It was the gentleness of it, she thought. The sheer gentleness and patience it must have taken to gain such trust from an intelligent creature like the parrot that had nestled in his strong hand. Traits she wouldn't have expected in a man who looked like Gunnar.

Lord, she groaned inwardly, was she truly her parents' child, judging him by appearance and life-style rather than for himself? She'd thought Marcus had taught her otherwise, but apparently it was more ingrained than she thought.

She knew he would be gone for a while. He generally swam the length of the marina and back, a feat Jill could only marvel at, especially since he was barely breathing hard when he came back. But she certainly wasn't about to complain, not when it produced a body like his.

You could use some exercise like that yourself, she told herself, although she knew from sad experience that all the dieting and exercise in the world wouldn't change the type of figure she had. She wished it would, that she could take off those extra twenty pounds. Maybe then she wouldn't feel so silly every time she had one of those lustful thoughts about him, knowing there was nothing more ludicrous than the idea of a man like Gunnar with a quiet, plump, brown little wren.

She sighed. She wasn't that strong a swimmer, anyway, and she didn't want him thinking she was trying to force her way into that private time of his. It was bad enough he hadn't really wanted her to come along on this test run and she'd uncharacteristically forced the issue.

She'd make up for it, she decided, by packing a great lunch to take along. Tuna sandwiches, cheese, chips, and the last of those brownies she'd baked the other day. They'd come out a little chewy in the *Black Sheep*'s sometimes tricky oven, but she liked them that way. She even had some grapes she'd bring for Kidd; she wasn't above trying to bribe the man by way of his pet.

By the time she had packed the lunch, pinned her hair up neatly, and found her hat, Gunnar was back and had rinsed off and dressed—thankfully, she thought—in a pair of jeans and a T-shirt. Her thankfulness faded when she saw how the pale green of the shirt lit up his eyes and the tightness of it emphasized the breadth of his chest and the muscles of his arms, and how the snug jeans hugged the tight curve of his buttocks.

"You didn't have to," was all he said when she handed him the bag of food and sodas with an explanation. "We won't be out that long."

She colored. "I just thought it would be nice."

He gave her a look that made her think he was regretting having said she could come. She busied herself with taking the lunch belowdecks and putting the sodas in the small refrigerator, hoping that her being out of sight would prevent him from saying she had to stay ashore.

The ploy seemed to have worked. When she went back on deck, he was getting ready to cast off. She tried to keep her excitement from showing; she'd been as far as Catalina Island with Uncle Marcus, but this seemed different. Very different. And as he neatly backed the cutter out of the slip and headed for the harbor entrance, she knew Gunnar was the difference.

To Jill's untrained ear, the diesel seemed to be chugging along nicely, but after they had been clear of the breakwater for a few minutes, he was cocking his head toward the open engine room door with an expression that told her he was hearing something he didn't like.

He looked up and glanced around. The surrounding sea was deserted except for a couple of small fishing boats far to the north.

"Here," he said suddenly, moving aside and gesturing to her to take his place at the wheel. "Just hold her steady while I go look at something."

Jill gaped at him. "What? I can't— I've never—"

"You've piloted the *Black Sheep*, haven't you? Under power, she's not much different. Just take the wheel and hold her on that compass heading. It'll only be for a few minutes."

He was gone before she could protest. She stared down at the compass mounted atop the pedestal that held the huge, old, varnished teak wheel. The spokes of the wheel felt solid in her hands, warm and oddly comforting.

Then he was back, and even Jill could tell that the sound of the power plant had smoothed out, become less noisy. Gunnar was smiling in satisfaction now.

"That's it. We'll just open it up a little now," he said as he reached for the throttle. The cutter surged forward seemingly at a touch, and the motor performed faultlessly as they headed out to sea.

Over the next two hours he tested it at all speeds, and shut it off and fired it back up so many times Jill started wondering about what kind of battery a boat like this had. At last, when they were far enough out that the shore was a thin line and the sheer, white bluffs at the south end of Catalina Island looked much closer, he shut it off and left it off. And suggested lunch.

"You were right," he said later, gesturing to the scant remains of the meal she'd fixed. "It was nice. Thanks."

She accepted the implied apology as she fed the last grape to Kidd, who had unbent enough to at least accept food from her. "You're welcome."

He studied her for a moment. "You don't get seasick at all, do you?"

She looked around, surprised that he'd asked. It was a moderate day, not glassy smooth, but not particularly rough, either. "Not that I know of," she answered. "But I've never really been in rough weather."

She wondered why he'd wanted to know, but his rather grim expression gave her no clue. And he said no more about it, just helped her gather up the wrappings.

When he moved back to the wheel, obviously preparing to start back, Jill stood. When he reached for the starter button for the motor, she started to speak then stopped. She'd pushed her luck enough for one day, she decided.

"What?" Gunnar asked.

I should have known he'd notice, she thought. She looked at him for a moment, wishing she wasn't so intimidated just by the looks of the man. But maybe she could ask, maybe he wouldn't mind—

"I wish you'd quit looking at me like...like I really was that pirate you keep talking about." He looked more uneasy than annoyed, a difference Jill didn't understand. "What were you going to say?"

She took a breath. "I... Do you need to test the motor some more?"

His brow furrowed. "No. It's fine now. Just needed some final adjustments. Why?"

"I just wondered..."

"Wondered what?"

He was being patient—to Marcus's silly little niece, no doubt—but the effort was showing. She took another quick breath and plunged ahead.

"If we could sail back."

For a long moment he didn't answer, just looked at her. Jill bit her lip, wondering if she'd somehow made him angry. Then, in a soft voice that sent a shiver racing down to her knees, he said, "I'll make you a deal. You take off that silly hat and let your hair down, and I'll run up all the sails you want."

Instinctively her hand went to the wide, floppy brim of the hat. "It's not—"

"Silly. I know. You told me." His voice became even softer. "It's your shield, isn't it? Just like the baggy, all brown clothes. Didn't anyone ever tell you that the sexiest things come in plain brown wrappers?"

Jill's breath caught in shock. No one had ever seen past her purposefully chosen armor, or if they had, hadn't cared enough to say anything. Especially not enough to suggest that she was sexy beneath the concealing wrapping.

"I never—" she began.

"I know. You think you're just some plain little brown bird—don't you?—just like Marc said." She felt color rise in her cheeks as his voice lowered. "And a plump one at that, no doubt."

Jill cringed inwardly. He was hitting too close to home. Sometimes Gunnar Royce was too damned perceptive. "I know I'm—"

"Soft. Curved. Tempting. Female. Just like you should be."

Tempting? Her? Jill stared at him, lips parted.

"And what about that tight little knot you pull your hair into?" he went on in that same soft, seductive voice.

She self-consciously reached up to touch the tidy bun at the back of her head. "I-it's neater that way."

"And we must be neat, mustn't we?" he said mockingly. Then, in a completely different, earnest tone, "Cut loose, Jill. If you can't do it with something as simple as your hair, you'll never be able to do it anywhere else." Her eyes flicked to his own hair, tossed, windblown and slightly wild. His mouth quirked at one corner in understanding. "Yes, I speak from experience."

Slowly, with hands that seemed to be shaking much more than the simple task deserved, she pulled off the floppy hat. She started to tug at the pins that held the bun, but her fingers didn't seem to be working.

Even more slowly, as if he were fighting the urge to do it, Gunnar lifted his hands to the back of her head. His lips parted slightly as he stared down at her, his fingers probing through the thick brown silk of her hair until he had released all the pins. She saw him let out a quick breath as his gaze shifted to the mass that fell free, tumbling over his hands nearly to her waist. She felt him thread his fingers through it, lifting, savoring.

"Hummingbird," he murmured.

"What?"

"Nothing. God, Jill...why do you keep it hidden?"

"I-it's just hair. Brown. Boring."

"It shines like satin. There are parts around your face that are almost gold from being in the sun these past two weeks. And it's so thick and soft, a man could—"

He broke off and, just as suddenly, pulled his hands back. "Sails," he said abruptly. "You wanted sails."

He started to move, and Jill saw the truth of her earlier words. He worked with a speed that was remarkable, yet never once looked as if he were hurrying. And he was as graceful as she had imagined.

The moment she felt the sleek cutter lift to the wind, she felt an echoing lift somewhere deep inside. When he let her take the wheel, she could feel the difference. The boat felt alive, eager, like a Thoroughbred tugging at the reins. It was as close to flying as she had ever been. The snap of the sails, the creak of the rigging, the sound of the bow cutting through the swells, it was all as she'd imagined sailing would be, and much more.

Much more, because it was a well-loved little ship that had been places she could only dream of. Much more, because she was here, her heart feeling as suddenly free as her hair flying in the wind. Much more, because there was a smart-mouthed, red-tailed parrot a yard away, shouting out nautical commands in the voice of an old salt who had once loved this boat. Much more, because Gunnar, who loved the boat as much as Cal had, was now her captain, and he suited her sleek lines and free spirit as no one else could.

It was much more because for the first time, when she caught Gunnar watching her, something in his eyes, something fierce and glinting, made her think that perhaps she wasn't so very silly after all.

Chapter Six

He'd been a damn fool to let her come along, Gunnar thought, and now he was paying the price for it. That moment when her hair had slipped free, sliding over his hands like warm silk, had sent his blood racing like a catamaran in a stiff breeze. The wren was disappearing, the hummingbird coming to life. He hadn't been able to stop watching her, standing there at the wheel, her hair whipped by the wind, her clothes plastered to curves that made his palms itch to trace them, her eyes glinting pure gold at the feel of the cutter leaping beneath her hands. Hands that he couldn't stop imagining touching him, in all the ways a woman touched a man she wanted.

And the hell of it was, she wanted him. He doubted if she even realized it, not in so many words, but he could see it in the way she looked at him, the way she shivered when he came close, the way she blushed every time he caught her watching him. He'd seen the signs before, he'd even taken advantage of them before. But not this time.

And that, he thought grimly as he furled the sails and took over the wheel to guide them back into the harbor, was the real hell of it. He wanted her, she wanted him, and neither of them was going to get what they wanted. There were too many reasons in the way. She was too damn innocent. She was Marc's niece.

Her conservative, rigid family would disown her if they found out. He'd soon be on his way to the next port. Alone.

And he wasn't sure he liked her reasons for wanting him.

The irony of it didn't escape him. For years he hadn't cared why women responded to him. He just knew it happened, and he had used that knowledge more than once. His looks had always been a tool, just as his brains were, just as his knowledge was. If using them in a certain way got the desired results, it was just another in a long line of successful negotiations. And if manipulating a woman's reaction to him was only part of a larger negotiation, so be it; it wasn't his fault if she felt used afterward. He'd been used a time or two himself, and it hadn't bothered him much, as long as the end result was what he'd wanted.

And now here he was, turning away from a woman he wanted so fiercely it almost frightened him, because he was afraid she wanted him for all the wrong reasons. Because he didn't like the idea that what she wanted was her romantic buccaneer. If she only knew, he thought grimly, how close to a true, brutal pirate he'd once been. With a reputation and nickname to match.

"Slow it down, ya bonehead," Kidd squawked as they turned into the channel.

"Shut up, bird," Gunnar snapped, already edgy from battling emotions he hadn't confronted in a long time.

"Cap'n, you—"

"Overboard," Gunnar warned the parrot.

"Uh-oh." Kidd's head bobbed. "Can't swim."

Jill laughed, and Gunnar couldn't stop himself from looking at her again. The shy, quiet woman hiding behind the tightly knotted hair and the concealing hat had vanished. This woman was a sun-kissed sea sprite, hair flowing free, cheeks pink, eyes glowing with a newfound joy. She was the hummingbird, bright and quick and full of life, no longer hidden. And she was damn near irresistible.

"Poor Kidd," she said. "I know how he feels. I can't swim worth a darn, either."

Gunnar stiffened. "Why didn't you say so? You should have had a life jacket on."

"I didn't want one. It felt too good to just be free."

"You can't be around boats if you can't swim."

He hadn't meant to sound so abrupt, but for once she didn't cringe away. She obviously was still feeling too good to let him ruin it, and said only, "I didn't say I couldn't, just that I don't do it well."

"Well, you should learn."

She hesitated, so briefly he wasn't even sure of it. "So teach me."

He stared at her. Lord, what had he gotten himself into now? He couldn't do that. He didn't want to do it. It would only make things worse, and they were bad enough already.

He was still telling himself that an hour later when, after docking and cleaning *The Toy Killer*, he found himself in the water playing swimming instructor.

It wasn't so bad, he told himself, as long as he didn't have to touch her. The water was cool, if not cold, and by dint of extreme concentration he was able to keep his mind on the task of swimming and not on the shape the modest gold suit covered but didn't hide.

When she'd arrived swathed in a huge towel, her hair once more pinned up, he knew she regretted suggesting this. And perversely, at that realization, he became determined to see it through. She'd blushed when he suggested she'd find it easier to swim without the towel, and made haste to get in the water once she'd discarded it. As he picked up the towel and tossed it aboard the boat, Gunnar didn't know if she was really that shy, or if she was just unhappy with the curves he knew some would find too lush—those who preferred the washboard-thin, angular women he'd had more than enough of in his old world.

For himself, he found her curves far too tempting, and he spent the better part of an hour fighting off the hundreds of reasons his mind supplied for touching her. Sometimes the reason was just too good, too logical—how could he show her how to float without touching her?—and the feel of her warm, soft body combined with the cool sea sent the blood surging to parts of him that were thankfully hidden underwater.

The lesson, which included swimming from the safety of one dock to the next, had them several docks away when Gunnar realized how dark it had gotten. He stopped, treading water.

"We'd better head back."

Jill looked around as if she, too, had just noticed the descent of the near-complete blackness possible only on water.

"Okay." She smiled. "I bet I can do it all at once."

He couldn't help smiling back. "Think you're a porpoise now, huh?"

"A guppy, maybe," she said with a little laugh that made him wish the water was a bit colder.

"You have gotten better, but don't push it," he warned. "Stop if you get tired."

She nodded and was gone before he could say any more. He watched her for a moment, absurdly proud of her smoother strokes. As she was, he thought as he started after her. It didn't take much to please her.

He nearly doubled over in the water, seized by a need as fierce as any cramp he'd ever gotten, as images of other ways of pleasing her shot through his mind. Caught off guard by the sudden clench of his body, he took in a gulp that was half air, half water, and nearly choked. It was a moment before he could level out and start to swim again.

She was still in the water, clinging to the cutter's boarding ladder, when he caught up with her.

"I told you I could do it!" She was smiling, he could see that even in the darkness that surrounded the stern of the boat. The marina lights hadn't come on yet, and in the silence it seemed as if they were alone.

"You did, didn't you?" he said.

Her lips were parted slightly for breath, and Gunnar instinctively reached out and pulled her over to where she could sit on the ladder step and rest. And regretted it the moment he realized that the move put her breasts at a level just beneath the surface and so close to his mouth he nearly took in another gulp of water as he sucked in his breath.

"Thanks for the lesson," she said, her voice husky. She was still breathing a bit heavily, and suddenly Gunnar realized it had nothing to do with exertion. And everything to do with other lessons he wanted to teach her.

"Jill," he began. He'd meant it as a warning; it came out like a plea.

"Yes."

His mind knew it was merely an answer to her name; his body heard only an answer to the plea. Before he could stop himself, he had moved, grabbing the uprights of the boarding ladder on either side of her and pulling himself up to her level. He didn't think she even realized what she was doing when she parted her knees, at least not until his body came up against hers, floating intimately between her thighs.

"Gunnar," she whispered.

He heard a touch of both wonder and fear in her voice, but he had no choice now. He was too close, she was too soft and curved and woman-warm, and he'd wanted this for too long. He moved his head slowly, giving her every chance to evade him, but she only tilted her head to give him access to her parted lips.

He brushed them softly with his own, his muscles tensing against the sudden flare of heat. He did it again, unable to quite believe the fierceness of it. He tasted warm skin, the salty tang of the sea, and some undefinable essence that was Jill alone. It was the last that sent him over the edge and the next kiss was hot and hard and deep.

He thought the moment when she opened to him, letting his tongue in to taste the hot honey of her mouth, was going to be the sweetest. But the instant the tip of her tongue tentatively stroked his in return far surpassed it, and the realization that she had shifted her arms to around his neck, bringing her body hard against him, her breasts pressing against his chest, taught him the true meaning of sweetness in one swift, fiery rush.

He freed one hand from the ladder and slid it down her back, barely aware of the water except for how it made it easier for him to guide her body. He pressed her hips close to his, knowing he shouldn't, knowing he was so aroused already he was liable to scare her, but unable to stop himself. When, instead of pulling away, she let her legs float up to wrap around him, bringing his swollen flesh up against the softness it craved, he groaned low and deep in his chest. Convulsively he rubbed against her, groaning again at the sweet friction.

He drove his tongue forward, as he wanted to do with his body. His hand slid upward over the thin fabric that was no barrier at all for the heat of her body, for the softness of her curves. He reached and cupped her breast, lifting, savoring the tiny shocked breath that broke from her beneath his lips. It became a gasp that vibrated through every part of him when his thumb crept up to flick over a nipple already drawn tight.

He'd been telling himself for days on end that this couldn't happen, but all his warnings vanished in a flare of heat as her hips shifted against him, enticing, luring. Breathing heavily as he broke the kiss, he drew her arms from around his neck, his fingers catching and dragging the straps of her suit down over her shoulders. She stiffened when her bare breasts floated free, but he quickly cupped one in his palm and lowered his head to the other. When his mouth closed urgently over her nipple, she let out a tiny cry that made him jerk convulsively, his hips driving his rigid flesh against her.

He suckled her deeply, savoring the pebble hardness of that rosy peak. With his fingers he plucked at her other nipple, teasing both until she was twisting against him, low moans rising from her with every gentle twist of his fingers, every flick of his tongue.

"Gunnar," she gasped. "Oh, Gunnar, I..."

The pure, wondering shock in her voice rang in his ears, refusing to be ignored as his own self-warnings had been. He wasn't sure where he found the strength to do it, but he let go of her and pushed himself away. He sank below the surface of the water for a moment, telling himself it was to cool off, but not completely certain it wasn't just because he wanted to drown right here and now.

When he surfaced again, she was staring at him, her arms crossed over her breasts, one hand pressed to her lips as if to hold back a cry.

"I'm sorry," he muttered as he took hold of the ladder with one hand again, careful to keep from touching her.

"Why?" Her voice was tiny, muffled by her hand.

"I'm not."

"You should be."

"Why? I—I wanted it."

Eyes narrowed, he turned her question back on her, an edge he couldn't help in his voice. "Why?"

She looked startled. "I . . ."

"You can't tell me you do this kind of thing regularly," he said, voice still tight. "Why me?"

She took in a quick breath, biting her lip. She lowered her gaze. Then, as if she'd only just realized how exposed she still was, she tugged hastily at the straps of her bathing suit, covering her breasts. "I guess it's obvious I'm not very good at this. I never have been, not at doing anything . . . unconventional."

"You still haven't told me why—" He stopped short as it hit him. *You look like a . . . a pirate or something,* she'd said. *Something wild.* "No, I guess you just did explain why me. You wanted something unconventional? Something wild?"

She didn't answer. He reached out and lifted her chin with one hand, making her look at him.

"Is that why, Jill? I'm . . . what? A summer fling? An adventure you want to grab at, because I'm the wildest thing you've ever seen?"

He could see she didn't want to answer, but when she did, he knew it was honest; he could see it in her face.

"Or ever will see," she said softly.

If you only knew, Gunnar thought, fighting the unexpected stab of pain that jabbed him. *If you only knew that I used to be the picture of the conservative traditionalist. A cookie-cutter yuppie. A man your parents would love to use as an example, three-piece suit, fancy office and all.*

"So that's it, " he said, aware of the sharpness of his tone, angered by the fact that he couldn't control it. "I'm some kind of...sexual experiment for you?"

Even in the darkness he could see her eyes widen, see the hurt flicker there. He felt her stiffen, as if drawing herself up straight with an effort. He released her chin, knowing she wouldn't look away now. When at last she spoke, he had the feeling he couldn't even begin to guess at the courage it took for her.

"I... If experiment means exploring something I've never known before—" Her lips began to tremble; she stopped the movement with a visible effort. "Then, yes, I suppose you're right. But I didn't mean it the way you said it. Not . . . cold, like that."

Her painful honesty clawed at him like Kidd's talons, like desire had the first time he'd laid eyes on her. "You don't know the first thing about being cold, Jill Brown. And you don't know the first thing about me."

"I know . . . enough."

"You don't know a damn thing," he bit out. "You don't know what I am, what I was, what I've done. If you did, you'd hate yourself for even being here."

She was staring at him now, wide-eyed. "No," she protested, her voice sounding quiet after the fierceness of his. He wasn't getting through, he realized. He had to stop this now, before it went any further, before another night like this happened and he couldn't find the strength to stop himself from taking what she was so innocently offering.

"Yes," he said flatly.

He lifted his hand, the hand that had so gently lifted her chin. His fingers curled into a fist and he slammed it against the stern of the cutter, just below the lettering painted there.

"This name? *The Toy Killer?* It's not for the boat. It's for me. I'm the killer, and you're in way over your head."

With one swift movement he grabbed the ladder and hoisted himself out of the water. He'd fired the big gun, and he didn't want to be there to see the aftermath.

Chapter Seven

"I'd like an explanation, please."

Jill still couldn't quite believe she'd had the temerity to ask. It had been a long time before she'd recovered enough to straighten her swimsuit and climb up the boarding ladder, and by then she'd been chilled enough to shiver repeatedly. She had grabbed her towel from where Gunnar had tossed it and wrapped it around herself. Then she had stood there, uncertain, torn between wanting to run for the shelter of the *Black Sheep* and needing to know just how big a fool she'd been. Deciding things couldn't get much worse, she had gone down into the cabin, where Gunnar sat slumped at the table in the soft glow of the brass kerosene lantern that hung overhead, his face buried in his hands. Kidd, seeming to watch his owner with concern, was perched on a branch fastened to a nearby bulkhead for just that reason.

Jill watched Gunnar go rigid when she repeated her request for an explanation.

"I'm not who you think I am, Jill." He sounded so weary she suddenly felt much colder.

"How do you know who I think you are?"

His head came up then, and he gave her a look that was as weary as his voice had sounded, yet at the same time incredibly gentle. "Honey, it's written all over your face."

The endearment made her catch her breath, until she realized it had been said in the same tone Uncle Marcus had used when she had run away to him at twelve and he had told her she had to go home to her parents. "Gunnar—"

"I'm not some flashy buccaneer, Jill. I'm not a romantic vagabond sailing the world for the sheer love of it. I'm not even like Marc, some quixotic hero trying to carve his own way in the world."

It was a moment before she could trust her voice. "Now that you've told me what you're not, why don't you tell me what you think you are?"

"I'm one of those sharks we talked about. One of the biggest, with the sharpest teeth. And when a shark is in a feeding frenzy, no one and nothing is safe."

"A very cryptic shark. And I'm just a silly little school librarian." *Lord, how silly,* she thought, remembering how quickly she had melted at his kiss, how willingly she had given herself up to his touch, how easy it would have been for him to take her right there in the water. That he hadn't done it told her a great deal. Including that he wasn't quite the conscienceless shark he was trying to convince her he was. "You'll have to make it clearer for me, Mr. Royce."

He winced at the "Mr. Royce." It was a moment before he spoke, and in that moment Jill wondered if he, too, was thinking of those moments in the water, those moments when his mouth had been on her body, when she had felt the unmistakable press of his arousal against her.

It was that memory that enabled her to control the furious blush that threatened. She'd never known the rush of feminine sexual power before, and it gave her strength. No matter what he said, he couldn't deny that he had, at least for that moment, wanted her. She kept her gaze fixed on his face. And for an instant she saw admiration flicker in his eyes. Then it faded, overtaken by bitter self-contempt.

"Three years ago, before I sold out and walked away, I was a takeover specialist," he said, his voice as bitter as that look in his eyes. "A corporate raider. One of the biggest, ugliest sharks out there. I even had a nickname. Gunnar the Raider. Hostile takeovers, leveraged buyouts, I did it all."

Jill hid her surprise. Of all the things she might have suspected, this was the last. "I suppose somebody has to do those things," she said carefully.

"But I did them with...enjoyment. I loved watching people squirm. The harder the target fought, the greater my pleasure was. And I didn't give a damn about anybody but the investors who backed me. If some little people got hurt, went bankrupt, or were forced out of their jobs, it was just business." His mouth twisted sourly. "If they couldn't play with the big boys—like me—they didn't belong in the game." He stopped.

After a moment Jill realized by the look on his face that he was waiting for her to say something, probably something condemning. She struggled to take it in, to picture the Gunnar she knew as one of the predators of the business world. It shouldn't be such a big step, she thought; after all, she'd half pictured him as a pirate, hadn't she? It wasn't the predator part that was so difficult, she decided, it was the shark part, the ruthless, cold, killer part.

Killer. *The Toy Killer.*

"What," she said, managing to keep her voice even, "does that have to do with the name of your boat?"

He looked a bit taken aback, as if he'd expected something else from her. An aghast retreat, perhaps? Then his jaw tightened, as if he were steeling himself.

"Everything," he said flatly. "I was moving to take over McDuff Toyworks, a small company about to hit it big. I had it wrapped up, it was a done deal. McDuff fought hard, but he didn't have a prayer." His expression went blank, as if he felt nothing—or too much to show. "He killed himself."

Jill smothered a gasp. Not so much at the grim fact of a suicide, but at the realization that all Gunnar's world rambling, all his sailing, had been done on a sea of guilt. With the name of his boat as a constant, daily reminder.

"It wasn't your fault!" Her reaction was instinctive, quick. And again he looked startled. "I mean," she hastened to go on, "you didn't do anything illegal, did you?"

His mouth twisted again. "No. Not illegal. Unprincipled and immoral? Yes. I gave up both of those luxuries early on in my illustrious career."

Jill frowned. "Maybe he was already... unstable. Maybe—"

"Maybe I was the last straw?" He laughed mirthlessly. "That company was all he had. It was his life. When I took it, I ended both."

"And your life, too," she said in sudden understanding. He had ended his own life, as he knew it, just as completely—and as purposefully—as McDuff had ended his. And still it hadn't been enough to ease his guilt. Jill lifted her hands helplessly. "I . . . don't understand much about business. All that takeover stuff. But surely you're not to blame—"

He cut her off. "If I hadn't . . . been what I was, he'd still be alive. Don't try to defend me."

For a long moment she just looked at him. Then, quietly, she said, "I can't help it. Because what you said is true."

He blinked. "What?"

"Past tense. It's what you *were*. Not are. Even if you were . . . so awful, you've changed. You said you walked away. You've left that world."

"But it hasn't left me. I lived and breathed that world. I loved it. It's still there, waiting. It always will be. Waiting for me to break down and go back. Waiting for the Raider."

"But—"

"I tried to smother him, Jill. The Raider, I mean. But I can't." He shook his head. "He's not dead. He's just . . . caged. And every damn day I wonder if that cage is going to hold."

"And as long as you wonder, it will."

Gunnar stared at her. "Marc was right. You are the eternal peacemaker, aren't you?"

Jill colored. How often had Uncle Marcus told her to stop trying to force an armistice between him and the rest of the family? "If you mean, I'd like to see you at peace with yourself, then I suppose I am."

He let out a long breath, almost a sigh. "I am, most of the time. But I can't ever forget. I don't want to forget."

"You won't. You don't need that name—" she gestured toward the stern of the cutter "—as your hair shirt."

For a long, silent moment, they just looked at each other. Something had changed, Jill thought, something in the very atmosphere between them. His expression reminded her of the way her father had looked at her when she had first accused him of being jealous of his brother's free spirit, as if someone he'd thought he knew well had suddenly turned into someone else. But Gunnar's expression was different; he looked as though he'd turned over a plain, unpretentious stone to find a new, wondrous facet.

"Hummingbird," he whispered.

Jill stared at him. That was what he'd said before, she thought in sudden realization, when they'd been sailing back to the harbor. Why? And why did he look so odd when he said it, half entranced, half…scared?

Jill shook her head sharply. The idea of Gunnar being scared of her was only slightly less ridiculous than the idea that he was entranced with her. But he had responded to her, touched her with tenderness—

Hormones calling to hormones, she told herself sternly. The question was, was she willing to settle for that?

She stood there, looking at him, for a long moment. He was still the man she'd been practically infatuated with at first sight. He was still just as sexy, just as breathtaking, just as wild. And even more tempting, now that she knew a little of what had shaped this . . . reformed pirate. Even more tempting, now that she knew the exotic exterior hid a man capable of deep emotion, a man capable of changing his entire life, at a cost she couldn't even imagine.

No, she thought with a sudden rush of self-knowledge, the question was, was she willing to give up this chance at a taste of the freedom she craved? Even knowing it could only be a secondhand taste? And temporary? Was she willing to walk away from Gunnar and the vivid colors of his life to go back to a world where her only exciting memories came from her beloved books?

Her common sense told her to do just that. Her heart, every emotion within her, cried out no. And for the first time in her life, those emotions won.

"So," she said softly, "I'm too innocent for the Raider, is that it?"

His expression changed, as if she'd reminded him of a painful truth. "Exactly."

"It's a good thing you caged him, then. Besides, I much prefer the current version of Gunnar the Raider."

His eyes widened. And in the green depths, Jill saw the longing she'd felt in his touch. Never had a man looked at her in just that way. Or perhaps someone had, and she had never noticed. Or cared.

But she cared now. More than she had ever cared about anything in her life. The realization frightened her at the same time as it thrilled her. It also left her incapable of speech. So she moved instead.

As she slowly crossed the space between them, a distance that seemed vast when in fact it was only the width of the boat's main cabin, Gunnar rose to his feet.

"Jill," he said, voice low and taut.

She knew it was meant to be a warning, but all she heard was the undertone—a combination of yearning, desire and, incredibly, hope—that drew her inexorably.

She came to a halt before him, bare inches away. Her peripheral vision told her his arms were stiffly at his sides, his hands clenched. He seemed to loom over her, tall, solid, strong. She felt the old shyness creeping up over her. But it was no match for the urge she felt to reach out and touch him, to run her fingertips over the bare expanse of his chest, to kiss the scar that marked his abdomen. When she raised her gaze to his face, it was as if he had read her thoughts, and heat flared in his eyes, enabling her to go on.

"You can tell me to go away if you don't want me," she whispered. "But for no other reason. Not who you were, what you did then, or if you don't think you've atoned enough yet."

He swallowed. "Jill...you don't know what you're doing."

She gave him a smile tinged with ruefulness. "You want to take responsibility for me, too? I may be a fool, but if I am, it's my problem. Only one reason, Gunnar," she repeated.

"Jill, no."

"You don't want me, then?"

He let out a short, compressed breath. "You know better than that," he said wryly, his gaze flickering downward.

She did. She'd been aware of the change in his body since she'd come so close; it was what had given her the courage to ask the question. And it was what gave her the courage to move now.

She lifted one hand and pressed it, palm flat, in the center of his chest. She felt him suck in a breath and hold it. His eyes closed, his lips parted. Jill felt a tremor go through him as she looked at the thick, dark semicircles of his lowered lashes. She slid her hand downward, lingering for a moment over the thin ridge of scar tissue before continuing to stroke her fingers through the path of soft hair that began at his navel. She felt the muscles of his belly ripple under her hand.

"You move another inch," he said hoarsely, "and this discussion is going to be academic."

She moved that inch, the tips of her fingers sliding beneath his waistband. When his eyes snapped open, she made herself hold his heated gaze. She was quaking inside, but the feel of another tremor rippling through him as she flexed her fingers slightly shored up her fragile confidence.

"It always was," she said simply.

Gunnar groaned, low and deep in his chest. His hands came up, gripping her upper arms and pulling her hard against him. His head came down with the fierceness of the raider he'd been called, plundering her mouth, tasting her, drawing her into a whirlpool of fiery sensation.

She welcomed the plunge of his tongue, tasting him back, thrilling to the quiver of sensation that rippled through her. His hands tightened, but she felt no pain; there was no room for anything except the heat cascading downward from his mouth on hers, searing her on its way to pool inside her, somewhere low and deep. And achingly empty.

How could she feel so much, and still feel empty? The paradox puzzled her, and she leaned into him, knowing instinctively that he held the answer. Abruptly he broke the kiss, and she heard him take in a sharp, rasping breath.

"Jill—" another harsh breath "—you're heading into blue water."

"And sweet winds," she murmured.

He shuddered, as if her words had been a feather up his spine. "Oh, Jill." Then he held her away from him, staring down into her face, his eyes alight with heat and need. "You're at the point of no return, lady. If this is just some kind of...experiment you're going to regret later, you'd better run like hell. Now."

"I don't know what it is," Jill said honestly. "But I know I don't want to run."

"Why? You should. Or is this your brand of mutiny against your family?"

Jill stared at him. He couldn't really think that, could he? But as her eyes met and held his, she saw the flicker of uncertainty there. That hint of vulnerability tightened something in her chest, making it hard to speak.

"I'm not a rebellious child, Gunnar," she said finally. "My family has nothing to do with it. Not even

Marcus. This—'' she slid her hands up his chest ''—is for me. For the first time in my life, it's for me.''

She felt him shiver again, but his jaw was set with determination. Determination to scare her off? she wondered. To make her change her mind? To back away?

"Are you on the pill?"

Yes, Jill thought, that's exactly what he was trying to do, to reduce it to cold, clinical facts, perhaps not to scare her off, but to make her see irrevocably what she was doing. She fought down the color she felt rising. "No. I... there was no reason."

His expression remained harsh, forbidding, but she felt the pounding of his heart beneath her hands. That racing pulse gave him away, and suddenly it hit her; if he wanted to stop this, all he had to do was say the simple words she'd told him were the only reason she'd accept. All he had to do was tell her he didn't want her, and she would walk away, would retreat to try to salvage what was left of her pride. But he never said the words. And his heart was still racing beneath her fingers.

"Are you a virgin?"

It was blunt, almost curt, but Jill saw it for what it was, and wondered that she'd ever found him hard to read.

"That's not your responsibility, either," she said softly. "People make their own decisions, Gunnar. I've made mine. Now you make yours."

His eyes closed for a moment as he drew in a deep breath, then swallowed. When he opened them again, his expression was rueful. "I just wondered," he said, his voice rough, "how badly I'd hurt you if we wound up right here, up against that bulkhead."

Jill blushed furiously at the image, all her cool certainty vanishing in a surge of heat. "I . . . You . . . I'm not," she finished in a rush. "There was one time. . . I think."

Gunnar blinked. "You think?"

"I mean, I tried. It . . . hurt. I'm not sure if . . ."

Her voice trailed off as she lowered her gaze. Her confidence had been a frail, brittle thing, after all, she thought. It couldn't even stand up to a pair of piercing green eyes that saw too much.

A tiny gasp escaped her as strong arms swept her up off her feet.

"I swear you'll be sure this time," Gunnar promised fiercely. And the Raider carried the librarian into his pirate's cabin.

Chapter Eight

Jill thought she had learned about flying when they had sailed the cutter home. Now she knew that had been merely sailing; she was learning to fly beneath Gunnar's hands, mouth and body.

He was relentless, caressing every inch of her, first with his hands, then following the path he'd blazed with his mouth. She heard herself cry out again and again as he found some ultrasensitive spot and lingered there; the back of her knees, the hollow of her throat, the small of her back. When at last he moved over her, she was clutching at him, opening for him before he asked, desperate for the feel of his aroused body joining hers.

He paused for a moment that seemed to last far too long, opening the foil packet he'd gotten from a small cubby in the head. That he hadn't had them handily by the bunk was a realization she would take time to appreciate later; by now, after the thrill of his sudden action, and the kisses he'd rained down on her as he carried her, she was already too eager for him to think about it.

When he rolled back to her and she felt the first probing of his rigid flesh, she moaned again, wanting. Yet still he waited, beginning the slow, lingering caresses again, as if he were starting over. And he whispered to her; sweet, praising words that her mind tried to write off as things any man would say under these conditions, but that her heart clung to with joy, that she had at last found a man who truly meant it when he said he liked the gentle curves of her and the way she was soft where he wasn't.

Soon she was crying out anew, little sounds that startled her with their sheer, ravening hunger. Involuntarily her body twisted against him, begging without words for him to fill the emptiness that had grown unbearable the moment his mouth returned to her breasts, suckling, flicking, teasing each nipple until her body arched convulsively. Her hands slid down his sleek muscled back to his hips, trying to urge him home. Still he withheld himself, until she was fairly writhing. He had, she realized dimly through the haze of pleasure and need, turned her into some frantic creature she'd never seen. He'd made her wilder than she'd ever thought he was.

It would have amazed her, this capacity for wildness he'd somehow sensed and freed in her, had he not at that moment shifted his body, at last moving to fill her with a slowness she was certain would kill her.

"Please, Gunnar," she gasped.

His answer came punctuated with panting breaths that told her how much effort it was taking for him to go slowly. "Don't...want...to hurt...you."

"You're killing me," she said on a moan, her fingers tightening, digging into the taut muscles of his buttocks.

He swore, low and deep under his breath. "Oh, I can't...when you do that..."

He became the wild creature then, driving himself home with one fierce thrust, making her cry out her joy at the sudden wonderful fullness. Jill watched in wonder as he rose above her, watched the rippling of his muscles as he buried himself in her again and again, saw the golden sheen of his body as he moved, the dark wildness of his hair, watched the tensing of the corded muscles in his neck and the slightly feral flaring of his nostrils when he threw his head back.

So entranced had she been with the sight of him it caught her almost unaware, the sudden surge of heated sensation, rolling over her in wave after wave, building, rising, making her cry out his name in astonishment. Gunnar's jaw tightened, his mouth twisting into a fierce smile of male satisfaction. He shifted slightly, keeping himself deep inside her as he moved further upward over her body, then rocked his hips. Her eyes widened as she felt her body clench around his. That rolling wave surged once more, higher, more intense. When at last it broke, so did Jill.

"Oh, Gunnar!"

She moaned it out again and again, clinging to him as release swept through her. He stayed still, until at last she eased her grip slightly. Only then did she realize he was holding himself so rigidly he was shaking with the effort. The moment she relaxed, he was moving, thrusting fiercely, sending little aftershocks of pleasure darting through her again and again.

She heard him give a throttled groan. He ground his hips against her, driving deep, every muscle going rigid as her name broke from him on a stunned gasp. She felt him shudder, almost violently, and his head went back as his body arched into hers. Her name came again, and Jill knew suddenly that not for anything, not even for the frenzied pleasure he'd given her, would she trade the look of him now, and the shimmering, sweet sound of her name on his lips as he collapsed against her.

"You were right." Jill snuggled closer against his side.

"Hmm?"

"I'm definitely sure this time." Jill felt the chuckle before she heard it; it was a sound that echoed that utterly male smile of satisfaction she had seen in the instant that flood of new, amazing sensations had overtaken her. "You don't have to sound so...so smugly male," she grumbled, more teasing than serious.

"Do I?"

She smiled into the darkness at his innocent tone. "Yes. But I don't mind. You should be. You made me feel things I didn't know were possible. Made me see things in myself I didn't know were there."

There was a long, silent pause. Jill slowed her hand's stroking of his chest, fearing she'd somehow angered him.

"I...did some learning of my own, too," he said at last. "I didn't know I could...feel like that. That much."

Jill let out a breath she'd barely been aware of holding. "I'm glad," she said simply. And meant it; that tentative admission thrilled her to her soul.

She began her stroking again, savoring the sleek smoothness of his skin and the strength of muscle beneath. He didn't seem to mind, in fact was stroking her hair in much the same rhythm. He stopped only when her fingers brushed over the scar.

"Gunnar?"

"I suppose you think you have the right to know, now."

Jill stiffened at the cold words. They were so unexpected that there was a moment of almost numbness, as if her brain was refusing to take them in. But she knew the hurt was hovering, and she started to pull away. Gunnar's arm tightened around her, holding her to his side.

"I'm sorry," he said. "I didn't mean that the way it sounded. It's just...it's all part of what I used to be. It's hard for me to talk about."

Jill relaxed again. She wasn't sure being shut out of his past hurt any less, but she said nothing. Gunnar sighed.

"I... It was..." He let out a compressed, short breath. "I'd just confirmed the stock buy that put me over the top in McDuff. I had the controlling interest. I was getting ready to meet with my investors, to give them the news."

He shifted, as if the slight pressure of her fingers against the scar hurt. When he went on, the flat, measured pace of his words told her how clearly he remembered every second of what he was telling her.

"I got up from my desk. Got my suit coat from the rack. Leaned over to pick up my briefcase." His stomach muscles jumped, as if they, too, remembered. "The next thing I knew, I was on my knees. Throwing up blood. A lot of it."

Jill sucked in her breath. "Oh, Gunnar."

"It kept coming." He went on doggedly, as if determined to finish it now that he'd started. "My secretary found me a while later. Lying in a pool of it. She thought I was dead. The emergency room doctor said if it had been ten minutes longer, I would have been."

Jill couldn't help herself; her arms went around him and she hugged him fiercely. He stiffened; then, slowly, as if making himself do it, relaxed.

"Turns out I had a perforated ulcer. It ruptured. They had to operate." She felt him shrug. "In a hurry. That's why it's not . . . real tidy."

"My God, Gunnar, didn't you know something was wrong?" Water and fruit juice, she thought suddenly. Why that was all she'd ever seen him drink made sudden, painful sense.

"My stomach always got a little restless on a tough deal, but it was no worse than normal that time."

"Restless? Your stomach's so eaten away it ruptures, and you call it restless?"

"Okay, it hurt. But nothing a couple of antacid tablets couldn't handle."

"Gunnar, stop. You nearly died."

She heard him swallow, a tight little sound in the dark. "I know."

"And this is the life you love? Even though it almost killed you?"

"I can't explain it, Jill. It's like . . . an addiction. I do love it. I can't deny that. It's why I can't go back. I might not be able to walk away again."

"When you . . . collapsed . . . that was when you decided to walk away?"

"No. It was later—"

He stopped. Jill sensed the sudden tension in him. "Gunnar?"

"Never mind."

"What happened later?"

"Nothing."

The old Jill would have let it go, but something in her had changed, some barrier had fallen, seared to ash by Gunnar's fierce loving.

"Nothing happened. But you walked away from your career, your life." She added a guess. "Alienated your family."

She felt the jolt that went through him as if it had gone through her, as well. Remorse filled her for prodding a wound she knew would never heal; she should have known better after years of watching her parents and Uncle Marcus.

"I'm sorry," she said. "I shouldn't have pried. Or mentioned your family."

"It's just that . . . you'll think I'm nuts. Hell, half the time *I* think I'm nuts."

There was an undertone in his voice that told her he was only half kidding. She said the only words she could think of to say. "I *know* you're not."

For a long moment he didn't speak. Just when she had resigned herself to his silence, he broke it.

"I . . . had a dream. In the hospital. Kids at a picnic, having fun, laughing, clustered around a man. It was McDuff, with his toys. The minute they saw me, the kids ran away crying." He let out a mirthless chuckle. "Guilt-inspired, I guess. Don't know why. I'd never felt guilty before."

Jill waited, sensing this wasn't the whole story. "And?" she prompted at last.

"I . . . When I woke up that morning, McDuff was there. In my hospital room. He didn't talk, just looked at me, shaking his head, this . . . horribly sad expression on his face. I'd never seen anyone look like that. I tried to ask him what he wanted, but he just looked at me. It shook me."

"That's when you decided to quit?"

"No," he said, his voice taking on that undertone again. "I was too damn stubborn to take the hint even then. I quit when—" He stopped, then it came out in a rush. "I quit when I found out McDuff had killed himself the night before."

A chill raced up Jill's spine and goose bumps rose on her arms. She shivered.

"Yeah," Gunnar said dryly, "that's how I felt. But I swear, Jill, he was there. And I was awake. A nurse heard me talking, and came in. I looked up when she came in, and when I looked back, he was gone."

Jill let out a shaky breath. For the life of her, she couldn't think of a thing to say.

Gunnar let out a rueful breath. "I knew there was a reason I've never told that to anyone."

A little thrill zipped through her at his words. He'd never told anyone, but he'd told her?

"It wasn't just a . . . hangover from my dream, Jill. I could feel everything, the IVs in my arm, the damn ache in my belly. I could hear all the hospital noises, smell the smells. . . ."

"I believe you," she said softly, still tingling from his words, although she was sure he didn't realize what he'd admitted.

"I . . . you do?"

"I don't pretend to understand it, or how it happened, but I believe you saw him. You're not crazy, Gunnar."

She felt the tension that had filled him when he'd first begun to tell her fade. His body sagged, relaxed, and she was moved by how much he had apparently wanted her to believe him. She moved her hand, fingers once more tracing the scar.

"I'm glad he came to you," she whispered, "if he made you leave a life that almost killed you."

"The question is, why? By rights, he should have been there to finish the job."

Jill pulled herself up on one elbow. The only light in the cabin came from the small portholes, but her eyes were adjusted now and she could see the contours of his face if not his expression. She didn't have to see it; she knew it by the wry tone of his voice. She was suddenly glad of the darkness; perhaps it had made it easier for him to talk, to tell the secret he'd told no one else.

"Maybe he knew that you would punish yourself far more than he ever could." Gunnar went very still. "When is the debt paid, Gunnar?"

Even without light she knew he was looking at her; she could feel his gaze like a physical touch.

"I . . . don't know." Silence again. Jill waited. "I think . . . part of the reason I fought you so hard was . . . I didn't think I deserved this. Or anything so . . . sweet.

But then you said…this was for you, and I thought…
Hell, I don't know. I don't know anything anymore.''

"I know one thing." Jill's voice was husky.

"What?"

"I'll never be the same again," she said, sliding her
hand down his belly until her fingers found and curled
around him. Gunnar sucked in his breath, then
groaned as she began to stroke him.

"Neither will I, Jill."

His arms came around her, pulling her on top of
him. And in the Raider's cabin, Gunnar once more
gave Jill all the wildness she had ever craved.

Chapter Nine

The shrill jangle of a telephone shattered Jill's sleep. She tried to go back to the dream she'd been having, like so many before, an erotic dream of Gunnar naked beside her, that beautiful body within her reach, even eager for her touch—

"Hello? Hello?"

Gunnar's voice. The lingering mists cleared abruptly. She sat up, staring down at herself, at the nude body that told her in no uncertain terms that this time it had been no dream. It had been real, every hot, steamy minute of it; the sensual ache between her thighs was undeniable. The image of Gunnar filling the empty place inside her was unforgettable.

"I'm sorry, Dad."

Jill's head snapped upright. She knew Gunnar wasn't in the room, but she could have sworn—

Kidd. The parrot sat on a perch about three feet away from the foot of the bunk that ran sideways across the stern of the boat. Jill nearly laughed aloud when she realized that the bird had made the telephone sound with deadly accuracy, and smiled when he again mimicked Gunnar's voice.

"I know what you think of me."

The smile faded. It was odd, she thought, listening to the parrot's one-sided version of what was obviously a phone conversation. And not a pleasant one, from Gunnar's tone—or Kidd's, she corrected.

So where was Gunnar? She hadn't heard him leave, or bring Kidd into the stateroom from the main cabin where the bird had apparently—since she hadn't heard any earsplitting singing—spent the night. Not that she would have...

Jill blushed, was seized with her old shyness even though her only company was the bird who had now lapsed into silence. She didn't know what to do. She didn't know what to say when she did see him. The only clothing she had here was her bathing suit, so reluctantly she began to pull it on.

"She's driving me crazy, Kidd."

Jill stopped in the act of tugging the straps over her shoulders and stared at Kidd. It had been Gunnar's voice again, oddly coming out as the bird addressing himself in his owner's voice. Who was the "she" that had driven Gunnar to say those words often enough that the bird had learned them?

"I know she's Marc's niece, but damn, I want—"

Kidd even had the abrupt cutoff of words imitated perfectly, but Jill barely noticed. Her. God, it was her. He *had* wanted her, even before.

Joy filled her, and her shyness vanished as she unlatched the door and went into the main cabin. Gunnar wasn't there, but she heard sounds from the cockpit and headed that way. And stopped dead when the sounds coalesced into words.

"...long do you think you're going to keep up this farce?" The male voice was harsh, angry. And not Gunnar's. But the next voice was.

"Look, Dad—"

Oh, God, Jill thought.

"Look, nothing!" The other voice again, angrier yet. "Do you think I broke my back sending you to college to see you waste your life like this? To be ashamed of my own son—"

"I can't go back, damn it! Can't you see that? That world, it's like a disease...like alcohol to an alcoholic, for me. I'd get sucked up into it again, turn into a shark again."

"And what's wrong with that? Better a shark than a...whatever you are now."

"What's wrong with it?" Jill heard Gunnar laugh, but it was a pained, sober sound. "You mean, besides the fact that it almost killed me?"

"Everybody in business gets an ulcer sometime," his father said dismissively. "Yours was just a little worse. Comes with the territory."

Jill wanted to race topside and slap him, he sounded so uncaring about his own son's life. Only the realization that her sudden appearance might make things worse held her back.

"You were the best, Gunnar." The voice had changed now, become coaxing, almost pleading. "I was so proud of you. The Royce Group made more money in a shorter time than any buyout house in history."

"And you got your share," Gunnar said dully. "Why can't you just let me go?"

The snap was back, biting, acidic, as his father said, "Because I refuse to have a worthless bum, a good-for-nothing, long-haired piece of scum for a son, that's why."

Jill smothered a cry. God, she couldn't stand this. She was going up there, she didn't care if—

"Well I'm afraid that's what you've got, Dad."

"The hell I do." The voice was vicious now, and Jill shivered, suddenly unable to move. Even her own self-righteous family had never been vicious. "I talked to the members of the group. Things haven't been going as well as we hoped. They said they'd be willing to take you back, even after all this time. But you've only got two weeks to make the decision, Gunnar. You come back in two weeks, or—"

"Or what, Dad?" Gunnar's voice was low and so full of pain that Jill couldn't believe the other man didn't see it.

"Or I no longer have a son."

She heard the sound of heavy, hard-soled footsteps moving away, no doubt digging into the carefully maintained teak decking. Furious at what she'd heard, not even caring that it would be obvious she'd been eavesdropping, she started up the steps to the cockpit, hand lifted to slide the partially open hatch the rest of the way.

"Gunnar, please listen to him."

The soft, feminine voice stopped Jill in her tracks.

"Listen?" Gunnar's voice was bitter. "Like he listens?"

"He just wants you to come back to us."

"No, Mother. He doesn't want me. He never did. He wants Gunnar the Raider back."

"You really won't . . . do as he asks?"

"I'm sorry. I can't."

"But...you were very good. And you liked your work, I know you did."

"That's the problem, Mother. I liked it too much. What I didn't like was what I turned into."

"Please, Gunnar, just think about it? It would make him so happy."

"My father," Gunnar said carefully, "has never been happy, that I can remember."

"But he was so proud of you. Please, just say you'll think about it. If I tell him that, he'll calm down."

A long pause made Jill ache to know what was happening, an ache that intensified when she heard the incredible gentleness in Gunnar's voice, even after the emotional wringer he'd just been put through.

"If it will make it easier for you, tell him what you want. I won't deny it."

"Thank you." The relief Jill heard in that soft voice made her wonder uncomfortably what this woman would be facing when she left here. "If you don't change your mind, you won't...leave, will you? Without telling me?"

"I'll call you. I promise."

Jill heard movement then, a rustling and some whispered words she couldn't hear. Then footsteps, lighter, but sounding like high heels that would do even more damage to Gunnar's flawless decks. Jill waited, trying to rein in her fury, giving Gunnar a moment to get a hold on what she was sure must be battered emotions. And waiting until she was fairly certain his parents were out of sight; she didn't want to see them. She wasn't sure why, except for some nagging fear that if she did, they would remind her too much of her own parents, her father, authoritative and self-righteous, her mother, quietly being towed along in his wake.

And they would react to Gunnar in exactly the same way. They would never understand why he had walked away from what they would consider a perfect world, one of wealth and power. And they would condemn him for it, just as his own father had. And suddenly she was ashamed of them all.

At last she slid the hatch all the way back and started up into the sunlight. Before she reached the top step she could see him. He was sitting on the cockpit bench, slumped forward, eyes tightly closed, elbows on his thighs. Between his knees his hands were clenched into fists, one on top of the other, pushing against each other with a fierceness that whitened his knuckles. Her heart twisted inside her and her throat tightened until she could barely breathe.

Dear God, she loved him.

The realization hit with the force of a gale wind. Her fury at his parents' treatment of him, her shame at the thought of her own parents' certain agreement, should have warned her. But it wasn't until she saw him now, until she felt her own agonized response to his inner pain, that the truth overwhelmed her. She loved him, just as he was; wild, exotic, unconventional, and as far away from the business waters he'd once swam in as could be imagined. It was a moment before she could take that last step.

His head came up sharply the moment she set foot on deck. He took one look at her face, and the stiff-

ness went out of him like the tautness of a mainsail
when the halyard let go.

"You heard," he muttered.

"It was...hard not to." She walked over to him and
sat a careful foot away, sensing he wouldn't welcome
right now the fierce hug she longed to give him.
"Gunnar, I—"

"Everything all right over here?"

Jill gasped. Gunnar groaned. And neither one dared
look at the other as Marcus Brown climbed up the
dock steps and boarded *The Toy Killer.*

Her uncle looked as he always had, Jill noted rather
numbly, a bit out of the mainstream in his baggy white
pants, brightly colored print shirt, and worn deck
shoes with no socks. But his mustache was still his
pride and joy, a long, curved, gray handlebar that
curled into a complete loop at both ends, carefully
groomed in a way his tousled, still thick gray hair had
never been.

"Ah, there you are," Marcus said, smiling at Jill as
calmly as if he'd expected to find her nowhere else. He
bent to give her a kiss on the cheek. Then he looked at
Gunnar. "I woke up to some rather heated voices. Are
you all right?"

"Fine." Gunnar's voice was flat and utterly uncon-
vincing. Then, suddenly, his gaze shot to Marcus's
face. "You woke up...?"

Marcus nodded. "Mm-hmm."

Jill paled. "You— When did you get here?"

"Oh, late, I'm afraid. Nearly midnight, anyway."

He said nothing about Jill's absence from the *Black
Sheep,* but her paleness gave way to a furious blush as

she thought of where she'd been—and what she'd been doing—at midnight. And eleven. And ten... *Lord, please don't let him ask,* she prayed silently.

She risked a glance at Gunnar. He met her gaze for an instant, his eyes full of the same memories. When he turned away to give Marcus a wary, sideways look, Jill was grateful; the images were far too intense and she was blushing enough already.

"So," Marcus said blandly, as if he hadn't even noticed their discomfiture, "I gather the man with the booming voice and the extremely unhappy expression was your father?"

"How could you tell?" Gunnar's tone was sour, and Jill wondered if this subject was any improvement.

"He looked just like my brother when he's listing my multitude of sins."

Gunnar looked startled. Then, with a halfhearted smile, he acknowledged Marcus's conclusion. "I guess you could tell, couldn't you?"

"He's much worse," Jill said vehemently. "At least my father would never want me to go back to something that nearly killed me."

"Jill—" Gunnar began.

"I don't care," she said sharply. "Maybe I shouldn't say anything because he's your father. But right now I'd like to disown the lot of them, yours and mine."

"I've often thought of filing for divorce, myself," Marcus said, his tone so studiedly nonchalant Jill felt a little fanatic by comparison. As usual, Marcus had read her expression perfectly. "It's old, old ground, honey. Not worth wasting energy on." He tugged on one waxed end of his luxuriant mustache, and turned his gaze on Gunnar. "Take it from an old hand, my friend. You can't change them. Only they can do that. The best you can do is not let them change you."

Gunnar didn't answer, but after a moment he nodded, a wry smile curving his mouth.

"Well," Marcus said briskly, getting to his feet, "I believe I'll go and have some breakfast before I head back."

Jill's eyes widened in surprise. "You're leaving? Already?"

"I have to get back to work. I only stopped by to pick up some papers on the *Black Sheep.*"

"Papers?" Jill rose quickly. "You're not really going to sell her, are you?"

Marcus hesitated. Then, quickly, "It's just for an appraisal, honey. Don't worry about it."

He turned to go. Jill watched him, biting her lip. Marcus had never lied to her, but he seemed awfully worried.

"Marc."

Jill looked at Gunnar when he spoke. Oddly, he was looking at her, not Marcus. But when her uncle turned back, he shifted his gaze to the older man.

"Just how bad . . . are things?"

"Times are tough everywhere," Marcus said with a shrug.

Gunnar grimaced. "Just how tough are they at New Endeavors?"

"Let's just say I'm glad Gunnar the Raider is . . . retired."

Gunnar stared, shock evident in his face. "I..." He stopped, then tried again. "You...knew?"

"Who you are? Of course. Even someone as oblivious as I am couldn't be in the business world for long and not hear about the Raider. You're a legend, Gunnar." Marcus grinned. "A legend enhanced, I might add, by your dramatic and somewhat mysterious disappearance from that world."

Gunnar looked a little dazed. Jill was feeling a bit that way, too. She'd heard Gunnar's story, she'd believed what he'd told her, but she hadn't quite realized what size shark he'd really been. That even Marcus, who paid little attention to the traditional workings of business, was well aware of Gunnar and his reputation told her volumes. She felt a shiver of dread; the excitement, the seductiveness of the world he'd left was suddenly dangling visibly in front of her, and even she could see the allure.

"I...never set out to be a legend," Gunnar said, his voice low.

"I don't suppose legends ever do." Marcus smiled. "And I would guess it's harder to stop being one than it is to become one. Especially—" he glanced up the dock where Gunnar's parents had gone "—when some people don't want you to."

Jill recognized the expression on Gunnar's face; she'd worn it often enough herself around her uncle. It was relief, the sheer relief of talking to someone who understood. And didn't judge. She tried to quash the foreboding that had overtaken her when she'd realized just what kind of power Gunnar had once wielded. And the price he was paying to turn his back on it.

"Yeah," Gunnar muttered. Then he seemed to draw himself up straight. "What's happening at New Endeavors?"

"No, Gunnar," Marcus said softly.

"What?"

"If I was going to ask for your help, I would have done it when I first realized who you were."

Gunnar's brow furrowed. "Why didn't you?"

Marcus's gaze lowered to the scar that marked Gunnar's abdomen. "Because I heard one version of the Raider legend that matches that scar," he said quietly. "And if a man has come through the abyss and survived, no one has the right to ask him to walk back into it again."

Chapter Ten

Gunnar lay in the sun on the cockpit seat, in wonderfully sated exhaustion, wondering what had come over Jill last night. Not that she hadn't been incredible the night before, more sweetly responsive than any woman he'd ever known, but last night had been ... different.

He'd never felt the way she had made him feel. Precious, somehow, although the word made him uncomfortable. Treasured, maybe. That was closer, he thought. It had been there in the way she had gently but insistently taken charge, pressing him back in the bunk, making her desire for him to just accept clear without words. It had been there in the way she had touched him, gently yet urgently, tracing long, sinuous paths over his body that had made him shiver. It had been there in the way she had followed the paths blazed by her hands with her mouth, until he was moving crazily, desperately beneath her, managing to keep from begging her to end it only by thinking of how incredible it would be when she finally did.

When it happened, when she had at last straddled him and sank down upon his aching flesh, he'd bucked violently, unable to stop the movement any more than he'd been able to stop the harsh cry of pleasure that had broken from his throat.

Yes, Jill had been the wild one last night, and he had responded to it as fiercely as she had the night before. And he smiled ruefully when he remembered his arrogant thought that she wanted to learn of wildness from him; she knew more than he ever would, it had just been buried away under years of neglect. His hummingbird had truly learned to fly.

And he didn't want her to crash, Gunnar thought, his brow furrowing. *I'll pull out of this, you know. Jill will be taken care of. She won't have to depend on those... ironhanded, pigheaded Browns.*

Marc's words had been nagging at him since he'd heard them; now they haunted him. Especially since he'd managed a brief moment alone with Marc before he'd left, just long enough to ask him who he planned to leave the business assets to when the time came. The answer had come as no surprise.

He liked Marc. Admired him. And greatly appreciated the fact that he hadn't said a word, even though Gunnar knew he had to have guessed where Jill had been the night he had arrived; it was almost as if he'd expected it, although that seemed crazy. But as grateful as he was that her uncle hadn't embarrassed her, Gunnar had to admit the man was blissfully ignorant of the brutal side of the corporate world. And seemed happy that way. *It's none of your business,* Gunnar told himself. *You're out of that game. You made a vow you'd never go back, and you're going to keep it.*

He stretched massively, wondering if it was worth the energy to turn over. He supposed he should, or Jill would come back from the store to find him in the exact same position she'd left him in. He'd offered to go with her, but she'd insisted she had plans for a special dinner and wanted to surprise him. And far be it from him to deter her from this new urge to pamper him, especially if it involved a home-cooked meal he didn't have to fix himself.

She'd come so far in such a short time, he thought, as he remembered how she'd looked when she'd left. She'd turned golden—her skin, the shapely legs left bare in the shorts she had taken to wearing. The sunny streaks in her hair, now worn down and free, tempted him to thread his fingers through it every time she came close enough.

He sat up suddenly. Maybe he should have gone with her. Others might not have seen the reality in the brown wren disguise, but his hummingbird was flying free now and no one could miss her beauty. He grimaced, wryly aware that he was wishing for the impossible, for her to stay this way, yet be his own personal secret at the same time. It couldn't be. He would live with it, he thought, rather than have her go back to the way she was.

She won't have to depend on those ironhanded, pigheaded Browns.

What if she did? At least he could afford his independence. What if the day came when Jill couldn't? Would they trample her down again, smother her, stamp out that spirit until she was just another pale, lifeless copy of themselves? The thought knotted up in his belly with a fierceness that rivaled the worst of that long-ago pain.

He couldn't let it happen. He wouldn't let it happen.

* * *

At first Jill thought it was Kidd, because it sounded like another one-sided conversation.

"How much stock?"

She shifted the two bags of groceries and stepped aboard *The Toy Killer*. That name, she thought, had to go.

"Just enough to rate a seat on the board of directors?"

Maybe it wasn't Kidd, she thought, when the voice paused.

"No, I'm not clairvoyant. It's a common move. Next will come a proposal for a more independent board, people who don't work for the company."

Definitely Gunnar, Jill realized. Clever as the imitative bird was, she thought that last sentence was a bit much. She stepped carefully down into the cockpit.

"Who is this group?"

Jill listened for the now familiar sound of an answering voice coming over the radiophone, but heard nothing.

"Headed by Becker Cosgrove?"

Jill stopped moving; something had come into Gunnar's voice, something sharp-edged and alert.

"You've got trouble," Gunnar said ominously. "He was an up-and-comer three years ago. Engineered the Lexco takeover."

She set the bags down on the cockpit seat. Her stomach had started to churn; something about the way Gunnar sounded made her uneasy. She didn't like the idea of eavesdropping yet again, but couldn't stop herself from peeking down into the cabin.

Gunnar was standing near the main salon table, holding what appeared to be a cordless phone, although Jill couldn't remember having seen one aboard the cutter. At least it explained the one-sidedness of the conversation.

Then he straightened. Instinctively Jill ducked back out of sight, but not before she'd seen Gunnar's eyes go oddly unfocused, as if removing himself from the distraction of his surroundings so he could concentrate.

"You'll have to move fast," he said into the phone. "Has he filed the request with the SEC yet?" Then, with a note of strained patience, "The Securities and Exchange Commission. They have to file the proposal."

A pause. "Never mind. He probably has."

Jill heard his footsteps, heading away from her. She leaned forward again, the uneasiness becoming apprehension. She saw Gunnar stop at the navigation station, where he drummed his fingers on the chart table for a moment, then turned and walked back to the center of the cabin. "You have anything special coming down the pipe?" Another pause. "Don't count on security." He paced back to the nav station, then turned again. "There are ways to find out even the best kept secrets."

He walked back to the other end of the cabin, his stride quick and measured. Jill watched him, the churning in her stomach becoming nausea. He was changing before her eyes. His fingers were drumming against his thigh now, an outward sign of the surging energy she could almost feel.

"Have any of your stockholders been approached about a possible tender offer?"

He turned toward her just as the answer came, and Jill couldn't stop the shiver that ran through her at the fervent, fierce look on his face. He was so intent, he never even sensed she was there. And she was too riveted to move, like a swimmer who wasn't quite sure what that shadow in the water over there was.

"Well you'd damn well better find out." Gunnar's voice was short, sharp. His eyes were narrowed. Jill stifled another shiver; instinctively she knew this was what he'd been like—fierce, intent...ruthless. She knew she was looking at the man who had become a legend.

After a second of listening, Gunnar nodded sharply. "All right. I'll accept that—for now. You're the kind of man who inspires loyal friends," he said in a flat, assessing tone. "If Becker's as smart as I remember, he'll know that. Maybe it isn't a hostile takeover attempt."

Whatever the person on the phone said, Gunnar made it clear what he thought of it. "Don't be an idiot. If it's become obvious enough for you to notice, then something's going on."

Jill felt a chill sweep over her. He seemed a stranger to her now, a fierce, controlled predator, not the wild, tender lover he'd been. Her knees began to feel funny, and she backed up to sink down on the cockpit seat.

"We could be looking at greenmail." At an apparent question from his listener, he repeated the word. "Greenmail. A form of corporate blackmail. Becker could be bluffing. Threatening a takeover, when what he really wants is to sell the stock back at a high profit. He makes the money and your other stockholders pay the price."

It sounded as if he had stopped pacing, but his voice kept up the rapid clip. "Get me that information. Fast. I'll need your last annual report. Make sure the inventory accounting method is there. And an accurate balance sheet. I've got to know those ratios, so I can see if you're undervalued enough to make Becker start circling. And a copy of the 13D report they filed when they bought the stock—"

Gunnar broke off, heaving a sigh, then said, with patience clearly running thin, "It's the report anybody who buys five percent or more of another company's stock has to file with the SEC. Check with your stockholders, even your friends. They may have been approached, kind of a trial balloon before any overt move that has to be announced."

Jill shivered yet again and wrapped her arms around herself. It didn't help; she couldn't stop the shaking any more than she could quell the queasiness in her stomach. Crazy, she thought inanely. She felt seasick, and the boat wasn't even moving.

"Don't have time now. Just get the stuff to me. I'll call you when I've got some ideas."

Jill heard an odd, sliding sound, then realized it must be the antenna of the cordless phone. A couple of moments later she heard a faint thump, then the closing of a cupboard door, made distinctive by the snapping of the latch that held it closed in high seas.

High seas. It felt like that, spinning, merciless, and utterly out of her control. She'd had little hope of holding a man like Gunnar, anyway, but ever since he'd told her his story, Jill had known she couldn't compete with the lure of his old world. But she'd comforted herself with the hope that, for his own reasons, he would never go back to that world.

His father had shattered that hope. She'd been a fool, she thought, to think anyone could resist the demands of a man like that. Not when he laid down an ultimatum no son could ignore. Gunnar had had no choice. He'd had to go back, or loose his family completely. Forever. So instead, Jill had lost her pirate. And the Raider was back.

Chapter Eleven

For the second time, Gunnar was wondering at Jill's fierce, erotic, utterly draining lovemaking. He lay atop her, still sheathed to the hilt in her soft, caressing body, his own body still shuddering at echoes of the explosion that had rocked him to his very core. Between his gasping breaths he tried to move, then gave up the battle and sagged once more against her.

She clung to him with an almost desperate strength that concerned him. She'd been acting so oddly since she'd come back this afternoon; edgy, tense, looking at him as if she expected him to pounce on her at any moment.

And then, after the huge, delicious meal she'd fixed, it had been she who had pounced on him, driving him uncomfortably close to frantic before he had at last carried her to his bunk and eased the need that was near pain by driving deep into her body.

His breathing finally slowed to normal, and he slid off of her to one side before she asked, her voice strangely subdued, "Who were you talking to this afternoon?"

Damn, Gunnar thought. She *had* heard. He had wondered when he'd found her sitting up in the cockpit moments after he'd stashed the phone back in the cubby where he kept it, since he used it so rarely. But she'd said nothing, insisting she was merely resting after lugging the groceries all the way down the dock. Now he wondered just how much she'd heard. And if what she had heard was the reason behind this odd mood. The promise he'd made suddenly seemed like the proverbial albatross around his neck.

"I, er, I called about having the boat hauled and scraped." That much was true, he thought. He had made that call. Before the other one.

She sighed, a tiny breath of sound that made him cringe inside. Had she heard too much? Did she know he was evading the truth?

"Jill—"

"I'm tired," she said quietly. She rolled away from him. Or turned her back on him, he thought grimly. He reached out and slid his arm around her torso, pulling her back against him, into the curve of his body. He felt her stiffen for an instant, but then her body slackened, giving in.

He thought she was only feigning sleep, but he was too glad she hadn't asked any more questions to push his luck. He didn't think he could lie to her if she asked him again, yet he'd promised not to say a word about what he was doing. He was thankful when, after a while, her breathing took on the deep, even rhythm of true sleep.

He didn't like lying to her. Why that should bother him, after all the years he'd spent saying whatever was necessary to get what he wanted, he wasn't sure. He just knew that he didn't like lying to Jill. And he hated the way she'd been looking at him all day, like a surfer who'd just spotted a dorsal fin.

He yawned, wishing his mind would slow down. He tried not to think about the task to come, but the only thing that had the power to take his mind off it was Jill, and right now he didn't want to think about her, either. She unsettled him too often, she disconcerted him, she never quite did what he expected. And she made him think such crazy things. Like now, sleepily wondering what it would be like to do the proverbial sail into the sunset with company this time.

He didn't know how long he'd been asleep. He knew only that this was the most pleasant way he could ever think of to wake up, with Jill's soft voice in his ear, saying his name in that breathless way she always did when he first slid himself into her welcoming heat. He reached for her, already hard, already aching. And sat up, suddenly, completely awake.

He was alone. Except for Kidd, who sat on his perch, his head cocked sideways as he looked at Gunnar.

"Damn," he muttered, embarrassed both at the bird's arousingly accurate imitation of Jill's voice, and his own reaction to it. "If she ever hears that, you're one dead parrot."

"Walk the plank," Kidd agreed.

"If you're lucky," Gunnar warned. He slid out of the bunk and walked, naked, into the main cabin, contemplating the chances of making his half-waking dream come true.

The cabin was empty. The hatch was closed.

Maybe she was in Kidd's stateroom, he thought. She seemed to get such a kick out of it. And, he admitted

with some abashment as he headed that way, out of
the fact that he had designed and built it.

The parrot's retreat was empty. The entire boat
seemed to echo with the hollow sound of emptiness.
He walked slowly back to the main cabin, brows furrowed. Maybe she'd gone to the *Black Sheep*. Most of
her stuff had wound up over here, but perhaps she'd
needed something. She could have—

He saw the note on the salon table then. Relieved,
he picked it up and read the oddly shaky handwrit-
ing. And read it again. And again. The words never
changed.

Gunnar,
I have to go home.
Thank you for everything.
Please take care of yourself.

                                   Jill

What the hell did that mean? *I have to go home?* He
knew she was off for the summer, but he'd never really asked how long she'd intended to stay here. He'd
kind of assumed it would be the whole summer. *Take
care of yourself.* What was *that* supposed to mean? He
always did, didn't he? Although he hadn't, once. And
she knew that.

He grimaced at the other phrase in the note. *Thank
you for everything?* For what? The stories? The sail?
The swimming lesson? His stomach knotted. The sex?

She didn't mean that. He knew she didn't. It hadn't
been like that, not the kind of sex you gave a casual
thank-you for in the morning and then went on your

way. He might be capable of that, had, in fact, done it on occasion, but not Jill. She was the kind of woman who had to have it all dressed up as love.

The word hit him like a runaway boom. It hadn't been just sex. Not for Jill. And not for him. For the first time in his life, not for him. It had been so much more, all tied up with tenderness and her soft heart, and the wildness she'd sought in him, the wildness he'd set free in her.

In the wake of this realization came another. And another, one chasing the other the way porpoises chased each other in play. He thought of the way she'd looked at him yesterday, warily, nervously. He thought of the wonder he'd seen in her face as she'd changed from wren to hummingbird before his eyes. He thought of the way she'd reacted when he'd told her of his collapse, the look on her face the day his father had come, and the tone of her voice when she'd asked him last night who he'd been talking to. And then he read the note again. Including the unwritten words between the lines.

I have to go home.
Because I don't know you anymore.
Thank you for everything.
For setting the hummingbird free.
Please take care of yourself.
Because I know you're going back to the world that nearly killed you.

"I'm not," he burst out, as if she were there to hear him. He knew now that she'd heard far too much of

that phone conversation yesterday, more than enough
to guess that he was breaking his long-held vow, that
he was diving back into the shark-infested waters
where he'd once reigned supreme. And because of his
promise, he couldn't tell her the truth about why.

The truth. Damn.

"Face it, Royce," he muttered under his breath.
He'd been kidding himself about his reasons, telling
himself he wanted Jill to be free of her family. That
much was true, but it wasn't the real reason. He
wanted her with him. He'd broken his vow to himself
never to go back to that world; he'd volunteered for
the job—and agreed to the promise—for the simple
reason that he loved her.

He looked at the note once more. And the last realization tumbled into place. The last of the unwritten words that were now as clear to him as if she'd put
them there in her shaky hand.

I love you.

Jill tuned out her father's rantings; she'd become
quite good at it in the two weeks since she'd left Gunnar. Her mouth twisted into a bleak smile; her life
seemed to be measured in parts now, the time before,
the dream with, and the time after Gunnar.

She'd had to do it, she told herself firmly as she
forced herself to eat another bite of ham from the
plate her mother had placed in front of her. She'd
barely eaten at all at last Sunday's customary family
dinner, and she didn't want to face another round of
her mother's questions. Especially in front of Uncle
Marcus, who had made an unexpected appearance

today, as casually as if he came every week, when in fact he'd stopped coming years ago, making Jill wish she had the nerve to do the same. And now that she did have the nerve, she thought ironically, she didn't care.

She'd had to leave Gunnar. It was for the best. There was no point in staying any longer, in falling more in love with him, in making it even harder—as if it were possible—to leave. Never mind that it didn't seem fair; life wasn't fair. If it was, her parents would have left her alone to fly her own path; Gunnar's father never would have set down the ultimatum that had driven his son back to the world he had tried so hard to escape. And the man she loved would still be there, instead of buried beneath the ruthless surface of Gunnar the Raider.

The only good thing that had happened lately was that Uncle Marcus seemed to have pulled New Endeavors out of whatever problems had been plaguing it. She wanted to know what had happened, but knew she'd have to wait until her father, still lambasting his brother for his support of a rather eccentric inventor, wound down a little. When she saw Marcus glancing at his watch with some regularity, she began to wonder if he would leave before she had the chance to ask.

"New kind of sponge, for God's sake! Really, Marcus, you've always been a fool about things like that, but this is ridiculous."

He paused for a breath. Jill took advantage of Daryl Brown's momentary silence. "I understand it has great potential as an absorbent material for oil and chemical spills." Marcus had told her this long ago; he'd always been pleased at her unfailing interest in the work he tried to do. "And that the government has expressed a great interest."

Her father gaped at her, much as if one of the chairs at the table had spoken. Jill stared right back at him. He didn't know the first thing about this project, but that hadn't stopped him from mouthing off about it. Jill was a little startled at even thinking that kind of thing about her father, but she suddenly realized it was true, and had been true all of her life; her father was at his most arrogant when he was the most ignorant. She glanced at her mother, who sat looking at her plate, and wondered how—and why—she had stood it for so long.

"Yes," Marcus agreed, winking at Jill as he tugged on one end of his mustache. "It could turn into a real money-maker."

"Will it..." Jill hesitated, not wanting to give her father any openings for more lectures, but Marcus was looking at her with such a twinkle in his eyes, she knew it was all right. "Will it solve your problem?"

"Oh," Marcus said breezily, "that's already solved."

"It is?" Jill smiled in delight for her uncle.

"Completely." After another glance at his watch, Marcus turned his gaze on her father, which Jill thought was odd, since she knew he didn't care what his brother thought. "At first we thought it might not be a true takeover attempt, but a sneaky move to milk all the ready cash out of us—using us as a 'cash cow,' I believe they call it. But it turned out someone had their eye on one of our prime assets," he explained kindly to his brother, who was now gaping at him much the way he'd gaped at Jill. Even her mother was staring, although she kept silent, as always.

Jill was gaping a little herself. She'd never heard Uncle Marcus talk like this, didn't even know he knew such things. He usually despised the business side of his business. But he sounded nothing less than elated about this. He also, she thought with a pang, sounded like Gunnar that day on the phone, the day she knew she'd lost him to his old world, the day that had brought her silly dreams crashing in around her.

"We thought about a 'poison pill' but I really didn't want to issue more stock," Marcus said. "That's what got me into this in the first place."

"A poison pill?" Jill's father asked, a little faintly.

"Yes." Marcus's voice became even kinder, as if explaining to a person of limited mental capacity. Jill smothered a giggle. "If there's a run on stock and you suspect a takeover effort, you issue more stock, that your current shareholders can buy at half price, thus reducing the percentage gained by the suitor."

After a moment of savoring Marcus's grin and her father's bewildered look, Jill asked, "What *did* you do?"

"I found a white knight. A rescuer. He explained about what they call a lockout, to combat the unfriendly takeover. We agreed on a stock option on possible future shares as part of the deal. And he agreed to buy out and continue to fund the environmental research division."

"The sponges?" Jill asked.

Marcus nodded, laughing. "Quite a name, isn't it, for one brilliant man in a lab? Anyway, since that was what the raider was after, when the white knight bought it out, we suddenly weren't so attractive anymore."

The raider. Jill smothered a sigh.

"You've never known a thing about business on that level," Daryl sputtered, angry, Jill supposed, that the sponge project he'd dismissed as ridiculous had been far from it. Or that she and Marcus had seemingly banded together in their insubordination.

"Nope," Marcus agreed cheerfully. "Hope I never have to."

"Then how—?"

"I consulted an expert," Marcus said, grinning as he interrupted his brother, a man who rarely stood for such impudence.

"I didn't know you knew any," Daryl said snidely.

"Oh, I know several. None quite as good as this one, though. He had a plan of action ready in a day, and carried it out in two weeks." Marc flashed a grin at Jill. She got the feeling it was expressing more than his relief about his business, but she couldn't guess what. "He also showed me how to revise the company charter to make it harder for a hostile bid to work in the future, by changing the proportion of shareholders needed to approve a merger, and by limiting their right to call special meetings."

"So, you did what I always said you'd have to do," Daryl said, the satisfaction in his voice grating on Jill's already tender emotions. "You sold out. To one of those rich men you have such contempt for."

"Not exactly," Marcus said, his voice suddenly as harsh as his brother's. "I sold to a man I trust. A man who feels the same way I do about what I'm doing. A man who will turn it all back to me when the threat is gone, for no more than what he paid for it."

"You're a bigger fool than I thought if you believe that. No man as rich as this one must be would sell for his cost."

"This one will."

Her father gave a derisive snort. And suddenly Jill wondered why on earth she put up with his pomposity.

"So who is this paragon?" Daryl asked in the same tone.

Marcus looked at his watch again, as if the answer was there. "I have a feeling you'll find out soon enough," he said. And he grinned at Jill again, and again she got that feeling that he was telling her something far beyond this rather stormy, if entertaining, discussion.

"What's that supposed to mean?"

"It means, dear brother, that you're about to learn a long overdue lesson."

Jill watched her father's brows shoot upward. Marcus had always enjoyed poking at his brother's rigid conceits, but she'd never seen him do so much of it as he had tonight.

"What do you think—?"

A slam echoed through the room, so fierce the windows rattled. Jill jumped, startled. It had unmistakably been the front door, and Jill's father leapt to his feet as her mother gave a little scream of fright. Marcus, Jill noticed, never blinked. This, along with the realization that a burglar or the like would hardly slam the door after him, eased her momentary alarm.

"You asked about the white knight?" Marcus said as the sound of swift, steady footsteps followed the slam. "Well, you're about to meet him."

Except for Jill's, all heads turned toward the sound. Her gaze lingered on Marcus for a moment. He was grinning so widely, her heart took a little leap. Then she, too, turned to look, just in time to see the man who appeared in the doorway. Her mother gasped. Her father's jaw dropped. Jill let out a tiny but joyous cry.

It was Gunnar.

He looked...extraordinary. He looked tall and broad and strong. His hair was down and loose and shining over his shoulders. He wore a pair of tight, dark pants, and a billowing white shirt, open at the neck to show enough of his tanned, muscled chest to make Jill's pulse begin to pound. Kidd was perched on one shoulder, his talons hooked around the collar of the shirt, and as the bird bobbed his head and tugged at Gunnar's hair, she saw the glint of gold. God, he even had the earring on, Jill thought, shivering at the impact this man had on her.

He was her pirate come to life; the living image of her fantasy. The only thing missing—a pair of knee-high boots. She barely stopped herself from crying out to him that she didn't need that fantasy anymore, that it had long ago been replaced with reality, the reality of the man standing before her.

He stood rock-solid in the doorway, body tense and unmoving as he scanned the room. His gaze lingered for an instant on Marcus, and an echo of Marcus's grin tugged at one corner of his mouth. Marcus lifted a hand in salute, a motion Jill saw only peripherally, since her gaze was riveted on Gunnar. It was a moment before she put it all together.

"You," she breathed. "You're the rescuer."

"That he is," Marcus said, looking at Jill now.

"Him?" Daryl nearly shouted in his disbelief.

Gunnar strode across the room, ignoring Daryl. He came to a halt beside Jill. She stared up at him, and what she saw in his eyes made her rise to her feet. She felt that same spinning sensation, that feeling she was about to plunge into swirling green depths. Only this time she wanted to jump, and she stepped forward instead of back.

"What the hell's going on?" her father roared. "Who is this derelict?"

"Jill, what are you doing?" Her mother's voice was shocked. "Do you know this...this person?"

She ignored both her parents. Gunnar's gaze never wavered.

"I found your note," he said. "You were wrong."

"I was?"

Her parents' protests grew in volume, but Jill never even looked at them.

"I never intended to go back to what I was."

"You didn't...?" Her brow furrowed. "I didn't write that."

"Didn't you?"

She saw in his eyes the knowledge of everything she hadn't written in that painful goodbye. "But I heard you, on the phone..."

"I guessed that. I'm sorry. I was talking to Marc."

Understanding flooded Jill. "Why didn't you say so?"

"I'm afraid that's my fault, honey," Marcus said, still grinning despite his apologetic admission. "I asked him not to. I was afraid if you knew how bad the trouble really was, you'd be turning your savings over to me."

Jill's eyes widened as she glanced at her uncle; more than once that very thought had crossed her mind.

"Uh-huh. That's what I thought." After a moment Marcus went on, still grinning. "He did it for you, you know, not me. He knew I meant the business to go to you, eventually. He didn't want you to ever have to depend on them." Marcus dismissed her angry parents with a nonchalant wave.

Daryl glared at him. Jill's mother was still staring fearfully at the piratical man standing so close to her daughter. Gunnar had yet to acknowledge their existence, and he didn't now.

"It felt good, working with Marc to save New Endeavors," he said. "I thought... this was something I could do, and not get sucked back into the insanity. That maybe I could fight it by doing the opposite of what I used to. By being the shark hunter instead of the shark."

She sucked in her breath when Gunnar suddenly took her hands in his. Heat shot through her. She heard her father bellow something; she paid him no more mind than did Gunnar. Marcus simply told his brother to be quiet. Kidd abruptly echoed the sentiment with a crude phrase that made her father flush and her mother gasp anew. Marcus, with a forcefulness that further astounded his brother, ushered them both out of the room. Gunnar never looked away from Jill.

"That sounds...wonderful," she said softly after a moment.

"But it still scares me, Jill. That world..." He shook his head. "You understand what it is to me. What it could do to me again. I can only do this if you're there to...keep me anchored. Marry me, Jill. I can't do it without you. Hell, without you, I don't want to do anything."

"Oh, Gunnar," she began.

"You don't belong here, Jill." He sounded a little urgent, as if he felt he had to convince her. "Not with them. Not anymore."

"I know," she said softly. Gunnar's eyes widened. "I knew right after I left you that I couldn't live like this anymore. I'm far too much like Marcus to tolerate this any longer. I was just...waiting, to decide what to do."

"Thank God," Gunnar breathed.

"I want to keep my job, for the part of it that I love. But," she added, "I've also learned I'm like you. I want to see what you've seen, Gunnar, go where you've gone. And never gone."

Gunnar smiled, a joyous, breath-stealing smile. "Then we will. Keep your job, love. I'll work when you do, helping companies like Marc's. But every summer we'll set sail for...somewhere.''

Jill's eyes misted at the easy way he used the endearment. "And I'll take a year off, now and then, so we can go farther."

Gunnar grinned. "Anything you want. Just say yes."

"Yes," she said fervently.

"Cast off," Kidd said enthusiastically.

Jill giggled. "Aye, aye, Cap'n Kidd," she said, throwing the bird a smart salute. Gunnar's grin widened. Then it faded as Jill turned a suddenly solemn face to him and said, "*Anything* I want?"

"If I can do it," he said, equally solemn.

"Oh, you can. If you will. It would only take a paintbrush."

Gunnar's brow furrowed. "What?"

"For a boat that needs a new name. They do that, don't they, when an old name doesn't fit anymore?"

Gunnar's brow cleared. He hesitated, then let out a long breath, accepting her words. "Yes. Yes, they do." His mouth quirked. "What did you have in mind?"

Jill smiled her relief; she'd been half-afraid he wasn't yet ready to give up his self-inflicted punishment. "*The Rescuer?*" she suggested.

Gunnar smiled, a smile that changed from rueful to satisfied as Jill watched. "All right," he said, "as long as you realize one thing."

"What's that?"

"That it's named after you, not me." Jill blushed. Gunner put his arms around her at last, pulling her close. "I love you, Jill," he whispered against her hair.

"I love you, too," she said, her voice muffled as she snuggled against his chest.

"I know. I saw it in your note."

"I didn't write that, either."

"The hell you didn't."

She hugged him then, long and tight. And let her imagination finally run free as she pictured herself and the man she loved, accompanied by a smart-aleck parrot, sailing into the sun for the adventure that would be their life.

* * * * *

Dear Reader,

For many years now, summer has been the one season of the year I did *not* look forward to. If you can't imagine how that could be possible, try working for a police department in a southern California beach town whose population quadruples in the summer—with, of course, no increase in the number of law-enforcement personnel to deal with said quadrupled population.

Our summers are personified by the Fourth of July, when normally sane people seem inspired by our country's birthday to do things they wouldn't be caught dead doing at any other time. My July Fourths have consisted of back-to-back, crazed, twelve-hour work shifts for the duration of the often four-to-five-day holiday period for so long that I've almost forgotten the truly joyous occasion it can be.

The rest of the summer generally isn't much better, from our viewpoint. (My editor had to remind me what a summer vacation was— "Picture yourself not working at *either* job." I could only sigh at the thought.) We come to work in mid-June, and the next time we have a chance to breathe, it's September. If you think *parents* cheer when their little darlings go back to school...

When Silhouette asked me to do this story, with its theme of love in the summertime, I wondered if I could. I wondered if I could think of summer as something to welcome, not dread. Summer as it used to be for me. Summer as it still is for that quadrupled population. And not just summer, but summer in a place people come hundreds of miles to visit. Summer in a place of gorgeous beaches, great waves, flying sails and cool sea breezes. Summer in a magical place, where anything—or anyone—could happen. And before I knew it, my imagination was sizzling and my story was launched.

For the moment, I'm afraid this story is as close as I'll come to a summer vacation. But you know what? I had a great time. And isn't that what summer is supposed to be all about?

Justine Davis

In Silhouette...

MORE GREAT ROMANCE FROM THESE BESTSELLING AUTHORS...

JACKIE MERRITT
NEVADA DRIFTER—
Silhouette Desire #866 in July 1994
Jude Colter intended to find out what her sexy handyman, Chase Sutton, was up to. He had easily stolen her heart. What else was the handsome drifter after?

ANNETTE BROADRICK
IMPROMPTU BRIDE—
Silhouette Romance #1018 in July 1994
Graham Douglas swept into a foreign country to rescue reporter Katie Kincaid. Running for their lives, they had no choice but to become instant groom and blushing bride. Would these hasty nuptials lead to a lifelong commitment?

JUSTINE DAVIS
LEFT AT THE ALTAR—
Silhouette Intimate Moments #586 in October 1994
Part of our Romantic Traditions program, *Left at the Altar* is a timely take on the classic story line of the same name. Sean Holt had never forgotten the pain of being jilted five years ago. Yet runaway bride Aurora Sheridan had had her reasons—dangerous reasons that had just turned deadly.

Look for these three exciting titles coming your way.

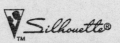

MONTANA Mavericks™

Stories that capture living and loving beneath the Big Sky, where legends live on...and the mystery is just beginning.

Watch for the sizzling debut of
MONTANA MAVERICKS in August with

ROGUE STALLION

by Diana Palmer

A powerful tale of simmering desire and mystery!

"The powerful intensity of Diana Palmer's storyline is exceeded only by the sizzling tension between her protagonists." —*Affaire de Coeur*

And don't miss a minute of the loving as the mystery continues with many more of your favorite authors!

Only from 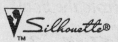 *Silhouette*®

where passion lives.

MAVT

Silhouette Books
is proud to present
our best authors, their best books...
and the best in your reading pleasure!

Throughout 1994, look for exciting books
by these top names in contemporary
romance:

JULIE ELLIS
The Only Sin in May

FERN MICHAELS
Golden Lasso in May

DIANA PALMER
The Tender Stranger in June

ELIZABETH LOWELL
Fire and Rain in June

LINDA HOWARD
Sarah's Child in July

When it comes to passion,
we wrote the book.

BOBQ2

Silhouette®

Fifty red-blooded, white-hot, true-blue hunks
from every State in the Union!

Look for MEN MADE IN AMERICA! Written by some of
our most popular authors, these stories feature fifty of
the strongest, sexiest men, each from a different state in
the union!

Two titles available every other month at your favorite
retail outlet.

In May, look for:
KISS YESTERDAY GOODBYE by Leigh Michaels (Iowa)
A TIME TO KEEP by Curtiss Ann Matlock (Kansas)

In June, look for:
ONE PALE, FAWN GLOVE by Linda Shaw (Kentucky)
BAYOU MIDNIGHT by Emilie Richards (Louisiana)

You won't be able to resist MEN MADE IN AMERICA!

IT'S OUR 1000TH SILHOUETTE ROMANCE, AND WE'RE CELEBRATING!

JOIN US FOR A SPECIAL COLLECTION OF LOVE STORIES
BY AUTHORS YOU'VE LOVED FOR YEARS, AND
NEW FAVORITES YOU'VE JUST DISCOVERED.
JOIN THE CELEBRATION...

April
REGAN'S PRIDE by Diana Palmer
MARRY ME AGAIN by Suzanne Carey

May
THE BEST IS YET TO BE by Tracy Sinclair
CAUTION: BABY AHEAD by Marie Ferrarella

June
THE BACHELOR PRINCE by Debbie Macomber
A ROGUE'S HEART by Laurie Paige

July
IMPROMPTU BRIDE by Annette Broadrick
THE FORGOTTEN HUSBAND by Elizabeth August

SILHOUETTE ROMANCE...VIBRANT, FUN AND EMOTIONALLY
RICH! TAKE ANOTHER LOOK AT US! AND AS PART OF THE
CELEBRATION, READERS CAN RECEIVE A FREE GIFT!

YOU'LL FALL IN LOVE ALL OVER
AGAIN WITH
SILHOUETTE ROMANCE!

CEL1000

Rugged and lean...and the best-looking, sweetest-talking men to be found in the entire Lone Star state!

Diana Palmer

LONG, TALL TEXANS

In July 1994, Silhouette is very proud to bring you Diana Palmer's first three LONG, TALL TEXANS. CALHOUN, JUSTIN and TYLER—the three cowboys who started the legend. Now they're back by popular demand in one classic volume—and they're ready to lasso your heart! Beautifully repackaged for this special event, this collection is sure to be a longtime keepsake!

"Diana Palmer makes a reader want to find a Texan of her own to love!"   —*Affaire de Coeur*

LONG, TALL TEXANS—the first three— reunited in this special roundup!

Available in July, wherever Silhouette books are sold.